He'd thought he loved this woman, but now she was a prime suspect in a murder...Did he really know her at all?

Faith grasped Tony's hand with a grip so firm it caused him to wince. But Faith only squeezed more firmly still, the pain feeling close to a physical assault.

He almost admitted, "You're hurting me," but somehow could not get the words to come forth. He kept expecting her to soften her hold on him, but she seemed to be already in some other place. He looked to her for relief and saw her eyes, her whole countenance, bearing the beginning signs of rapture. The press of her hand remained steady, strong, but somehow the pain decreased, or transformed as he seemed to feel her spirit seeking to investigate his own. After another moment, Faith, with her grip still inescapable, took Tony's hand and placed it under her sweater and onto her heart, where he felt the slow and then slower beats of a perfect sinus rhythm. He had no access to time, as he was incredulously drawn to an ecstasy of something that, if not divine, was still certainly other worldly. Faith's will seemed to envelop him and her eyes brightened at last with the knowledge of how she had fully enraptured him. When she finally released him, his tea was cold and his hand felt as if it were on fire.

"We'll get there Tony—the two of us together. But you still have so much to learn."

She gave him a long, tender kiss on his cheek before her eyes bade him farewell for the evening. As he drove back to his apartment, he wondered, with a kind of stunned sadness, why he had never before suspected Faith could be a leader of the new alumbradas.

When Monsignor Martin Heamey is found strangled just after a debate with Tony Cupelli, a former monsignor and present professor at Smith College, Tony's detective brother Mike seeks a possible link between this murder and the apparent suicide of a Carmelite nun in Brooklyn. The brothers uncover a growing cult of young women devoted to dark interpretations of the teachings and life of St. Teresa of Avila, a cult the brothers seek to prove guilty of the crimes, even as more possible victims of the devotees are revealed. When not one, but two, of Tony's present love interests are included among the most likely suspects, his own life is at risk unless, and until, the Cupelli brothers can decipher the clues awaiting in the secret writings of St. Teresa.

KUDOS for *Saving St. Teresa*

Saving Saint Teresa, a sequel to *The Monsignor's Wife*, is a compelling mystery with an intricate plot, intriguing characters, and complex themes. Tony Cupelli, the protagonist of the first novel, now a professor, no longer a monsignor, is once again a sleuth on a perplexing series of murders with his detective brother, Mike. The two brothers face a labyrinthine puzzle of suspects, centered mostly on a heretical cult based on the secret writings of St. Teresa of Avila. As he becomes increasingly involved in investigating these murders, Cupelli's life becomes more and more endangered. From page one to the end, Benevento's novel ramps up the devious, the sinister, the macabre. ~ *Jack Smith, author of* Hog to Hog, *winner of the George Garrett Fiction Prize, and* Icon

Joe Benevento follows up on his brilliant debut in *The Monsignor's Wife* with another Cupelli Brothers tour de force that combines an academic element worthy of C. P. Snow with a dexterity in plotting that would do Raymond Chandler proud! The author takes you through authentically described settings as varied as NYC and New England on and off campus, his potent narrative propelled by a cast of vivid and singular characters, and by his deep knowledge of Catholic history, and you will neither leave the edge of your seat nor guess the killer! Saving St. Teresa is an extraordinary blend of visceral action and serious intellect, and another grand tradition in American crime writing is being established before our eyes. ~ *Lee Slonimsky, author of* Bermuda Gold, *co-author of the Lee Carroll* Black Swan Rising *trilogy, and seven time nominee for the Pushcart Prize in poetry*

In *SAVING ST. TERESA*, Joe Benevento shows himself to be a highly talented novelist, unafraid to explore the philosophical and literary boundaries of the mystery genre while, at the same time, weaving a gripping mystery that is the epitome of a page turner. Benevento is a writer of such depth that, even while he goes deep into the history of Catholic mysticism for one plot element, he shows himself to be well versed in all manner of contemporary social issues in other elements. But he is, most of all, a terrific storyteller. Each new and unexpected plot twist will draw you further in. *SAVING ST. TERESA* is a must read for mystery and non-mystery readers alike. ~ *Carol Goodman, author of Hammett Prize winner* The Seduction of Water *and other novels*

ACKNOWLEDGEMENTS

My thanks to Jack Smith and to Kate Kort for being first readers of this novel in draft form. Their insightful suggestions for revision went a long way towards making this book publishable. Thanks also to the astute editors at Black Opal, who helped me take *Saving St. Teresa* the rest of the way to its present form.

Saving

St. Teresa

Joe Benevento

A Black Opal Books Publication

GENRE: CHRISTIAN/MYSTERY-DETECTIVE/THRILLER

DEDICATION

To all my friends and family from the old neighborhood, particularly those who remember me as an adolescent, trying to entertain them with scary stories I had made up, as we sat many a summer night on one or another of the stoops of 130th Street in Queens.

"I saw in his hand a long spear of gold, and at the iron's point there seemed to be a little fire. He appeared to me to be thrusting it at times into my heart, and to pierce my very entrails; when he drew it out, he seemed to draw them out also, and to leave me all on fire with a great love of God. The pain was so great, that it made me moan; and yet so surpassing was the sweetness of this excessive pain, that I could not wish to be rid of it."

~ *Autobiography of Saint Teresa of Avila*

"Lord, either let me suffer or let me die."

~ *The motto of Saint Teresa of Avila*

Chapter 1

The slippery white silk of Faith Covington's camisole was close to disappearing under the dark blue dress she had laid out on her bed when Tony Cupelli entered the room. As he approached, Faith needed no words to understand what Tony wanted. She accepted his embrace but then pulled away.

"Not now, Tony. It's almost time to get to Graham."

"Well, maybe if we took the car instead of walking?"

"The walk will be good for you, for all the usual reasons, but also to clear your head before the debate," Faith said with confidence, inviting no further argument.

"That's just it, though. I'm pretty nervous about all this. I'm not sure a walk is going to work. But love, that's good for about any situation, don't you think?" Tony's tone was playful, though maybe already colored with a touch of resignation.

"Love is 'a pure, divine affinity,'" Faith quoted, "not a release for physical tension. And I thought we were making progress."

"Progress?" Tony asked, even as he thought of how

nicely Faith's stylishly short, light-brown hair framed her near perfect face and large gold-green eyes. "Not taking time out for love is progress? How? It's not like we're a married couple, right?" Tony joked, even as he realized how little his humor had a chance of working. Still, life-long habits were hard to forsake so he continued. "I mean, 'pure, divine affinity' is fine when you're alone in a cabin and it's too cold to walk to Concord anyway. But, let's face it, the one flaw in Henry David's program is his preference for solitude. I mean, he was like the Transcen-dentalist Garbo. Only an occasional squirrel ever snug-gled in his cabin at night, not a woman like you."

"This is no time to debate Thoreau," Faith said with a half-smile that seemed almost involuntary, like a moth-er amused more than she should be by her child's antics.

An assistant art professor at Smith College, Faith was a teacher and potter by profession, but also an ardent, if eclectic, eco-feminist. Tony understood how she saw herself as a virtual disciple of Thoreau, whose chapter on "Higher Laws" from *Walden* she took as a central verse in her personal bible culled from all the important spiritu-al teachings of the world—our progress in life was ever away from the gross appetites and onto the wholly spir-itual ones.

That her potential soul mate and sporadic lover of the last several months would both joke about and question one of the great books of American literature should have made her upset. Instead, she settled for ending the con-versation with another chaste kiss and the definitive movement of her dark blue dress off the bed and onto her body.

He laughed. "Okay, but if I freeze up on stage, it'll be your fault."

"You'll find some heat once you're on stage fighting that fascist Monsignor Heamey. You'll channel all that desire into defeating sexism. I can't wait to see you return to the field. There will be plenty of time to celebrate later," Faith promised as her eyes flashed with real conviction.

It was a cool, early November night in Northampton, with a frost warning in place for the hours approaching dawn. It was a bit over a mile from Faith's apartment to the Brown Fine Arts Center on the Smith campus. Since she and Tony had begun dating in June, Faith had pushed him to find more ways to fit exercise into his daily routine, even as she encouraged him to begin the process of detoxification that would come from the eventual abandonment of meat, processed sugar, alcohol, caffeine, and most of Tony's other oldest and closest culinary companions. So far, he was making more progress with exercise than with diet, but Faith still seemed optimistic for the long term. He had gotten back down to one hundred and ninety pounds on his six foot, two inch frame, or four pounds lost for each month with Faith. He joked that if they stayed together long enough, he would disappear. Tony walked alongside Faith's brisk pace with all the energy of a former athlete not ready to admit he was well past his prime, though sixteen years his companion's senior, at forty eight.

When Faith and Tony reached their destination, they were happy to have a difficult time getting past the stream of an arriving audience even larger than their expectations. Monsignor Martin Heamey was already near the podium. He was talking intently with Tony's boss and friend since high school, Henry "Hank" Gallagher, a large balding man with light blue eyes and a dark gray suit. A Renaissance scholar and, for the past five years, the English department chair, Henry was a consummate politician. This explained how he could be a mostly popular male chair within a department where the majori-

ty of his colleagues were not only females, but ardent
feminists. While some of Hank's published writings nodded with respect toward contemporary feminist interpretations and criticisms of the church during the Renaissance, his Irish-Catholic background seemed to make him
equally comfortable handling Heamey. Next to Dr. Gallagher, Tony spotted other colleagues, including a large
contingent from the Religion Department at Smith. He
focused more on the one woman among the faculty he
didn't recognize, but before he could ask anyone about
her, Faith ran up and embraced her.

"Oh, Veronica, I'm so glad you made it."

"Well, of course, Faith, I told you I would. And is
this the infamous Antonio Cupelli?"

"How do you mean?" Tony asked. "Have you been
reading my books or has Faith been talking 'out of
school,' so to speak?"

While Faith gave Tony an eye roll, her friend's laugh
seemed genuine.

"Your books. I've read all your books, actually. I've
even taught the one on the Holy Spirit," she informed
Tony in a voice with a slight, perhaps Mediterranean lilt
he could not identify more specifically. "I'm Veronica
Teuma, I teach in the Religious Studies program at Holy
Cross. Faith was my student when I was at Brown."

With that introduction, Professor Teuma reached out
to shake Tony hand. He noted her hand's warmth and the
pleasant firmness of her grip, something he missed
among most academics. Veronica seemed to radiate a
confidence connected to some internal reservoir of calm
conviction. And her eyes' darkness seemed belied by
their steady suffusion of light.

"Teuma, Teuma, at Brown? Yes, you've done what I
thought were really fair reviews of my last two books.
It's nice to meet you." Tony smiled. He felt immediately

comfortable with Veronica, comfortable enough to ask her a potentially troublesome question. "But why leave the Ivy League for Worcester?"

"I wanted to be someplace where I didn't have to apologize for my Catholicism." As Veronica responded, she lightly fingered a thin, string necklace whose pendant was hidden from view in her black sweater. For just a moment, her dark sweater and modest black skirt gave Tony the impression of a beautiful nun. Her hair was also dark, almost black, and just lightly touched with gray, but Tony guessed her to be at least a few years younger than he. She was not quite as slender as Faith and was a few inches shorter at about five feet, five inches tall, but Tony found her every bit as beautiful as he listened to her add, "I'm anxious to see how you and the monsignor will handle that here at Smith."

"Tony's no longer a practicing Catholic," Faith assured her friend.

Veronica looked a little disappointed, both at the news and the level of proprietary smugness with which it was delivered. But there was no time to continue the conversation.

The debate topic was simple and twofold: whether women should ever be allowed to be Roman Catholic priests and whether both men and women priests should be able to marry. Faith had done most of the leg work to bring Heamey to campus, so Tony could debate with the monsignor on the merits of his controversial tome, *A Better Role for Women,* which one Catholic feminist critic had proclaimed "set back women's progress in the Catholic Church to before Vatican II." The book had been written in almost direct response to Tony's best-selling title of three years before, *The Holy Spirit: Restoring Respect To the Sacred Feminine.*

At Smith, an all-female college and one of the original "Seven Sisters" of higher education for women in America, Heamey, a Jesuit and professor at Loyola in Chicago, had to know the deck was more than stacked against him. Still Heamey had eagerly accepted the invitation, so eagerly that Faith had voiced to Tony her fear the priest might have some secret method to crumple women's rights both within and outside the church, even within the halls of a Seven Sisters school.

Monsignor Heamey looked typecast from any number of old movies featuring an Irish Catholic priest. He had cottony white hair and plenty of it; blue, only slightly bloodshot eyes; and a commanding overall presence in spite of being a half foot shorter than Tony. What Heamey lacked in literal stature he made up for with a brassy tenor voice and a readiness for combat that did his Jesuit roots proud.

"If it isn't the former Monsignor Antonio Cupelli himself."

Heamey bowed, thereby grabbing an immediate tactical advantage by reminding anyone within earshot that Tony was a fallen soldier. He had been permanently suspended from the priesthood, due not to his ultra-liberal church politics, but for his relations with women. Tony had even been a suspect in the murder of his long time secret lover, Maggie Rosario. Though he had been completely cleared of that killing, the ensuing scandal had left him shamed, guilt-ridden, and unable to continue his work for women's rights within the church. Only three years past Maggie's death, Tony was actually taking to the podium for the first time since and had hoped Heamey would be unwilling to open old wounds.

Tony nodded. "Yes, it's good finally to meet you, Monsignor. I appreciate your taking the time to visit with us."

During the debate itself, Heamey took a higher road,

sticking to a presentation of the Catholic Church's traditional positions with vigor and conviction, despite the clearly unsympathetic attention of his audience.

"Of course, if Christ had intended for women to represent him as priests, he would have named women among his twelve apostles. Professor Cupelli rightly points out that women did have a role, a meaningful role in Jesus's life. There were his friends Martha and Mary for example. Even more to the point, Mary Magdalene, who far from the reformed prostitute some mistakenly depict her as, was instead a close friend and an even more faithful follower than those flawed men. So, yes, one might even call her a female 'disciple' without inaccuracy, but she was not one of the twelve specifically called upon to come and follow Christ. Christ's intentions seem clear. He sees a different, though not lesser, role for women in the church to be. I—"

"But, Monsignor." Tony could not stop himself from interrupting his opponent, as his old fervor for righting injustices against women within the church came back to him in full force. "Judas was one of the twelve, so clearly, there is nothing inherently good or priestly in being one of the first chosen. Beyond that, one has to take into account the times Christ lived in and the culture he inhabited. Women are not in the same place in the social scale that they were back in the days of Christ. This 'separate but equal' claim you are trying to sell to this audience, this 'different role,' makes no better sense than it did for African Americans in the pre-Civil Rights south."

Heamey shook his head and cast his blue eyes around the room. "It's clear to me that too many of you in this room want easy answers to difficult questions. But the Catholic Church seeks answers that are not restricted or defined by present politics or fads. Christ selected twelve men, in a purposeful, meaningful way. Unlike

Christ, they were flawed men, even as we of the present priesthood are flawed. It has never been the Church's intent to even imply that men are better suited for the priesthood because they are better than women. When John Paul II reiterated the church's position on the impossibility of a female priesthood, he affirmed the dignity and absolute equality of women in the Church's eyes. He pointed out the simple and clear fact that Christ, who had his own perfect mother and a future saint in Mary Magdalen to choose from, clearly decided not to choose a woman for a priestly role. As unpopular as that must be in this room, in this place, it's the simple truth."

Tony tried to stay calm. "Please, Monsignor, it's the truth as promulgated by men for men. Recent scholarship has unearthed how the gospels that made it into the contemporary Christian bible were chosen, making it clear to anyone who looks at things objectively that if Christ had chosen Mary Magdalene or one of his other female followers as an apostle, the men who decided what would remain from Christ's life for us to read about, could have easily suppressed those choices, even as the early men of the church ignored the female nature of the Holy Spirit, ignored Christ's use of the feminine word *ruach* for the Spirit, his references to the Holy Spirit as she, just so they could displace the feminine from a share in the Triune Deity. Since we know that to be true, we can easily surmise they must have picked and chosen that recounting of the events of Christ's life, which set before us a false image of his selection of men only for the holy priesthood."

Tony scored applause with this remark, but Heamey pressed on. "If you're going to question the veracity of Holy Scripture, than there's little point really left for us in common to debate about. As a former priest yourself, surely you understand that the Catholic Church believes in the New Testament as the Gospel, the good news from God himself."

"Monsignor, surely you can't be suggesting that anyone who advocates women's rights is going against God?" Tony asked. He was beginning to feel uneasy over his overwhelming advantage in the sympathy level for his point of view within the increasingly vocal audience.

"No one who works for the good of his neighbor is in danger of going against God," Heamey responded with the first hints of anger in his voice.

"But why then do you and the Catholic Church support such inequitable treatment of your female 'neighbors'? Tony challenged.

"I assumed, Professor, that you had actually read my book, as I have carefully read and reread yours. My support of women is clear throughout those pages, my admiration, for instance, of the leading female doctors of the church, most especially St. Teresa of Avila. And I admit injustice and inequity in the church regarding women over the years. I'm not one who tries to underplay the many errors men have made. Still, there is no getting around Christ's clear preferences. As Pope John Paul made clear, as so many others before and after him make clear, we have no choice in the matter—we cannot disregard the Lord's own will on this issue."

"Where in the New Testament does Christ insist that no woman can ever be a priest?" Tony demanded. "What is a priest, anyway? I have huge doubts that Christ ever would have conceived of the priesthood at all the way the Catholic Church has configured it. And if we're going to debate those preferences further, can you show me where in the New Testament it shows Christ advocating a celibate clergy? With a female priesthood, you at least have the apparent proof in the New Testament that all of the original twelve Apostles were men. But on what Biblical basis can you support celibacy? How can you possibly invoke Christ's will on the matter, since the Roman Catholic Church is presently letting in married Episcopalian priests? You can't have it both ways. If Christ is against a married clergy, show us where, if that is the word of the Lord that cannot be undone, let us see it for ourselves. But then please explain why, in certain special and convenient circumstances, you are now allowing some relatively few Roman Catholic priests to be married?"

"I never maintained a celibate clergy as the will of God, so I don't have to defend that argument," Heamey insisted. "As to maintaining a celibate clergy, certainly I'll agree there is nothing inherently wrong with a married priest. We both know that priests were often married within the very early church, but there are sensible, clearcut reasons why celibacy is worth maintaining. These arguments are, again, clearly not indictments against women, but instead come from a sincere conviction that celibacy is, in itself, a noble calling, one which both men and women are invited to within the church. The church recognizes and values the married life, but also the celibate life, one which is best for those who want to serve God most directly. No one who loves a wife or a husband or his or her own children aptly can model love for all equally the way a true celibate can. I—"

Tony again interrupted his opponent, his own enthusiasm temporarily getting the best of his courtesy. "Wait, Monsignor, the church's reticence regarding sex is well established and based on its fear of women and of sexuality. Women are depicted throughout the early Church as temptresses, taking men away from devotion to God. Sex is tolerated, at best, as a necessary evil for procreation. It's no coincidence that the Catholic Church not only insists that Christ had to come from a Virgin birth, but that

Mary remained a virgin throughout her life. This deep-seated bias against women is what drives celibacy. Priests can show their purity by resisting women's snares and nuns can show their shame in their sexuality by covering themselves up and never tempting anyone. It's a design flaw in the whole fabric of the church, not a higher calling."

The audience applauded Tony loudly, as they had more and more throughout the debate. When Monsignor Heamey sought to respond, they even began to boo him, until Tony strongly signaled them to be quiet.

"I never called celibacy a higher calling. Though you scoff at the idea of 'separate but equal,' I'm saying there is a truth there regarding this topic. It is equally important to have literal and spiritual fathers and mothers. Each is too important, too all-consuming a role, in the Catholic Church's view, to be attempted by the same person. As to your remarks regarding the Church's attitude toward sex, I'd counter that contemporary cultural mores, which make sex a cynical thing and allow the procreative function to be aborted at will, are the very kinds of things the Church is proud to stand up against, no matter how unpopular it may be to most of you."

Monsignor Heamey's remarks drew more boos from the audience. He tried to ignore them, looked for Tony to help him, then waited another beat before shaking his head again, and continuing. "I don't mind losing a debate, but it's the hardening of your hearts, the willful misreading of what is sacred that troubles me, that makes me wish I was more eloquent to take you all to a better, more generous place."

"Monsignor Heamey, I don't think you suffer at all from a lack of eloquence. I really believe it's the church's inflexibility that is ruining its chances to reach any really sensible person. The archaic rule of celibacy came close to ruining my own life, but it's the lives of those still within its grip I'm worried about. The church has to stop condemning reasoning adults from making decisions based on their own moral compasses rather than tired dogma."

The applause got louder as did the subsequent cat calling when Heamey tried to counter. Tony waited longer than he should have to calm the audience down. Martin Heamey looked at him too much like a Judas for Tony not to recognize how much he was letting his fervor for the cause knock out his normal preference for fairness.

"I'm afraid we are making a mockery of debate. No fair exchange of ideas is possible in this atmosphere," Heamey said as he literally threw up his hands in resignation. "There are only two great commandments—love God completely and love your neighbor, all your neighbors, even old priests, I might add, as yourself. Nothing else really matters. And I will pray for you all, as I wish you would be willing to pray for me."

Heamey's last lines caused a loud chorus of boos, hisses, and exclamations to emerge from the overflowing crowd. Tony this time made an immediate effort to quiet down the crowd, but it was pointless. Monsignor Heamey had walked off the podium and hurried away toward the exit. No one tried to get in his way.

Tony sat down at his seat by the podium, feeling far more shame than triumph. Faith struggled through the milling, energized crowd and grabbed tightly onto his hand.

"You beat him, Tony, completely. He had nothing— that's why he fled."

"Did he flee or did he just abandon us in despair?"

"That's crazy. You can be a force again—you beat their best. He ran from you, from the truth. Oh, Tony, I'm so proud."

Tony felt the fervor of Faith's pride in him through the firmness of her continued hold on his hand. After her approach, many others followed, all expressing their disappointment in Monsignor Heamey. Eventually, Hank had his turn with his old friend.

"See what happens when we try to bring in the other point of view? That was crazy. Next time let's forget the controversy and bring in someone the students can relate to." Hank offered, even as he patted Tony's shoulder and his blue eyes twinkled with a seeming appreciation for his friend's victory.

"Maybe Veronica would honor us," Faith offered as she saw her friend approach the podium.

"I'd be happy to give a talk here, but I'll leave the debating to you competitive sorts," Veronica said. "Really, I'm worried about Monsignor Heamey. That just wasn't like him. He really seemed...I don't know...just so troubled."

"You know him, Veronica?" Faith seemed surprised.

"Yes, a little. As a matter of fact, we've been in correspondence lately regarding St. Teresa. She's someone I've written about and he's wanted to talk with me about some of the finer points of *The Interior Castle,* particularly."

"Well, I don't think he'll be attaining the seventh level any time soon," Faith joked, showing off her familiarity with the text in question.

Tony, though getting the joke, was in an unusually unfunny mood.

The reception that followed in the adjoining room was far more animated and engaged than dozens of crab puffs, mini cheesecakes, and other appetizers otherwise would have warranted. Tony soon grew weary of all the approbation and longed to get away from any form of celebration. When he and Faith did make it back to her apartment, after walking through a light drizzle that was contemplating sleet, they were only inside a few minutes when the opening lines of the old Spanish love song, "Solamente Una Vez," signaled a call on Tony's cell phone.

"Tony, Tony I'm glad I caught you," Hank cried.

"Hank? What's the matter? You sound strange."

"Something terrible has happened."

"Terrible? What do you mean, I—"

"I tried calling up Heamey, make sure everything was okay, you know. He was staying just over at the Autumn Inn so—"

"Oh, no. Is he sick or something? Veronica Teuma said he was acting strange and—"

"No, no, Tony, you don't understand. He didn't answer, but the clerk was sure she saw him go into his room. You know it's a small place, so when he didn't answer again, as a favor to me, she went to knock on his door, but, but they found him—he, he was dead."

"Dead, dead? Oh my God! What, what happened? I mean, did he have a stroke or something? Oh, God, do you think it was the debate?"

"The debate? No, of course not. But, it wasn't any stroke. He's been murdered!" Hank shouted.

"Murdered?" Tony gasped. "How can that be? Oh, my God." He paused to hear more details, but when Hank hesitated he continued. "How are they sure it's murder? Was he shot or something?"

"No, nothing like that, no blood, but—"

"But what?" Tony shot back. "How do you know it wasn't just a heart attack?"

"Well, because they're telling me it looks like he was strangled," Hank reported in a voice as unlike his normal, calm, kidding tone as conceivable.

"Who told you this? How can they know?"

"The clerk told me, right before she called for the police. She was hysterical, of course, but she told me he had a set of rosary beads wrapped around his neck."

"Oh my God," was all Tony could offer.

"Oh my God is right. The monsignor's been murdered, practically on our campus."

Tony dropped his cell phone to the floor. Tears welled in his eyes as he worried, suffused with guilt, over how much his uncharitable part in Monsignor Heamey's last debate had had in inviting this murdering rage.

Chapter 2

So what the hell have you gotten yourself into this time?"

Tony couldn't believe who entered his office at Smith the following Monday, just moments after his American Romanticism seminar. Or, rather, he could believe it, but he didn't want to.

"What are you even doing here, Mike? I knew you were homicide now, but, in case you hadn't noticed, this isn't New York."

"Mom wanted me to check on how you were holding up. The papers, even in far off NYC, are having a field day with this latest mess of yours. 'Disgraced Monsignor Questioned in New Murder.' You know, just the kind of thing that an invalid in her 80s needs to start her day off with."

"That's awful, after all I've put Mom and Dad through already. But I've told the police and reporters all I know. *The Daily News* knows there's no story here, but when did that ever stop them? Plus, I feel terrible about the poor man being killed, and especially after coming here to debate me. But I don't know any more about who might have killed him than you do."

Mike Cupelli nodded impatiently at his brother's words and did not wait for Tony to offer him a seat. He chose a chair positioned at a strategic distance and angle from his brother's, a chair normally meant for student-teacher conferences.

"How come you get the soft swivel job and your students have to sit on this hard metal number?" Mike chuckled. "So you can wheel closer and they can't move away? You gettin' any co-ed action, Romeo?"

"They're not 'coeds' here. This is Smith," Tony corrected, as he fell into his normal give and take with his sibling. "There are no Eds at all, only Ednas."

As if on cue, a young woman, blonde, with confident blue eyes, walked into the office, then did an old-fashioned double-take when she noticed the man sitting in the seat next to Tony. Her surprise must have come from how much this stranger resembled her professor—the same large, very dark brown eyes, black hair streaked with gray, neatly trimmed salt and pepper beard, and the same aquiline nose. Hearing the stranger speak, however, she had no trouble distinguishing who was who.

"Hey, am I interrupting something?" Mike asked her, with a slight exaggeration of his working-class Queens accent. "You two got some, whaddayacallit, 'conferencing' to do?"

"Dr. Cupelli, I just, well," the student stumbled, in the face of this intruder, "It's my regular work-study hour, I was just—"

"Sorry, Nicole. I wish I had had time to text you. I'm afraid we'll have to cancel for today. My brother just surprised me with a visit. Come by tomorrow and I'm sure I'll be back on my regular schedule."

"Don't be too sure, brother," Mike countered.

But Tony refused to engage in more repartee in front of his student.

The young woman kept her eyes solely on her mentor, but then snuck a look toward his seeming doppelganger before heading out of the office without speaking another syllable.

"So why didn't you introduce me? You ashamed of your roots?"

"Listen, I know you can never resist giving me hell, but there's no need to get poor Nicole in the middle of that—she's a nice kid. And I still don't understand why you drove all the way up from Queens. You never heard of the telephone?"

"Listen, man, I just got into town and figured I'd find you here. We need to talk—there are things you need to know about."

"Things? What things?"

"We can't talk here. Who knows who will show up next? You got room for me at your place the next few days? Or do I need to find a motel?"

Tony wheeled his swivel chair right up to his brother's seat, put his right arm around the detective's shoulders, and said in his best imitation-sincere voice. "Mikey, it's so good to know you care. Maybe I could just take a week off from classes and we could tour New England together."

Instead of pushing his brother away, Mike put his own face even closer to his just younger brother's, as if he were about to kiss him, before deadpanning his reply. "That would be sweet, but I think I'd rather stay here and get a start on solving a pair of murders. And, as much as it pains me to admit it," he continued, but not before kicking his brother's chair so that it, and his brother, both wheeled off away from him. "I need your help."

"What pair of murders? Somebody else has been

killed? This is awful. But how could I possibly help you, Mike, I mean really, I—"

"All in good time, Professor," Mike interrupted, as he idly fingered the copy of Borges's *Ficciones* that was ever present on his brother's desk alongside a green leather bound edition of *Leaves of Grass.* "I told ya, I ain't talking here. The less anyone else knows about this for now, the better. Am I staying with you or what?"

Tony saw how serious his brother really was, read past the usual edgy humor and sarcasm, and knew there could be only one response.

"*Mi casa es tu casa, hermano.*"

"Yeah, I doubt that, but thanks. I'll meet you there after your work day's over, which is when?"

"Actually I'm done with classes for today, but I do have a meeting at three, so let's make it 4:30."

"It's not even noon and you're done with classes? This is an even softer gig than being a priest was." Mike shook his head. "Pizza any good around here?"

"No, not up to NY standards. I'll take care of dinner. And you can stay as long as you want, but I still can't see what I can help you with that would take days."

"You let me worry about that, ace. It'll all be a lot clearer when I have time to explain."

"Explain what? C'mon, man, I—"

"Make something nice," Mike interrupted, as he got up to leave, before adding, with a final leer. "One thing you could always do was cook."

Tony had a fairly spacious, two-bedroom apartment just six miles from the Smith campus, in the subdivision of Mill Valley Estates. He preferred to have the bit of privacy not being in walking distance of campus afforded, and his previous success as an author and present gig as a professor made him well able to afford the $1,650-per-month price tag. His brother seemed impressed, though he acted a lot more interested in Faith, who insisted on making it three for dinner. Tony wasn't happy about her decision, but he knew it was useless to try to dissuade her once she had made one.

The first thing Faith's inclusion complicated was what to make for dinner. Tony knew what Mike would enjoy—a steak, or maybe a nice piece of veal, marsala, piccata, scallopine, or parmigiana. Mike would be more than okay with any of those choices.

But since Faith was a vegan, meat and cheese were both out, and that saddened Tony, not only because he still held to the code that a guest, even, or maybe especially an annoying brother, should always be offered the best you could provide, but also because he too was looking forward to a retro night where he could eat the flesh of a cow, old or young, without recrimination. Instead, he settled for falafel with pita bread and all the trimmings, the feta cheese an option Faith could pass on. He knew Mike would mock him, but he didn't see a way around it. He just hoped his two guests wouldn't be at each other's throats before they could even fill them with food.

Dinner was only the first of the surprises the night would hold. Faith came to dinner more dressed up than he'd ever seen her for a midweek meal at his home in a tastefully elegant yet revealing black dress. Tony didn't have to guess how much Mike approved of that choice, but he was close to shocked to discover that Faith found his older brother, scruffy in an old Jets green and black sweatshirt and faded jeans, more intriguing than exasperating. She encouraged Mike to share stories from the old neighborhood, particularly ones in which Tony played a less than heroic role. She even seemed to be flirting a little with the detective lieutenant, often rolling her gold-green eyes at Tony's defensive remarks, but opening them wide to whatever Mike offered, as if the better to take in every syllable. She even poked fun at what she considered the "odd décor" of Tony's apartment—the mismatched, outdated, furniture and the signed, framed photos of Groucho Marx and of Willis Reed.

To which Mike simply responded, "Yeah, you don't know the half of it. The truth is, he's always thought of himself as some odd combo of those two—a sharp and funny guy with a post game and a soft jumper."

As Tony was removing the dinner dishes, without help, to make room for dessert, he could no longer contain his curiosity.

"I'm glad you two are hitting it off so well. Mike, I know, never saw a pretty face he wouldn't try to make, but, Faith, what exactly is it you find so charming about the lieutenant here?"

"Oh, I'm sure he has the politics of a caveman, but one rarely meets anyone in academia so honest, so comfortable in his own skin."

"Yeah, I'm plenty comfortable." Mike laughed, as he made a gesture to loosen his belt. "Plus, she must think I'm good-looking, since you look so much like me."

Tony laughed. "Yes, there's that."

"You're not complaining, right?" Mike asked. "I mean would you like it better if we weren't getting along? I thought at first maybe you cooked up this fried chick-pea slop just to bug me, but it was a hell of a lot better than I ever would have guessed."

"You never had falafel before?" Faith marveled.

"Only garbanzos I ever ate before were in 'pasta fazol.' That's poor people's food, though, and I'm guessing you never had any."

"Actually, Tony's made it for me more than once. It's vegan friendly."

"Yeah, yeah, me too." Mike laughed again, while Tony set the dessert bowls down on the table.

Tony knew the only dessert Faith ever ate was fruit, since processed sugar was just as big an enemy to good health as a hamburger. But in November in New England, few fruits were in season, and Faith also objected to eating produce not locally grown. For her, then, Tony only had some spiced apple sauce. For himself and his brother he had whipped together a zabaglione, something that had been a Cupelli favorite for all their years in Queens. As he served only two portions, Faith protested.

"Well, aren't you forgetting someone?"

"Oh, well, you can't have this."

"Whaddaya mean can't have? Give the girl some custard," Mike goaded.

"I don't mean she 'can't' have any—it's just not vegan, is all."

"Oh, yes, I know, but it looks too good to pass up," Faith reported, before reaching for the bowl with the custard and serving herself a healthy portion. "I guess maybe you're a bad influence on me, Michael." She laughed as she once again looked toward Tony's brother.

"That depends on what you mean by bad," he countered. "This zabaglione, it ain't bad at all."

Faith finally seemed to have had her fill, in most regards, a little after ten, making the inevitable notice of it being a "school night," as her ready excuse for departure. Tony made a gesture toward loading the dishwasher, but then placed the three dessert dishes back onto the table and turned to his brother, sitting smugly at that same table. "So that went a lot better than I ever would have guessed. Maybe even too well," Tony observed, recalling other times the two brothers had vied for the same woman.

"What? Can I help it if I'm irresistible? But, hey, don't worry, she ain't my type."

"Yeah, but what if you're hers? Faith is used to getting what she wants."

"You don't think she really liked me, do ya? If she did, it was like when you go to a movie so bad that it's good. That's probably what just happened here, I was her bad movie."

"Now you're beating up on yourself? This really has been a strange night."

"Me, brother, I've got no illusions. Now, you on the other hand,"

"Oh, now here it comes, I—"

"Listen, no offense, really," Mike interrupted, "but how can you even think to, not only go out with a girl that young, but then let her tell you what you should make for dinner in your own house?"

"I chose the menu myself. But why shouldn't I respect Faith's requirements?"

"Hey, believe it or not, I'm all for respecting women, but you can't make yourself into someone else just to please one of them. That just ain't gonna work. I mean this vegan stuff—it just ain't really you. I can tell this girl ain't shifting over to our side anytime soon."

"How do you know what's best for me, how—"

"Aw, come off it, I'm your brother, right? You gonna tell me you wouldn't rather have had a steak or something tonight? You telling me if you stick with this girl you're never gonna eat a meatball again? I mean, if she don't want to eat meat or fish or butter or eggs, that's her business, but how are you gonna stay happy pretending it's all okay with you? Besides, this whole vegan kick is just another way to feel superior to the rest of us, like—"

"Man, that's not fair, Faith isn't like that, she—" Tony tried to interrupt, but Mike kept going,

"—like being a well-off, high IQ, gorgeous WASP wasn't enough for her. Don't get me wrong. I kinda liked

her somehow. She's quick, but, really, she just ain't for
you, man. That's just not who you are."

"Listen, I care for and about Faith and she cares
about me. Everything I'm aiming toward, like eating
more healthy, it's all for the best. Maybe people can
change more than you think."

"That would be nice, but it's why or who they're trying to change for that makes the difference."

"I don't expect you to understand. And anyway, I'm
beat. I'm going to bed. I actually have a 9 o'clock class
tomorrow."

"Nah, man, that's where you're wrong again. You
can't go to bed yet," Mike assured his brother, as he left
the room for a moment, only to return with a file folder
marked, "Jesuit-Carmelite Case."

"What's that?" Tony couldn't help but be curious.

"It's why you and me are staying up a while," Mike
said, as he sat back down at the kitchen table. "Somebody's life might depend on it."

Chapter 3

So what's this all about?" Tony wondered, even as he moved aside a number of canisters from an upper shelf in his kitchen to uncover a small bottle of grappa. He set the bottle on the round, maple-wood kitchen table, along with two small glasses.

Mike laughed. "Hey, a little late for an after dinner drink, no?"

"Faith thinks I should stop drinking altogether, so I wasn't going to offer you any with her around."

"But now that the boss is away—"

"I guess you're just a bad influence on me, Michael," Tony smirked as he sat back down. "What's this folder about already? And the 'pair' of murders?"

"A couple a months ago we had a weird case back in New York, a young Carmelite nun committed suicide, poisoned herself, over at the convent in Brooklyn. It made the papers. You heard about it?"

"Yes, I did see that. That was really sad, but it was a suicide, wasn't it?"

"That's still what we're calling it, officially. But I've got my doubts, especially now."

"Especially why?" Tony wondered, as he took a small sip of brandy.

"Statistically speaking, nuns are way low on your high-risk professions for suicide. So I had my doubts from the start, even though there was a signed suicide note."

"Why doubt it then?"

"The note was typed except for the signature, and it isn't that hard to forge a signature, which was a little uneven at that, like she had a bad pen. Then there was the note itself claiming an overwhelming sense of shame. But from what little we could get from the other nuns in the cloister, that didn't seem to match up with the Sister Maria Dolores they knew."

Tony reached for the short, fat bottle of brandy and poured himself another shot. "Well, that's not a lot to go on, but if she was murdered, of course, I hope you find out who did it and catch them. But I still don't see what it could have to do with anything I could help with."

"This is the good stuff," Mike approved, as he reached his glass over for his brother to refill. "Anyway, when I got wind of this Jesuit getting murdered here, and they started mentioning your name—"

"But, like I told you, I'm not involved. I—"

"Shut-up already and listen. I know you're no killer. I knew that the other time, even when you thought I suspected you. The thing I remembered from the last time, though, was when we were trying out all the angles and you said that the Carmelites and the Jesuits had had some famous feuds over the years, and now we've got a questionable suicide of a Carmelite nun and an unquestioned murder of a Jesuit priest, so—"

"There's been no feud between those orders for centuries now. You're really reaching. For this you've had me worrying all day? I—"

"Just keep listening a little more. Sure it could just be a coincidence, but when I made a few phone calls to the locals here, when I found out about the scapular thing—I mean, it was the same brown one that—"

"What scapular thing?"

"Oh, yeah, well the nun, Sister Maria Dolores, she died clutching a brown scapular and the priest, he had the same kind, the brown one, on him when he died."

Mike then reached in his pocket and produced a brown scapular, with the familiar image of Mary, hanging from brown cord that was thicker than on most Tony had seen before.

"Well that just blows your theory before you even get started," Tony decided, as he fingered the thickness of the cord. "The brown scapular is for Our Lady of Mt. Carmel. It's the one all the Carmelites wear. So if Monsignor Heamey had on one like this, it shows he's friendly to the Carmelites, not opposed to them."

"Yeah, except he had the image of Our Lady of Mt. Carmel practically over his mouth when the police got there. I guess they didn't share that info with you though, huh? You like symbols, right? Maybe it was a sign he was being shut up and—"

"So you're thinking some nun uncloistered herself long enough to get revenge on one of the big shot Jesuits in retaliation for his *boys* taking out one of her own? This isn't the Mafia or the Jets and the Sharks—this is the priests and the nuns."

Tony's tone seemed to rankle Mike more than Tony would have guessed possible.

"Hey, I know it sounds weird, but weren't you mixed up in a multiple murder case over some weird church stuff? You're saying crazy shit only happens to you?

Who the hell else would have motive to silence some priest and take him out with rosary beads, of all things? And those were brown too, by the way, with unusually heavy beads and cord. Did you know the cops here assumed those beads were Heamey's, but now his priest buddies are saying he didn't own a pair like that? It's at least something to consider. Maybe the scapular wasn't his either, maybe—"

"Okay, sure, crazy things happen. But even if the one in Brooklyn is a murder, you're not showing me anything that proves the two cases are related."

"Yeah, but you're already giving me stuff I didn't know and that's why I'm here."

"What are you talking about?"

"First of all, the nun had her scapular outside of her clothes and people usually wear them inside, right? Next, if the brown one is, like, the Carmelites thing, don't you think it's a little more suspicious that the scapular and rosary on the priest were the brown ones? Especially, if I tell you, that like any good Irishman, he preferred, so they tell me, the green Scapular of Mary, the Immaculate Heart one?"

"Well, yeah, I guess that's a little odd," Tony conceded. "And I see you've already done a little research, but, still, it's not really enough to cause any real suspicion, is it? I mean, you don't have much yet, do you?"

"Again, man, that's why I'm here. There's a lot of things I don't know yet, but if there is a religious angle here, it would be a lot easier for me to piece it together if you helped, since you know way more about this stuff than I ever will."

Tony paused in the middle of what would have been his next line of rebuttal as what his brother had just said registered with him. Mike was actually asking for his younger brother's help, he was acknowledging Tony's expertise, he was not questioning, condemning, or ridiculing Tony's behavior.

Even Tony, after a long day and a quick, third shot of grappa, could not entirely ignore this novelty. Still, he wasn't ready to admit to being flattered. "What's your partner Klein think of all this? I see he didn't drag himself over here to badger me."

"Actually, Davey and I aren't working together any more. He requested to be reassigned. Can you believe it? So I'm kinda in between partners, 'indefinitely' is how Captain Rodríguez put it. Besides, there's no official investigation by the NYPD right now. I'm just nosing around on my own dime."

"But, still, Mike, really, what can I do? If you have questions about religious matters I'll try to answer them, but why did you need to come all the way here?"

"I want to do some of my own investigating here first. The locals are okay with it, even cooperating, but then I want you to come back with me to New York."

"New York? Right in the middle of the semester? Why is that?"

Mike looked into his brother's eyes, so much like his own, poured himself a corresponding third shot of brandy before replying. "I want you to use your connections to help me get in to talk to some nuns. You know, the ones who don't normally like to talk much."

Chapter 4

After a two day stay in Northampton, Mike returned to New York by himself. Though he had tried to convince his brother that solving a double murder, one committed by someone who might kill again, mattered a lot more than teaching students about "what a bunch of already dead guys wrote a long time ago," Tony had not been convinced he would be of any real help by giving up campus life to take up the career of an amateur sleuth. Tony knew that Mike wasn't one to give up happily, though, so he wasn't surprised when his brother put their mother on the case.

Rosa Cupelli, well into her eighties, was in constant ill health and getting worse by the week, at least according to Mike's reports. In the three years since the scandals that had removed her son from the priesthood, Tony had only seen her a few times a year—at Christmas and for her birthday in June. These were the only times he visited New York at all, as he tried to put all the shame and notorious publicity behind him. Tony was convinced that Rosa, a deeply religious Catholic, had never fully forgiven her once-favorite monsignor for all that shame. And he was far from convinced he really deserved to be forgiven. His mother's lack of insistence over seeing him more often seemed further proof of her real feelings. But the Sunday before Thanksgiving, Tony received a phone call.

"I want you home this Thursday," Rosa simply informed him.

"Thanks, Mom, but, you know, I'm so busy here this time of the semester, plus I'll see you next month at Christmas, okay?"

"No, it's not okay," Rosa countered, with the same sharp determination she had shown Tony all her life. "I need you here for Thanksgiving. I don't know if your father will make it to Christmas."

"What's wrong with Dad?" Tony's surprise and concern delivered an immediate quavering to his voice.

Angelo Cupelli, near ninety, walked with a cane, had some trouble hearing, and did little by way of diet or exercise to counter his type-two diabetes. But he seemed to go year to year without any really serious distress. Rosa, however, was in and out of the doctor's office frequently, the only time she ever left the house anymore.

"Nothing's wrong, nothing like that, his health's good."

Tony exhaled. "Well, what then, Ma?"

"He misses you," Rosa blurted, "especially on the holidays. He says it's my fault he never sees you. Can you imagine?"

"Mom, everyone knows it's not your fault. I—"

"Everyone but him. You know he'd never tell you himself, but I'm telling you, he misses you. Would it break your heart to come for the day?"

Tony had no excuse with which to counter his mother's request. Faith didn't believe in Thanksgiving, didn't

believe she, much less the whole country, should celebrate a bunch of sanctimonious Puritans—though her
family proudly traced its roots back to that same bunch—
in their beginning endeavors of imperialism and geno-
cide. She was actually planning to fast that day, in a kind
of penance for the sins of her ancestors. Tony had been
trying to figure out a way not to join her without insulting
her sensibilities. This offer from his mother, this overt
proof that his parents still valued his company, was the
best reason possible to pass on Faith's program:

"Okay, Mom, I'll come."

"Good, but none of this in and out like on Christmas.
Spend a few days—there's plenty of room."

"Sure, thanks, Mom, I will. Our last day of class is
Tuesday. I'll come Wednesday, if that's all right."

The familiar drive back to his parents' house, a modest, two-story home in South Ozone Park, a working class
section of Queens, whose other white denizens had fled
decades before, leaving the neighborhood to an eclectic
mix of blacks, Latinos, and, more recently, Asians,
brought back too many memories from Tony's past, including his last years as a monsignor while pastor at
nearby St. Teresa of Avila Church. His parents' house,
with its peeling light green paint on the outside and its
saggy ceilings and outdated paneling on the inside, only
made those bad memories more poignant. Still, his parents and especially his two maiden sisters, Rose Anne
and Beatrice, who lived with them, never took his visits
for granted. He only wished he could undo his past mistakes and feel like he had a full right to their regard.

His father Angelo's greeting felt very much like old
times. "Hey, look, it's *the genius* himself."

He laughed as he warmly shook his son's hand from
his usual post at a corner of the family's dark blue living
room sofa. Tony recalled when that nickname had been

used by his father to mock his lack of anything but book knowledge. Now it felt more like a blessing upon a prodigal son.

"Yeah, well you don't have to be too smart to know enough to get back to Ma's cooking for the holidays. Speaking of which, am I spelling pasta sauce right now?"

"Of course." Rosa nodded, even as she kissed her son as he bent down to her in her special recliner, which had controls to help boost her out of the seat the few times each day she needed to get up. "You know we have had macaroni every Wednesday since before you were born."

"Stuffed shells tonight," Angelo informed him. "Fancy. Anytime one of you kids shows up we always eat better. Now with the two of you here the same day, I'm surprised she didn't make the turkey early."

"One turkey at a time." Mike laughed as he entered the living room from the dining room, where he had been sitting with a few meatballs he had already pilfered from the kitchen.

"Look who's talkin', ya big *caffon'*." Angelo easily shifted to giving Mike his share of the hard time he always had ready for his sons. "Did ya ever see such a pair of *mort' di fams*?"

"Well, nobody's going to go hungry here," daughter Beatrice announced. "Dinner will be ready in a minute."

Of course Tony was not at all surprised that his brother Michael had not waited until Thanksgiving Day to show up at their parents' home. Since his divorce five years before, Mike had no one to question how much time he might spend at his parents' home. But Mike showed no inclination to rush Tony through his meal, stuffed shells being a favorite they held in common, nor even through the crumb cake with Bavarian cream filling his sisters had bought from Stallone's bakery especially for Tony. Still, not five minutes after the family had re-settled in the living room, where they spent almost every night watching network TV, he tapped Tony on the knee. "Hey, whaddaya say we go down in the basement and finally go look at the card collection, figure out if we have anything worth something, and then what belongs to who, okay?"

"I've been telling you boys for years to do that. That's a good idea," Rosa approved. "At least have one less thing down there."

"Just bring them up here and we'll all look at 'em," Angelo suggested, though, as usual, his deep-voiced request had more the sound of a command.

"Okay, sure, we'll do that, Dad," Mike assured him. "Though I guess we could go through some of that other junk while we're at it, huh, Ma?"

"Yeah, that'd be good." Rosa nodded. "Whatever you could take or better yet throw out."

Tony always considered it a kind of pun when his parents' basement was referred to as "half finished." The middle room's floor was covered with a worn, brown linoleum, and the walls with paneling equally tired and brown. But the laundry room before it and the storage space back room had never received those vain attempts at further civilization. Nothing downstairs was new, from the slightly sagging wooden beams, the old pipes and wires, and the stand-up brass lamp that would flicker on and then off again, to the loud freezer, keeping the extra meat and vegetables ready for use, and the old wooden armoire, also brown, which kept musty coats and blankets no one would think to wear or use again. The armoire was covered on its top not only by a thick layer of dust, but by numerous old baseball and basketball trophies, including Tony's high school basketball MVP award from Cathedral Prep. Inside the closet, in the far left hand corner, toward the back, rested an old Pan-Am carry-on bag, alternating white and blue stripes, containing maybe three hundred baseball cards, which Tony began to pull out to examine. In the basement it was at least ten degrees colder than the top two floors, so, on a night when the temperature was below freezing, it was uncomfortably cold for Tony, in spite of a green, heavy, woolen pullover. Mike seemed less bothered, though he wore no sweater, just a red and black flannel shirt, from the pocket of which he withdrew a folded piece of paper.

"Put down Tug McGraw and the rest of those old timers and take a look at something a little more recent."

What Mike handed Tony was a brief, handwritten letter.

> *Dear Sister Maria,*
>
> *I understand your predicament, but I do not understand why you should feel so guilty now, after having made the right decision. Since the time God inspired you to contact me, you have been back on the path of the true faith. Now that you have left the world of the alumbradas, your guilt should be past. I am fully prepared to use the information you have sent me, and once it becomes public, once the secret writings of St. Teresa have been more fully examined, we'll know more clearly how to proceed. I will certainly give you forewarning before I level specific accusations. I'll want to be sure of my footing. At that time we can again discuss the idea of relocation and a fuller opportunity for expiation of your sins. For now, the best advice I can give you is to "Pray unceasingly." I will be in touch again soon.*
>
> *Yours in Christ, Msgr. Martin Heamey, SJ*

"This Sister Maria..." Tony began, though the answer to the question he might have posed was already in his brother's face.

"Yes, it's the same nun, Maria Dolores, the Carmelite here in Brooklyn who supposedly killed herself."

"You still have no real proof she didn't, right?"

"I'm getting there. The fact that she knew Heamey and had a letter from him hidden away in one of her clothes drawers, the fact that they spoke of a need for 'relocating' her, like we do for our star witnesses who are in danger, makes it a hell of a lot more possible, don't you think?"

Tony absently shuffled through a few of the old baseball cards, looked at them, and stifled an involuntary shiver, realizing that each of the three photos of players he had visible from his deck—Tug McGraw, Tommie Agee, and Danny Frisella—all former Mets, were all already dead and gone.

"I guess so."

"You guess so?" Mike snorted. "And can I guess now that you're ready to help me out?"

"Of course, I'd want to help catch someone if he killed some innocent nun, but you don't seriously think I have any pull with anybody around here do you? I was kicked out, remember? How do you imagine I can help you?"

"Stop being so dramatic," Mike responded, with a sweeping upward gesture of his right hand, which inadvertently knocked some of the old baseball cards from his brother's hands. "You can help me plenty. I mean, as it turns out, it wasn't as hard to get in to interview nuns as I thought it would be, so I don't really need you for that, anyway. But I still need you."

"Why?" Tony asked, with a tone that betrayed an increasing level of interest in his brother's reasoning.

"Listen, I just stumbled on to this connection. The only reason I thought the two deaths were linked was because of what you told me once about the Carmelites and Jesuits feuding." Mike arched his eyebrows and aimed them at Tony. "But unless *this* monsignor was a great liar, these two were working together, and they each are dead because of what they were working on."

"Yeah, well, you're the detective. You're the one with the expertise and resources to figure this out, right?" Tony asked as he scooped up the cards that had fallen to the dusty linoleum and then sat down on an old wooden chair.

"But you're the one who knows about this stuff. You're both a priest and a professor. This is your line. I bet you know who these 'alumbradas' are, for example, and can tell me more about them than I could ever get from Wikipedia or the Catholic Encyclopedia, which, by the way, have really different spins on them to begin with. And I'm sure you know more about St. Teresa than I do, and maybe something about what this 'secret writing' of hers could be about. Plus, one of the murders took place on your turf. If it wasn't just some kind of hit man from out of town, maybe there's something going on by you that needs looking into, and I can't be two places at once."

"We have cops in Massachusetts too, I'm pretty sure."

"But none of them know this shit like you do, and none of them want to investigate a double murder when only I'm convinced so far that there's been one. So are you gonna help me or what?"

Before Tony could answer Mike, their sister Beatrice's voice came from the top of the stairs. "Hey, Mom wants to know what's taking you two so long? Did you find the cards?"

"Yeah, yeah, we found them. We'll be up in a minute," Tony assured her. He waited till she returned up to the kitchen before getting up from his seat. "Okay, yes, I'll help. As much as I'd like to believe there's nothing much to this, no double murder, no more murders ahead, I can't shake the feeling that you might be on to something. We'll talk about it later, though. Let's go up now and look at some baseball cards with Dad. I hear he's been missing me."

Mike nodded, almost smiled. "Lead the way, little brother. You can have all the cards, too, if they're worth anything to you. I've got all I wanted from down here already."

Chapter 5

S o the best I can make out, these alumbrados go way back to like the 1500s, and they caused a bunch of trouble with the church till the Inquisition cleaned them out. There was this one nun, Magdalene of the Cross, who had everyone convinced she was some kind of a saint, but once the Inquisition had their little talk with her, she 'confessed' she was in league with the devil, like all her other heretic friends. But what that has to do with a nun and a priest getting wacked this year, I can't begin to figure out."

Mike was explaining the present state of his investigation in between bites of a turkey sandwich and swigs of beer from a slightly battered looking ceramic Jets mug, to his brother, who sat directly across from him at the Cupelli kitchen table, also eating a turkey sandwich, though his brown liquid drink was apple cider and his mug the blue and orange of the Mets instead of the Jets green and white. Like most people, both brothers had overindulged at the Thanksgiving afternoon meal, but still found themselves, a little after eight o'clock in the evening, with room for more. A half-finished chocolate pudding pie rested to their left, awaiting its inevitable demise.

Though only the dining room separated the kitchen from the living room, where the brothers' parents and sisters were congregated, the loudness of the ever engaged television, a concession to Angelo's ever worsening deafness, eliminated any reason to worry about being overheard. Now that all the other company was gone, now that the dishes had been washed and put away, Mike could finally catch his brother up on the case.

"Well, I'm no expert on that time period in the church," Tony began, "but I have always been fascinated by the various heresies, maybe because of my own ideas on the married clergy and female priesthood."

Mike shook his head. "Yeah, a lot a good those ideas did ya, huh?"

"Exactly, so you have to be careful where you get your definitions from. You can't trust those more conservative Catholic websites. You probably noticed they make the Inquisition sound like it was no big deal."

Mike snickered. "Yeah, just some friendly questions and gentle persuasion."

"Anyway, the alumbrados, as far as I know, were dangerous to the church mostly because they claimed you didn't need priests or even to follow the usual rules if you could get to the level of contact with God they were selling through your own meditation and prayer. So the church wasn't going to let a group like that alone. Sooner or later they got them all to confess the error of their ways."

"Okay, that makes sense," Mike conceded. "But I still don't know what any of this has to do with today, or what these 'secret writings' of St. Teresa are about. Hell, I don't even know which St. Teresa they're talking about—there's at least two of them, right?"

Tony had finished his sandwich, so he got up, put his plate in the old stainless steel kitchen sink, reached for two smaller plates for pie, and cut himself a generous near-half of what was left. He was about to put the remainder on the other plate, when Mike stopped him.

"Don't bother dirtying another dish. I'll eat the rest right off the pie plate—get all of it that way."

Tony shook his head and handed the pie plate over to this brother.

"You know, Ton', I don't mind now, but when I was a kid I hated to eat at this side of the table, especially if I was in here sneaking some cookies or something, what with those eyes staring me right in the face."

Tony didn't need to turn around to know what his brother was referencing—a "Sacred Heart" picture of Jesus, taped to the kitchen door, in which a red heart was centered on Christ's chest, with shafts of lights emanating in all directions, yellow flame sprouting from the top of the heart, and a small cross centered in the midst of those flames. More to the point for both brothers was the long haired, green-eyed Jesus's penetrating visage, his glare of unwavering, humorless holiness, which had also served to make Tony feel guilty more than once when he was similarly occupied in the kitchen. But the two boys were now men, their mother was happy knowing they were in the kitchen eating more of her food, and, besides, it felt to Tony like he might be at the beginning of an opportunity to redeem himself by doing God's work.

"Well, here's the thing, Mike. It's almost certainly St. Teresa of Avila, because she was alive during the whole alumbrado thing, plus, really, the only thing that kept her from some grilling from the Inquisition herself was that she always was willing to go orthodox, spout the party line, whenever she needed to, because, otherwise, you couldn't have told her from an alumbrada without a score card."

"Whaddaya mean?"

"I mean St. Teresa was totally into all these levels of praying that led to the 'annihilation' of self and total union with God. She was a real mystic, going after most of the same stuff the heretics were going after. The only difference was that she always deferred to priests, always said that loving your neighbor was still a big part of the deal, always put herself down, even though she was a great writer and, eventually, the first woman 'doctor' of the church."

"Yeah, but so? I still don't see what this has to do with a Carmelite nun and a Jesuit priest getting killed." Mike launched into his pie with something close to vengeance, forking a sloppy bite that left a spray of white, whipped foam on his neatly trimmed black and white beard.

"Well, neither do I, of course, but you do have something to work with. It sounds like the two of them were working with some sort of 'secret writing' of St. Teresa. I've never heard anything about that, but, you know, St. Teresa is the one who founded the Discalced Carmelites in the first place."

"Discalced?"

"Shoeless."

"They wear shoes. I woulda noticed."

"Yes, but at first they just wore rope sandals, to emphasize poverty. Now, though, rope sandals are trendy and cost too much, so they've gone back to wearing simple shoes. But the Discalced ones live a very cloistered life—just spend all day working and praying, and don't get out into the world. So—"

"So what?" Mike interrupted, with a mouth still full of pie.

"So it's a good place to keep a secret, a cloistered abbey, and if Saint Teresa had some 'secret writings' it would be a big deal, and if those secret writings somehow align her more closely with the alumbrados than her published stuff does, well, that could be a real scandal for the church, so—"

"So how big? Big enough to kill someone?"

"I don't know. And then the other thing—Monsignor Heamey says, he says...show me that letter again, will ya?"

Mike put down his fork long enough to reach into his gray suit jacket pocket for the letter. Tony took a second and then quoted the line he had been trying to remember:

"'Now that you have left the world of the alumbradas,' I mean, what does that tell us? How can you leave a world that hasn't existed for almost five hundred years? Does he mean now that she has stopped studying them? Or does he mean somehow that Sister Maria was mixed up in something more recent? And would St. Teresa's secret writings shed any light on all this? Plus, why does he say 'alumbradas,' the feminine plural? In Spanish, if you want to talk about both men and women at once, and the old time alumbrados had both males and females, you use the masculine form. So why is he using the feminine form? Are only women involved this time? And only nuns at that?"

"Ya see?" Mike shouted, slamming his fork down onto his plate and accidentally spraying a bit of chocolate pudding across the small, wooden table onto Tony's purple cashmere sweater. "Here you've been putting me off all this time when we could have been getting somewhere with this case. You're all the way in, now at least, right?"

"Well, if I were, one thing I'd like to look at is what they found over at Loyola, like any letters from Sister

Maria to Monsignor Heamey or anything else to show he
was investigating all this."

"Yeah, well, as for that, the cops in Chicago didn't
come up with much, no letters from the nun, for example,
which means the monsignor had a paper shredder or else
maybe the Jesuits aren't wanting to let us see all he was
up to. Maybe they want to keep the investigation close to
the cassock. Maybe you could even help us there, if
there's a priest or two left that you haven't totally pissed
off. From what I've been reading, the Jesuits don't mind
going against the mainstream themselves, so maybe that's
yet another way you could help out. So, are you in?"

Before Tony could respond, their conversation was
cut into by the shrill ringing of a telephone. There was a
portable phone in the living room, so both brothers assumed the call would be answered in there and they could
continue their talk uninterrupted. But youngest sister Beatrice's voice, at a shout to get past the volume of the TV,
came to them clearly across the three rooms. "Hey, Ton',
it's for you!"

Tony picked up the dining room phone. "Hello."

"Well, then, Antonio, so you are in town. You
weren't going to come and go without looking me up,
were you?"

The voice was female, Latina, familiar. Though Tony knew at once who was actually calling, he could not
help but think of whose voice it resembled. But that
woman was dead and gone, as gone as any part of Tony's
past could be.

"Are you still there?" the voice teased him, enjoying,
apparently, this proof of the level of Tony's uneasiness.

"Yes, I'm here, Isabel. It's good to hear from you.
How are your parents? I was hoping to see your dad
while I'm in, but he said it wasn't going to work out."

"Yes, well, you know, Mom had a lot to do with that. But she's always been that way. How about I come by and represent the Goya family's better intentions? I'll pick you up for lunch, tomorrow, okay? I haven't seen your parents in years. Is noon okay?"

The longer Isabel Goya spoke the more she reminded Tony of his former lover, Maggie Rosario, to whom he could never say no—Maggie, the woman he had treated virtually as a wife through the later years of his priesthood.

"Yeah, sure, Isabel, noon will be fine."

"Okay, great, see you then."

"Who the hell was that?" Mike asked, a detective already beginning to read a clue, which could only disturb him.

"Isabel, you know, Fernando's daughter."

"Yeah, yeah, I know. You aren't getting mixed up with her now, are ya? She's young enough to be your daughter, even younger than green eyes back at Smith there. Isn't one cradle robbery enough? Plus, I thought we'd spend more time working on the case."

"This is only for lunch tomorrow. I have no interest in Isabel that way, even though she likes to think I do."

"Are you trying to convince me or yourself, Ton'? You need to keep your focus on this case now."

"Fine, we can keep talking now, for as long as you want. And you have to work tomorrow anyway, so me going to lunch with Isabel isn't a problem, right? We can talk again tomorrow evening if there's any reason to."

"Okay, sure." Mike nodded, his dark eyes gleaming already with suspicion. "Let's hope Izzy has enough sense for the both a ya." Mike was about to go back to his pie when he suddenly almost shouted, "And stop looking at me," to the picture of Jesus still in its perpetual stare. "I'm on your side this time, ace. Trying to figure out who offed two of your people. Stare at this *caffon'* here, if you wanna stare at somebody. Damn, Ton', are you actually reaching in there for another pie?"

The question was rhetorical, since Mike could see his brother pulling another glass pie plate from the crowded recesses of the refrigerator:

"I just wanted to try a small piece of the Dutch apple. I didn't get any this afternoon."

Chapter 6

Isabel Goya was only fifteen minutes late, a fairly re-markable feat, considering her usual casualness about promptness and the traffic in Queens on the day after Thanksgiving. Because of that traffic, Tony and Isabel opted not to try driving very far from his parents' house for lunch,

"Why don't we just go to that pizzeria my father al-ways raves about?"

"You mean Tommy's?"

"Yes, he's always saying you can't get anything like it out on the Island. I don't have a ton of time anyway. I'm actually working today."

Isabel's outfit reinforced that assertion. She had a long, stylish, dark-green overcoat over a black pants suit, with matching green silk scarf and leather gloves. She didn't bother taking her coat off as she greeted and made small talk with Tony's family. Perhaps she sensed a lack of warmth in Rosa's reception and knew its cause beyond her ability to repair.

Isabel just looked too much like her Aunt Maggie,

the aunt who had ruined everything in Rosa's priest son's life.

Isabel was driving a sleek, black Lexus GS 11 sedan. Tony's comment as he belted himself, "Nice car. You look good in black," made Isabel chuckle.

"It's not black. It's 'obsidian.'"

"Like the knives the Aztec priests used?" Tony scooted over a bit toward the passenger door.

"No, obsidian as in they can charge you more than for just plain black. Besides, green's your favorite color, as I recall. How do I look in green?"

Isabel touched Tony lightly on his left shoulder as she asked her question.

"Very nice." Tony nodded, stopping himself before saying anything he might end up regretting.

The drive to Tommy's didn't take five minutes. Tony appreciated the familiar warmth of the pizza ovens and the aromas they released as he and Isabel entered from the cold. Tommy's was doing a steady business, as always, but most of the pizza and calzone buyers carried the food off with them, so there was a red and white table waiting for Isabel and Tony at the back of the pizzeria. They got their slices, with a diet coke for Isabel and orange soda for Tony, and made their way back to sit down.

Isabel took her coat off, but finding no place to hang it she folded it carefully and placed it on the seat beside her, after wiping that seat carefully with two napkins. Across from her Tony noticed that the blouse under her black jacket was also green, and she further had an emerald pendant, which hung outside the blouse at chest level.

"Do you remember this?" Isabel asked, as she fingered the pendant.

"Should I?" Tony responded, almost immediately uncomfortable in a place where he'd been happy and comfortable many times before.

"You ought to, I guess. You bought it. It was Aunt Maggie's favorite."

Isabel, feature for feature, hardly was a perfect look-alike to her now deceased aunt. She was probably two inches taller than Maggie had been with darker hair and a nose from her father's Ecuadorian side. But her brown eyes were like her aunt's, strikingly similar in their dark shade and depth and their seeming level of interest in Tony. That interest appeared to be on the rise as Isabel entered her mid-twenties, and it was the feature most crucially linking her to her aunt, a woman who had been murdered mostly because she had refused to let the monsignor go.

"Yes, I remember it now. I bought that a long time ago," Tony responded, before taking the first bite from his Sicilian slice.

"Yes, I miss Aunt Maggie too," Isabel countered, spinning her way back to a subject Tony seemed intent on avoiding. "She was someone not afraid to fully identify with her sensual self. She didn't let the Catholic Church or other traditions keep her from who she really was. Nothing like my mother—it's hard to believe they were even sisters."

Isabel also punctuated her sentence with a first bite from her "regular" slice. Even the way she then chewed her food, with an intent look into Tony's eyes, seemed a conscious imitation of her dead aunt's former focus.

"So, Izzy, how are your folks?" Tony again gamely tried deflection, remembering Faith back in Massachusetts and also how little Isabel's father, one of his oldest and best friends, would approve of Tony and his youngest daughter together.

"They're fine, Tony, or as fine as anyone can be with how uptight my mother is. But I didn't invite you to

lunch to talk about them. I'd much rather talk about you,
about us, really."

Isabel seemed ready to reach across the table to
touch Tony on "us," but instead she just gave him another
deeply, darkly brown look.

"What us, Izzy?" Tony put down his slice. "You're
the daughter of a good friend, you're a young woman just
starting a promising law career here in New York. Me,
I'm an aging professor off in small town Massachusetts,
and, last I heard, we both had 'significant others.'"

"You don't listen well enough, then," Isabel rejoined, this time playfully tapping Tony on his left ear.
"Sergio and I broke up a month ago. I'm certain I told
you that in an email you never answered. As for my job,
I'm just finding my way in the law. I don't have to stay in
New York. Boston needs plenty of lawyers, or maybe
even smaller towns than Boston could use someone with
my skills."

"But Isabel, I've never encouraged you to be thinking of those kinds of things, and, after all—"

"There's this woman you're still seeing, Faith, isn't
it?" Isabel asked before having a long drink from her
coke.

"Yes, that's right."

"I hear from my father she isn't much older than me,
which makes our age difference impediment seem even
sillier. And if you're worried about my parents, I'm a
grown-up now—it's Isabel, not little Izzy. So I guess the
only obstacle left is little Miss Massachusetts."

"It's Ms. Massachusetts, definitely Ms.," Tony
joked, feeling a betrayal of Faith even in so small a joke.

"Tell me all about her," Isabel requested, this time
taking Tony's hand away from grabbing his slice again,
by holding onto his left hand with her right, as she awaited his response.

Tony felt very uncomfortable, wanting neither to embarrass nor encourage Isabel. Still, he also felt a need to speak up for Faith. "What can I tell you about her? She's beautiful, brilliant, and concerned about me in a long term way."

"I get the first two parts. I know you only become intimate with beautiful, brilliant women, after all, but how does she show her concern?" Isabel managed to ask that question, while simultaneously putting a firmer grip on Tony's hand and grabbing her pizza adroitly with the other, preparatory to another large bite.

Tony felt more and more defensive as he explained, "Faith's a vegan and an eco-feminist. Consequently she's very spiritual. She knows there's far more to life than physical desires and gross appetites. She isn't with me now because she never could have accepted the excesses of yesterday afternoon's meal."

"You mean the meal you enjoyed so much?" Isabel laughed. "Just like you're enjoying that slice of Sicilian a vegan makes taboo, just like you're enjoying the touch of a woman who understands, just like her aunt did, that we can only reach the spiritual by embracing, indulging, all our appetites, instead of trying to live in denial of their power?"

Tony wondered what Isabel might do, or propose next. He knew he should pull away, both literally and figuratively from any such proposal, but Isabel's questions about why Faith was his best option made too much sense to escape. Imagine never having another slice of Sicilian pizza at Tommy's, imagine denying the pleasure in simply holding someone's hand? Just then Isabel released his hand, the better to finish off her lunch and allow him to return to his.

A moment later she looked quickly at her elegant, gold watch before explaining, "I've really got to get back to work. Help me on with my coat and I'll get you back home before I scoot back."

Tony obediently stepped up to enrobe Isabel back in her dark green protection from the just-below-freezing weather outside. "Where is it exactly that you work, Izz—Isabel?" he wondered as he bent back into her $60,000 car.

"In Forest Hills, for a corporate firm right on Queens Boulevard. You know, not far from where Aunt Maggie used to live."

One more reminder of the niece's connections to his former lover was hardly necessary. He almost suggested getting together that very night, but he had promised his brother to leave that time for more discussion of the case, and he was driving back Saturday morning, having promised Faith to at least share the latter portion of the long weekend with her.

"So will you be back over the Christmas holidays?" Isabel asked.

"Yes, and probably for longer than the last few years. My Mom and Dad aren't getting any younger."

"No, none of us are, Antonio." Isabel smiled, a smile more like her Aunt Maggie's than maybe even she realized. "Not even me," she finished, before engaging her Lexus briefly in reverse, before putting it back into drive to quickly take Tony back to his old home.

"Of course, there's always tonight," Isabel noted, with her eyes briefly focused on Tony, before returning to the traffic on Liberty Avenue.

"Well, tonight, you see, Mike's supposed to be stopping by, and, well…"

"How long do you think he'll stay? You know, in New York, there are clubs that don't really get going until midnight. Do you like to dance, Antonio?"

Isabel put a hand to her long dark hair and flicked it

away from her face, before making the turn that would lead back to Tony's parents' place.

"Oh, no, I'm not much of a dancer. That late night clubbing—that's a young person's game."

"Well, you give me a call if you change your mind. You can meet me out in front of your house if you don't want your mother to know the company you're keeping. I think she thinks I'm dangerous or something."

Isabel delivered one brief kiss to Tony at parting, but it was on the lips and lingered long enough to promise many more to come. Tony felt himself close to reeling from the seduction of her beauty and her perfume, the same gardenia scent her aunt had always favored.

Before he could even try to make things good with his mother over his lunch date, she tersely informed him, "Mike called. He said it's real important. He wants you to call him back right away."

Tony dutifully punched in the number his mother handed him. Detective Cupelli wasted no time in delivering the urgency promised.

"There's been another murder, Ton'. I'm heading to the crime scene now. My CO finally is convinced this is worth pursuing."

"Another killing? This is just horrible. Was it a nun or a priest this time?"

"None of the above, man. A civilian, female, in Worcester."

"Then how come you're certain it's connected?"

"Well, it happened on the Holy Cross campus, another Jesuit hangout, if I got my facts straight. The vic was a student there, but, way more to the point, this poor kid also had the brown scapular."

"But, Mike, probably a million people have a brown scapular, and—"

"And how many of them who have one were also strangled?"

"Strangled? God, it's like a nightmare," Tony shuddered and then added, "But what was she even doing on campus during the Thanksgiving break?"

"Damned if I know. That's just one of the many things we're gonna go find out."

"We?"

"As in you and me, kid. We're going to Worcester."

"To Worcester? When?"

"What when? Now. If we leave now, we don't have to drive in the dark. I suppose you'll want to stop at your place first. Worcester ain't far from where you're at, so that's fine, but I want you to drive home now—as soon as you can pack. I'll meet you at your apartment in, what, let's say five hours? That should give you plenty of time. It's normally just a bit over a three hour drive, right, so no more than four if there's traffic, right?"

"Are you sure you really want me along?"

"Three people are dead and there's no sign of it slowing down. You can help save somebody or bodies' life. You're damn right I want you along."

Tony still doubted he would really be able to do anything that could help solve the case. But he no longer doubted his brother's belief, and that counted for something, even with all the sadness involved in the crime scene ahead.

"Okay, I'm on my way, Mike, as fast as I can make it. See you back at my place."

"Great, thanks, man. See you then."

Tony felt an overwhelming sadness for the poor Holy Cross student whose death he would soon try to help figure out.

But he also felt a rising anger, at himself for not having paid more attention to his brother sooner, and toward the unknown killer, whom he prayed he might help un-cover before anyone else died.

Chapter 7

The Worcester police and Holy Cross's own campus cops were cooperating in the investigation into the murder of Marissa Hitzel, a twenty-two year old senior whose body had been found in a second floor hallway in Loyola Hall, an upperclassmen dormitory on campus. Mike and Tony met up with members from both forces on campus and were soon at the crime scene, though only after some hesitation on the part of all the police to allow a civilian like Tony to be part of the process. But Mike was pretty persuasive, more skillful than Tony would have guessed possible, playing the big city cop in need of help from his Massachusetts brother officers just right, neither condescending nor deferential.

Once inside the "residence hall," an older though modernized building which had originally been a kind of rectory for the Jesuits who made Holy Cross the oldest Jesuit College in New England, the lead person on the Worcester police team, a Captain McCarthy greeted them. He appeared to be in his early fifties, his few pounds off his ideal weight somewhat hidden by his five-foot-eleven-inch frame, with a close to pug nose, receding gray hair and tired blue eyes.

He got right to bringing both men up to date. "Based on the forensic evidence, we don't think the girl died here. Looks like someone strangled her somewhere else, and, yes, Lieutenant, our people say a thick pair of rosary beads could have been the murder weapon, though none were found on the scene."

Mike gave his brother a quick look before refocusing on McCarthy. "Yes, and?"

"And then she was snuck in here some few hours later. The poor little thing hardly weighed a hundred pounds, so she wasn't all that hard to move."

"How easy is it to get in here unobserved and drop a body off, though?" Mike wanted to know.

"Well, like I told you over the phone, this particular dorm was shut down for Thanksgiving," a short, dark eyed campus cop in a predictable blue uniform, whose plastic name tag read, T. Crapanzano, responded, more than a little defensively. "We try to keep an eye on things, plus you'd still need a Crusader One to get in, but who's looking for anything to be brought in, instead of taken out?"

"A Crusader One?" Tony had to ask.

"It's the access card to get in the residence halls and other campus buildings. It ensures that only people who belong here can get inside."

"It mostly ensures," Captain McCarthy corrected. "Though I guess it's totally possible some student or students were the ones who killed the girl."

"But why in the hell would they bring her back to the dorm, then?" the campus cop questioned. "She didn't even live here. She was a local girl, from here in Auburn, lived with her folks. Why would the killers, if they were students, want to bring all the more suspicion on themselves? If you ask me, some local nut just wants to make our students look bad, like your newspaper's always doing."

"If your over-privileged, spoiled 'Crusaders' weren't always tearing up the town, drunk and high," Captain McCarthy responded, "and treating the citizens like dirt, maybe we wouldn't have to keep listing all their crimes in the paper, I—"

"Guys, we don't need this. We're working all together, right?" Mike reminded his colleagues. "I'm more convinced than ever we've got some kind of serial killer here. Three capital crimes in three different cities, all mixed up somehow with religion—which is why I brought my brother along."

"Religion? Oh, yeah, the first two victims were a nun and a priest," McCarthy remembered. "But this girl, she wasn't even studying to be a nun or anything like that. Her major was English, if I'm not mistaken."

The Cupelli brothers spent the requisite time with the local police to garner any other information they might find useful. But neither brother seemed hopeful that these men could provide much beyond the basic facts of the crime.

As they drove back to Tony's apartment, where Mike had again arranged to spend the night, Tony shared a theory for his brother's ears only:

"Three people killed in the last several months, all in possession of the Our Lady of Mt. Carmel scapular, two strangled by rosary beads. If you ask me, the reason the victim was brought back to a dorm was so she could be found, on campus. It's no coincidence, I'm betting, that they chose Loyola Hall, where the Jesuits themselves used to live, maybe so they could keep us thinking it has something to do with Jesuits, or maybe as some kind of a warning to others."

"A warning to who about what?"

"That's what we need to figure out, right? It's got something to do with the stuff about St. Teresa in that letter from Monsignor Heamey. I'm almost sure of it."

"Well, one murder ago I might have agreed, but this girl isn't a nun."

"That just means this thing is even bigger than we imagined, maybe."

"At least now *we're* imagining. I like that—that's progress."

The two men continued discussing the case for the ride back to Northampton and into their settling down for the night at Tony's place. But their conversation was interrupted by Tony's need to call Faith.

"Can't you ever think of anything besides food or women?" Mike lamented.

"Actually, this is all police business," Tony countered.

"Vice squad stuff, ya mean." Mike laughed. "Well, then, I don't wanna know."

Tony had already called Faith once that day, to let her know of his change of plans for Saturday. When he dialed her cell phone at 10:30 p.m., he worried she would already be in bed, but she answered on the second ring, with nothing sleepy to her tone.

"You need what?" she asked, with what sounded to Tony like equal parts interest and annoyance.

"I need Veronica Teuma's phone number. You have it, don't you?"

"Yet another woman?" Mike overheard and snickered. "And asking your own girlfriend for it? Have you no shame at all?"

"Oh, shut up, would ya? No, no Faith, of course I wasn't telling you to shut up. It's my brother here." He pointed, as if Faith could see. "Please, it's just I know she

could help us with this case I told you about. You know
we were just in Worcester. Do you know if she stayed
around for the break."

"No, no, I don't. We aren't super close or anything,
you know. Here's her home number. She doesn't have a
cell. Do with it what you will."

Tony was anxious to get off the phone and Faith
showed no desire to detain him.

"You think it's too late to call?" he asked his still
bemused brother.

"If it's gonna help the case, call away, ace. What's
the worst that can happen?"

This phone call did seem to awaken its recipient,
though once Veronica knew who was on the other end,
she seemed to perk up quickly. "Oh, hello, Tony. I'm really glad you're calling. This is about my student, isn't
it?"

"Your student?"

"Yes, Marissa, the young woman they found dead on
campus."

"I was told she was an English major."

"Actually, that's right, but she was a double major
with Religious Studies. Probably only the first major and
first advisor lists on her paperwork."

"But how did you know I would want to talk about
her?"

"Faith told me some days ago that you were working
with your brother on the possibility of Monsignor
Heamey's death being linked to that of a Carmelite nun in
New York, so, naturally, I assumed—"

"But, well, you couldn't have known about the obvious link. The police didn't make that public and I didn't
even tell Faith. So, why—I mean, this Marissa, she
wasn't a nun or anything."

"No, no she wasn't, but she was a Carmelite."

"What?" Tony blurted, too stunned to say anything more.

"Yes, a secular Carmelite—I was her sponsor into the Carmelite life".

"You, you're a Carmelite too."

"Why, yes, I thought maybe you knew."

"No, but, listen, there's a lot I still need to learn. Can my brother and I come see you tomorrow?"

"Yes, certainly. Perhaps we can meet for Mass. I usually go to the ten o'clock."

"That'll be fine. My brother and I were wondering when we'd be able to make Mass tomorrow." He nodded with an almost laugh at his brother's pained look. "Tell me how to get to the church, please."

Chapter 8

About four inches of snow, all of which had fallen between 3:30 and 9:30 a.m., complicated the drive to Worcester from Northampton. This made it just a bit trickier to get to the Catholic Church on the south side of town, which Veronica had directed them to. Our Lady of Czestochowa was a light tan building with white pillars in front and a modest steeple atop the far left side. Tony knew Teuma wasn't a Polish name, so he assumed Veronica just lived closest to this particular Catholic Church, one of five in Worcester. He was relieved to read in the church bulletin that the ten o'clock Mass would be in English, though the 11:30 was in Polish. It was too blustery to wait outside, but Veronica greeted the two brothers as they entered the church.

She was wearing a long black coat with a white, wool scarf and matching hat. Her coat was already unbuttoned, revealing a royal blue, knee length dress. She greeted Tony with a handshake that was, literally, warm and waited to be introduced to his black-leather jacketed brother.

"Mike Cupelli, Professor Teuma," Mike said, offering his name and hand.

"It's wonderful to meet you. Please call me Veronica."

Tony was surprised by his brother's deviation from his normal informality. He wondered if Lieutenant Cupelli was already thinking of Veronica Teuma as someone who would need to be interrogated rather than befriended. Tony kept that question to himself as the three found a pew toward the middle front of the church.

Both men spent time observing Veronica's demeanor and disposition during Mass, though perhaps from differing motives. In spite of the cold weather outside, the church was kept comfortably warm and, when Veronica took off her overcoat, her brown scapular was noticeably displayed over her blue dress. She seemed to be intensely engaged in every aspect of the Mass, from her reciting of the prayers to her intent and almost participatory listening to the homily by a sincere, but tired looking Polish-American father. Tony felt regret and remorse, a large part of him wishing he had never squandered the right to say Mass. His fine baritone voice tried to find consolation for his sorrow during the hymns, particularly on the chorus of one of his more recent favorites, "Christ be our light, shine in our hearts, shine through the darkness," during which he could not help but notice the beauty of Veronica's mezzo soprano. When he held hands with her, during the saying of the Our Father, and noted again the warmth and firmness of her grip, he might have been carried away even farther from his real reason for attending Mass in Worcester, if not for his brother's hand he held to his left, colder, though just as firm.

After Mass, Veronica invited the brothers to her home, a simple two bedroom ranch a few blocks from the church. Veronica had walked, but she joined the men in

Mike's car, so as to better direct them to her house.

"This seems like a nice neighborhood, better than right by the U," Tony noted. "Do you enjoy the Polish community here? I think I'd feel a little left out."

"Well, actually, I prefer any sense of ethnicity to none. I was born in Malta myself, which is, I'm sure you know, the most Catholic country in the world. But you also know Poles are pretty serious Catholics, with traditions I especially cherish during the holidays. Plus, this particular church's devotion to the Black Madonna of Czestochowa resonates with me a lot."

"Black Madonna? I ain't never heard of any black Polacks, I mean Polish people," Mike corrected himself, also unusual for him.

"Well, it's a famous painting of Our Lady, with a blackened face, which some say was caused by a fire, and scars on her cheek that also have various interpretations. But she's essentially the dominant form of the Blessed Mother in Poland, like Our Lady of Guadalupe in Mexico."

Mike nodded. "Or Our Lady of Mount Carmel, right?"

"Oh, here's the house now," Veronica noted, leaning forward from the back seat—she had insisted her five-foot-five-inch frame would be better suited to the back of the Mustang than either of the six foot plus brothers—and pointing to the right. "You can just pull into the driveway behind my car."

She insisted on preparing a "little lunch," for the brothers, though there was nothing little about the chicken salad sandwiches on homemade sour dough bread nor the incredibly rich pastry ring, *Qaghaq ta'l-Ghasel*, which awaited for dessert.

"I've heard of that, but I've never had it," Tony said admiringly. He was a food lover, particularly amorous of desserts. "You didn't make that just for us, did you? I mean, I only called you last night."

"It was a pleasure," Veronica replied with a smile that backed up her words. "I love to make this. It's a traditional holiday season dessert in Malta, but I wasn't going to make one just for myself. Luckily, I already had the ingredients. It isn't easy getting treacle around here, I can tell you, but I was in Boston for Thanksgiving."

"Oh, so when did you get back to Worcester?" Mike wondered.

"Just yesterday morning, actually, why?" Veronica asked with the memory of her smile still trying to linger.

"Oh, no reason," Tony interjected. "I'm sure he's just hoping we're not putting you out too much, right Mike?"

"Yeah, sure, we really do appreciate your taking the time to talk with us. Tony tells me you're a real expert on St. Teresa."

"Let's sit down and eat." Veronica pointed them to kitchen chairs. "I'm happy to help in any way I can."

Mike had already forewarned Tony not to give away any details of the crimes that were not public knowledge, though this had to impede the freeness with which they could quiz Veronica on what they wanted to know. Still, Tony's invitation to have Veronica share with both men her insights into the saint, particularly her writings and her connections, if any, to the "alumbrados" gave her license to present an almost mini-lecture on the topic.

"I'm sorry your interest in St. Teresa had to come from such awful circumstances, but I've already given some thought to all I know of her and how that might conceivably be helpful to you, and so I first want to share with you all the ways people have misunderstood her life and writings."

"Yes, that's just the kind of thing we need," Tony assured her.

"Have you heard, for example, that some people think Teresa's visions and ecstasies were just caused by epilepsy, that she didn't have divine contact with God at all, but just a disease?"

"Yeah, I have heard a little about that," Tony offered, like a good student who wanted to show he knew more than the teacher expected him to. "Wasn't there even a novel not too long ago where the main character was a Carmelite nun and she discovered what she thought were her mystical unions with God were all just really from a tumor giving her a form of epilepsy?"

"Yes, that's right. The writer used his fiction to make it seem by the end that that was all there was to it. That a simple operation would take away that nun's visions and, by extension, would have worked for St. Teresa, if she had only lived now."

"Yeah, that's a shame," Mike commiserated, as he reached to pick up his three-quarters-eaten sandwich again. "But I don't think epilepsy will help us that much. What else you got?"

Veronica seemed more bemused than upset by Mike's approach, so she continued without a shift in tone: "Well, Teresa had to always be wary because the mystical contact with our Lord that her contemplative prayer life created didn't seem that different from what the alumbrados were seeking. So more than once she came close to having to come before the Inquisition. But Teresa had two things in her favor. She knew how to appease men by always referring to herself as an 'ignorant woman' or 'just a woman' and, more importantly, unlike the alumbrados, she never forgot the two great commandments."

"I thought there were ten," Mike countered. "Which

two of them are so great?" he asked, just before taking his first bite of the rich dessert.

"Christ tells us to love God with all our hearts and souls and to love our neighbors as ourselves. If you follow those two precepts, everything else will take care of itself. The alumbrados seemed to think if you followed the first, if you were in spiritual union with God, how could anything else matter—whether you went to church, whether you committed adultery—but Teresa never made that mistake."

Veronica's voice stayed in a steady, sincere, and somehow humble register, as if even talking about St. Teresa was an honor she fully felt. Even Mike seemed a little impressed, but Tony was enchanted by this woman's quiet wisdom.

"I know Teresa was a great writer, and I've read most of her work, including the autobiography, *The Way of Perfection, The Secret Castle*. But I'm wondering if there are other works I'm less familiar with that might be important, or if you know of anything previously unpublished that has been uncovered recently."

Tony wasn't certain if Mike wanted him to allude that strongly to any "secret writings" by the saint, so he shot him a quick glance, but couldn't read whether his brother thought he had gone too far. Lieutenant Cupelli had his cop poker face on, showing he was less trusting of Veronica than Tony was becoming.

"Well, there are other writings, but those you've mentioned are probably the most important. Still, I wonder if you're aware of some of the nonsense and even pornography that has been created, inspired by a willful misreading of her life and work."

"Well, I've read some people have misinterpreted the Bernini statue as a representation of Teresa in sexual ecstasy, but that's still housed in a church, after all, so I don't think the church makes much of that."

"What's this sex business?" Mike asked. "She was a nun, no? And if she made it to sainthood, she wasn't fooling around, right?"

"Of course she didn't fool around," Tony shot back. "But the description of the mystical union with God, that's almost always described in what seems like sexual terms and that goes way back to the Song of Solomon."

"Yes, but it really has gone beyond that with Teresa," Veronica informed them. "Surely, you've heard of that awful movie that British film maker made, so offensive that the British government invoked an almost never used censorship law to stop its release. In it, they have all sorts of dreadful things, ranging from Teresa enjoying graphic, bloody, self-torture to her making love to Christ on the cross."

Tony nodded. "That really is sick."

"Yeah, sure, I agree," Mike said, "but when you think about it, that's what the nuns used to tell us—that they were married to Jesus. I mean, you can see why someone might go that way, since that's what married people do, right?"

"Mike, c'mon, I—"

"No, Tony, your brother is right to consider that point of view. You see, the reason I wanted to speak to you is precisely because Marissa had been saying some strange things about Teresa lately. She had been mixed up somehow in this idea that Teresa was a sexual creature, and that her writings do lead to conclusions not that far from what Nigel Wingrove created in his film."

Veronica was almost wringing her hands as she said these last words. The calmness of her demeanor had disappeared, replaced by an agitation of someone who might have a secret she hesitated to reveal.

"What are you saying?" Mike pushed. "Are you saying this girl was maybe mixed up in more ways than one? Was she mixed up with something involving St. Teresa that could have led to her getting killed?"

Veronica stood up, ostensibly to get Tony a refill of his coffee, but she paced a bit, her shoes tapping a nervous beat on the kitchen tiles. "I don't know what to think. Marissa Hitzel went from being a very religious, innocent girl, a Carmelite Aspirant in fact, to someone very different in the past semester."

"She was studying to be a nun?" Mike interrupted.

"No, not a nun, a secular Carmelite, like me."

"What's that mean? Tony told me you were a Carmelite, but 'secular' that means you're not a nun, right? But that's why you wear that scapular?"

"Well, yes, I've been part of the secular order for ten years now," Veronica responded.

"Well, I need to hear all about this. I didn't even know you could be one without being a nun or priest. But first tell me about the vic, I mean, this girl Marissa. She was gonna be one too, but then what? She lost interest?"

"Well, no, she still was intensely interested in St. Teresa, but her honor thesis ideas were more and more fixated on masochism, on the pain that never ends, a clever, complete perversion of Teresa's actual words. And I don't think she was just coming to all these new ideas on her own."

"Veronica, what are you actually saying?" Tony stood up too, as a sign of support somehow.

"I have no real proof, but I think there might be some kind of cult willfully abusing the sanctity of one of the great female doctors of the church. I think that the alumbradas are back."

"Alumbradas? Not alumbrados?" Tony questioned.

"Yes, as far as I can tell there are only women now, and St. Teresa has, through their perverse misreadings, become their patron saint." Mike remained seated, sipped his coffee, gave his brother a look whose darkness Tony could not quite decipher or define.

Chapter 9

The Cupelli brothers didn't leave Veronica's house before getting a complete explanation of the basis for her suspicions about a renewal of a cult the Catholic Church believed it had eradicated hundreds of years before. She had no direct proof, but she passed on to them Marissa Hitzel's honor thesis proposal, from which Veronica suggested Tony could surmise the dangerous straying Marissa had done from the path of Catholic orthodoxy. And Veronica also gave them names of women Marissa had mentioned, at least two of whom had also been Veronica's students at Holy Cross, who the brothers might question. While Tony came away from the meeting, certain they had found a promising ally and helpmate in solving the murders, Mike proved more skeptical.

"It's a good thing you ain't actually a cop. Any pretty face would throw you off, especially one attached to a body that can bake like that."

"What are you talking about? How could she have been more helpful?"

"Yeah, sure, she was plenty helpful," Mike agreed without agreeing. "Lots of things to think about, one of which, though, is her own motives and means."

"Are you crazy?" Tony questioned, both for what Mike had just said and for how hard he took a snowy turn on their return to Northampton.

The skidding was only moderate and Mike seemed to enjoy rather than be panicked by the slip, so his calm response was no surprise.

"Listen, dopey, here we got a Catholic from the world's most Catholic country, a woman who thinks that these girls are disrespecting her favorite saint big time, a religion professor who probably thinks the Inquisition should make a comeback. And maybe she's jump started that Inquisition herself."

"You are crazy." Tony shook his head and felt ready to plug his ears so as to not hear the blasphemy that was sure to follow.

"Just hear me out. For all we know she was back in town in time to ice her student. We know for certain she was on your campus the night the priest got killed, and we have no way just yet to say she wasn't in Brooklyn the night the nun checked out. After all, it's not that far a drive. So, minimally, I'm seeing motive and opportunity."

"Come off it. You're doing this just to aggravate me, aren't you? Even if your crazy notion that she wanted to punish her wayward student made sense, where's her motive for the other two killings—a priest and nun who both seemed to be fighting this alumbrada thing. They'd be in sympathy with Veronica, then, not against her."

Tony said his last line with a kind of voice punctuation to signal his confidence that the conversation was over.

Mike accelerated, causing them again to slide in the

slushy snow, and laughed at his brother's discomfort before countering. "You think you have me there, but your first mistake is being certain she's telling us the truth in the first place. For all we know, she's the head of these new nut jobs herself, and she had to off one of her disciples, this last student here, because she knew too much about the other hits."

"I'm telling you, there's no way Veronica's devotion to St. Teresa isn't genuine. There's no way she's an alumbrada."

"Really? Well, even if you're right, it only makes her better for the last murder. Let's figure there are two sides going at it, the first two murders by these alumbradas and now one for the other team, both equally wacky, just like they were back in the day when St. Teresa might have been playing both sides of the fence."

"You can't possibly be serious about that. You can't possibly take what these women are making up seriously."

"Well, that's the difference between me and you. Whatever side makes sense to you, whatever team you're on, that's the all or nothing. Me, I'm a cop. I've got to consider everything as possible until the evidence totally, totally eliminates my suspicions. To me, it makes no difference whether St. Teresa was getting it on with God or just had epilepsy or that neither thing is true. And, sure, this Veronica could just be a nice person who's gonna help us a ton, but if I don't at least consider that she could be something else again, then I risk not doing my job."

"It's a really sad job then, isn't it? Never being able to trust anyone."

"It's not for everybody, that's for sure, ace." Mike laughed, while pushing his brother's shoulder with his right hand. "But somebody's gotta keep the nuts in line." Mike's concluding words were said with a pseudo-maniacal leer and a feign at turning the steering wheel even more wildly than he had before, though he kept, instead, a steady course toward Tony's home.

The brothers arrived back in Northampton around six o'clock. Mike had to get back to New York, but he assigned his brother to do what he could to follow up on the investigation in Massachusetts. "Listen, this is all right up your alley. Find out more about this Professor Teuma and find a way to talk to these friends of the vic's without alerting suspicion. You can do that a lot better than a cop can. Do whatever other snooping you think of and let me know what you find."

"I will if you say so, but you just got finished telling me I was lousy for police work, didn't think like a cop."

"Yeah, well, what did I just say? Tell me what you find out and not what you think, or tell me both since you can't help yourself. I'll just mostly pay attention to what you find out, all right?"

In spite of the usual kidding, something about his just-older brother needing his help still was oddly attractive to Tony. Or maybe the attraction was to Veronica, a woman he was convinced had only virtue and faith, supporting his growing trust in her.

He didn't share that last possibility with Faith when he finally got around to calling her at eight o'clock. Though he was tired and totally unprepared for the next day's resumption of classes, he could not convince Faith he should call it a night. She not only insisted they get together, but that Tony be the one to brave the dark and cold to come to her apartment. He was at her place by 8:30.

Faith looked well-rested and comfortable in jeans and a tan turtle neck sweater. Over the phone she had made it clear she was unhappy about Tony's priorities of the past two days, and he knew she felt generous in even giving him the opportunity to re-convince her of the seriousness of his feelings toward her. Trying to be fair to her point of view, he was ready to be more apologetic in person.

As they sat together in Faith's living room on a very modern looking, and not especially comfortable, scarlet divan, Faith began to express her dissatisfaction. "I can't accept that you preferred to spend these last few days with your brother, someone you've always been critical of, instead of with me, when you knew I had blocked off these days to spend with you back here, when most everyone else was still gone for the break."

Faith's words felt like a lecture to a disobedient child. Tony felt the irony of her tone, not only because he was almost old enough to be her father, but because he was fatigued enough overall to become a little tired of her implicit sense of superiority over her misbehaving beau.

"Well, he is my brother, for better or worse, but like I told you, it wasn't like we were just sitting around downing beers and watching football—I was helping him with his investigation of three murders. I didn't volunteer. He asked for my help. Should I have said no?"

Faith's eyes sharpened at Tony's words, though instead of responding, she got up and walked into her kitchen to take the tea kettle off her shiny black electric stove, preparatory to making them both a cup of chamomile tea. The steam off the kettle seemed to dissipate her own, as she calmly came back to her lover.

"I guess I'd be pretty selfish if I insisted you be with me when you might be some help in catching a murderer, but why can't you at least tell me what it is you've been doing? We can't really take the final steps toward real intimacy unless there's absolute trust between us."

Tony knew Faith was too earnest and strong ever to feel the need to ply anyone with tears. Still, her words suggested to Tony that he held a key to the lock on her deepest affections.

"I'd like to reach that next level with you. You can only imagine how much, but I've also made a promise to my brother and I know you also value that kind of trust. I'll tell you what I can, though. Today we went to see Veronica Teuma because she knew the last victim and because we thought she might have some insight into some of the religious elements of the crimes. Surely, you've figured out that my brother thinks I can help because of my past as a priest, not because I'm some great crime-solver."

"Well, tell me then, Tony," Faith requested as she put her hand, warm from having just been on her hot tea cup, on Tony's hand, still somewhat cold from the outside chill. "What did Veronica tell you? Better still, are there things you need to know about Veronica? Maybe I could help you there."

Tony was taken aback by Faith's willingness to assume Veronica might have things to hide. Her eagerness to share information about Veronica reminded him of their old neighborhood's code, "Nobody likes a squealer," and further annoyed him in the way it aligned with his brother's conclusion that Veronica should not be ruled out as a suspect. Still, if Faith could help in any way to solve the crimes, he had to listen to whatever she would be able to reveal.

"Well, today in fact we found out that Veronica's a Carmelite, a secular Carmelite. Did you know that about her?" Tony asked.

"Well, yes, of course I knew. She was recruiting me for a while, if you can believe that." Faith's eyes opened wide with her remark. Tony didn't respond so she continued. "Of course I've always been interested in Teresa of Avila myself because she was such a strong woman and because of her reaching the ultimate through meditative prayer. Veronica is practically obsessed with Teresa and I knew she could teach me a lot about how to reach the divine ecstasy that comes through silence. But there was no way I could sign on for all the Catholicism—that woman suppressing, hateful religion that Veronica is so tied to, the religion you finally were smart enough to reject yourself."

With these words Faith seemed to be offering Tony a choice, an either or he could not get around with rhetoric. Was he really the ex-monsignor, true champion of women's rights and full equality, or could he again give into the allure of the church and all its rituals? Her right hand once again went from her tea cup to the fingers of his left hand and her gold-green eyes were as intent as a flashlight beacon searching for a child lost in the wilderness. And now the irony was that Tony did not feel inclined to reject whatever it was that Veronica might be about, but rather to suspect Faith's own motivations and desires. He knew his own feelings were somewhere in the middle, someplace where women could be respected and receive equal rights without abandoning what was best about the Church's teachings.

Still, he didn't want Faith to stop thinking they could be on the same side, so he responded. "That's what I've always wanted for us, Faith—a way to the divine, the ultimate. But you've always seemed so distant, so reserved."

"The way to the divine isn't through praying the Our Father with Veronica, it's through seeing to the ecstasy without gender, without sex, the connection with a God so completely free of human bondage that all the soul desires is its ongoing unity with the one that is all. Once we get there together Tony, anything is possible, nothing will be withheld from you, since we will be fully one. Isn't that the adventure we've really signed up for? Aren't we both made for 'higher laws'?"

As she said these last words, Faith grasped Tony's hand with a grip so firm it caused him to wince. But Faith only squeezed more firmly still, the pain feeling close to a physical assault.

He almost admitted, "You're hurting me," but somehow could not get the words to come forth. He kept expecting her to soften her hold on him, but she seemed to be already in some other place. He looked to her for relief and saw her eyes, her whole countenance, bearing the beginning signs of rapture. The press of her hand remained steady, strong, but somehow the pain decreased, or transformed as he seemed to feel her spirit seeking to investigate his own. After another moment, Faith, with her grip still inescapable, took Tony's hand and placed it under her sweater and onto her heart, where he felt the slow and then slower beats of a perfect sinus rhythm. He had no access to time, as he was incredulously drawn to an ecstasy of something that, if not divine, was still certainly other worldly. Faith's will seemed to envelop him and her eyes brightened at last with the knowledge of how she had fully enraptured him. When she finally released him, his tea was cold and his hand felt as if it were on fire.

"We'll get there Tony—the two of us together. But you still have so much to learn."

She gave him a long, tender kiss on his cheek before her eyes bade him farewell for the evening. As he drove back to his apartment, he wondered, with a kind of stunned sadness, why he had never before suspected Faith could be a leader of the new alumbradas.

Chapter 10

The contact with the divine is almost always described by Teresa as pain-filled, but it is a pain of ecstatic and ultimately joyful union. For this reason, many have mistakenly compared it to sexual union between a man and woman, but that ecstasy is, by definition, fleeting and unsustainable, with both the pain and ecstasy dissolving in coitus. Teresa's prayerful union with God and her careful directions for achieving that union need a far different paradigm than sex to be understood and duplicated. People are always quoting those lines where she compares divine contact to the thrusting of a sword in and out, which Bernini immortalized further with his sculpture, and which makes everybody turn to the sexual parallel. But how many people are familiar with Teresa of *The Interior Castle* who encourages us to 'annihilate ourselves,' detaching ourselves from all things, in order to receive that 'delicious wound,' that 'most precious grace,' that 'hurt that never heals'? Teresa once said, 'let me suffer or let me die,' because as the nineteenth century Spanish poet Bécquer also understood,

'*Padecer es vivir*,' to suffer is to live."

These words from Marissa Hitzel's honor thesis proposal were disturbing to Tony, not only because they indicated a dangerous path for a young woman who had, since penning them, actually been murdered, but also because he knew enough about St. Teresa's work to know she wasn't being misquoted, however much she might have been misunderstood. He hadn't actually read any of the saint's works in years, but he thought more and more that he would have to get back to her books in order to understand what might really be behind the three murders he had agreed to help investigate. It wasn't unusual for a professor to think he could catch up on his reading during the Christmas break, but could Tony really wait that long, when another potential victim's life might be saved with a little more diligence? And so he promised himself to get right to the library as soon as he returned to Smith in the morning. Yet as he was pulling out of his parking space, thoughts of Smith jogged his memory to the annual department holiday party Hank Gallagher was hosting, and he got on his cell phone to call in his regrets.

"What do you mean you can't come? You already cancelled our lunch a few days back. What the hell's going on, Tony?" Hank asked, sounding a lot more put out than Tony had anticipated.

"Something else came up last minute, Hank. I'm sorry, I—"

"You're sorry? What about me stuck with all these femi-Nazis and other drips without you to keep me sane? I was counting on you. Are you sure you can't cancel whatever else you got rooked into? It's not something Faith's dragging you to, is it?

"No, nothing like that. But I really can't get out of it."

"Get out of what, then?"

"I really can't say, Hank, sorry, I—"

"Must be some other pair of legs, then. You think I'd rat you out, ever, mystery man? Especially to Faith Covington?"

Tony decided it was no time to get into another argument over why he was dating Faith, so he instead responded, "Really, Hank, it's nothing like that. Listen, I gotta go—I shouldn't be talking and driving like this in the first place."

"Yeah, all right, I'll let it slide this time, but you owe me, then, big time," Hank decided, though still not sounding at all appeased.

"I'll just owe you all the more, then, Hank. Thanks for understanding."

Tony had gotten Nancy Temple's name from Veronica, with whom he had spent a few pleasant half hours chatting over the phone, unable to get away from Faith's attention for longer than that over the past three weeks since Thanksgiving. Though their sexual intimacy had essentially ended, the intensity of their relationship had still somehow grown, at least at Faith's end. She had become far more possessive, had shown up several times unexpectedly during his office hours, once just five minutes after he had gotten off the phone with Veronica, and Faith had spent every night with him either at his apartment or hers.

She only wanted to talk, though, to try to prepare Tony for a new level of commitment, one which would make conventional sexual relationships, if not irrelevant, than at least incidental. Tony felt guilty in feigning more interest than he actually felt. To him, Faith's leanings were worrisome and seemed more fanatical than inspired. Still, he needed to learn more about Faith's sources and outlets for her mystical ideas. He needed to pretend he was completely on board this metaphysical journey.

The main reason Nancy Temple and Marissa Hitzel's other closest friends had agreed to meet with him, he assumed, was because of his notoriety as an author and one-time rebel within the Catholic Church. She had, in fact, invited him to participate in a "study group" that was meeting at her house that very evening. What exactly the course of study would be, Tony was more than a little anxious to discover. That anxiousness even included some worry for his personal safety, so he had made sure to let his brother know about this latest investigation and was hoping to find a subtle way to let Nancy and her classmates know that people knew he would be spending part of his evening with them.

Tony's fears were not allayed when he arrived at Nancy's residence. Her directions had led him to believe she did not live near the Holy Cross campus, but he was surprised to find those directions sending him entirely outside the city limits of Worcester, to a wooded area where the houses were separated from each other enough to make the nearest neighbor invisible. The house itself seemed run down as Tony drove up to the driveway in December dusk. He could make out peeling, yellow paint, curled up old shingles, and, eventually, shaky wooden front steps in need of repair. Precious little light emanated from inside, and the big bay window, with its peeling insulation, no longer received any light from the disappearing sun. Tony went ahead and knocked, with an old brass knocker on a dirty, red wooden door. He didn't need to wait long before a young woman opened to him.

"Professor Cupelli?" the woman asked, rhetorically. "I'm so glad you found us. A few of my friends thought I might be making it up, having a celebrity join us for the evening."

Nancy's voice was soft, measured and calm, which belied a little her flaming red hair and bright green eyes.

Those eyes shone, somehow, in spite of the candlelight, which only semi-illuminated the living room into which Tony was ushered.

"Has the power gone out?" he wondered, hopefully. He wasn't surprised, much, though, by the response.

"No, not at all. We just like to have these discussions of Teresa without any of the conveniences she herself would not have known. Of course, it isn't always possible, but candles over electric lights—that's pretty easy."

Nancy kept sounding harmless to Tony and, as he looked around the room, he saw four other college-aged women, all of whom also looked pretty normal, much like the women he was now teaching at Smith. Tony decided not to panic unless there were far more reason than the lack of electric light. After introductions to the others, two dark haired, tall, thin women, Angela and Teresa, a short blonde named Sally and a possibly Indian woman, with very short, black hair and dark, intense eyes, named Shanti, Tony sat down on a slightly dusty, old, burnt-orange sofa, next to Teresa, who at a closer look was quite pale, almost gaunt. He then listened to Nancy apologize about the run down nature of their home, which she shared with Shanti and Sally and which had the advantages of being both relatively inexpensive and out in nature. The more everything coming out of Nancy's mouth seemed reasonable, the more Tony assured himself he had nothing to worry about, though he still did not have himself entirely convinced.

"I hope you don't mind my saying this," Angela, began from across the room, "but we're really excited to have you come speak to us. We've been debating if a man could really ever be in sympathy with St. Teresa's real message, but a few of us think, based on your book on the Holy Spirit, that if any man could join us, it would be you."

"That's Angela for you, always wanting to cut to the chase." Nancy laughed, a little nervously, maybe. "But maybe Professor Cupelli would like to relax a minute before it's time for an Inquisition."

"Nobody expects the Spanish Inquisition," the gaunt woman to his right deadpanned, a line he knew well from Monty Python, but which had a little too much Peter Lorre in its present intonation for his taste, including its concluding Lorre-like two syllable laugh.

"Maybe you'd like something to eat." Nancy pointed to some cheese and crackers and a bowl of honey-roasted nuts. "Or some wine, though we only have red. Oh, and don't worry—we're all over twenty-one."

Remembering that poison was what had killed Sister Maria Dolores made Tony neither hungry nor thirsty. "I just had a nice meal a little before I got here," he deferred. "I've still got to drive, and the older I get the less wine it takes to make me tipsy, so I'd better say no. Thanks, though."

"Okay, then," Angela asserted. "I was saying, just last week in fact, that your book on the feminine reality of the Holy Spirit fits right into everything our saint believed in."

Tony best-selling book *The Holy Spirit: Restoring Respect to the Sacred Feminine,* had argued, to strong controversy but with mostly excellent reviews, that Christ himself had always presented the third part of the Trinity as a feminine force, not only evidenced by the word for spirit, *ruah*, being feminine in both Hebrew and Aramaic, but also by the early, misogynistic church's conscious decision to choose in translation, the masculine word "spiritu" over the feminine Latin word "anima," as a part of a plan to go against the idea of referencing any of the Godhead as feminine. But rather than a belief in an actual "goddess," Tony had argued that God was, of course, without gender, though the only way to emphasize woman's equal role in and outside of the church was to be able to refer to God as either man, Father, or woman, Holy Spirit. He felt pretty confident that his present audience had read more into his book than he had actually intended. But he didn't want to share that suspicion with any of them.

"Tell me more. I'm really intrigued," he stated instead.

Though he almost felt Nancy's green eyes trying to pierce her friend Angela's intent enough to change it, Angela would not be denied.

"It's simple, really." Angela leaned toward Tony, the distance across the small room certainly insufficient to disrupt her intensity. "We believe St. Teresa could not afford to be fully frank about her truest beliefs because of the Inquisition. She saw what the priests did to the others, like Magdalena de la Cruz, who were less careful. But, at heart, we believe Teresa knew you didn't need priests, or any other men, to get to a union with God."

"But doesn't she use language about being Christ's bride. Isn't that who she seeks union with, and, after all, Christ was fully human and a man," Tony offered, but with a tone that implied he'd welcome correction.

"Just another diversion, we think," the woman on his sofa said. "Give the men what they want, we're just the brides of Christ. But, of course, there's only one God, one soul, and it's all spirit, all Holy, feminine Spirit, just like you say."

"So you really do think Teresa was no 'saint' in the orthodox Roman Catholic sense? You really think she was one with people who thought like Magdalena de la Cruz or later Isabel de la Cruz? What name did they have for them, I'm trying to remember," Tony feigned, hoping his acting was not too weak to convince.

"Illuminati in Italian, alumbrados, in Spanish, the ones lit up by the one true fire, the ones able to do exactly as St. Teresa describes in *The Way of Perfection*, to get to a pain that never ceases, a fire that never goes out, a union with God that is perpetual and that makes everything else unimportant. Her message is there. The wonder is how the church let her get away with it," Angela concluded.

"The wonderful thing is how great a gift she had as a writer that she could get us all the essential message and still seem orthodox enough to actually be designated the first female Doctor of the church," Tony's sofa companion added.

The enthusiasm of those two speakers did not seem to be shared by Nancy and her other two friends. Shanti, in particular, seemed to be sending dark daggers with her eyes at Angela and Teresa.

Tony nodded. "You know, it's not like I haven't considered some of these same things myself. I've often wondered if Teresa might just be paying lip service to the idea of loving one's neighbor, while really focusing on how to get to union with God wholly on your own. It makes me want to reread her work more carefully."

"You see, he is in sympathy," Angela practically cheered. "I knew he would be."

"It's one thing to consider, another to believe," Nancy cautioned. "Not that it matters, of course, whether you agree with us or not—though, frankly, Professor Teuma is unsympathetic to the point of bias. And when she's your professor, that can't be a good thing."

"Are you all students of hers?"

"Only Angela and I have had that pleasure," Nancy smirked.

"Well, ladies, you are going to a Catholic school. Over at Smith things are very different. There's no overt bias to any particular point of view, but you can't expect that same treatment at a place called 'College of the Holy Cross.'"

"No, that's certainly true," Nancy admitted, a bit ruefully, Tony thought.

"Did Marissa feel the same thing? Did she feel Professor Teuma wasn't being objective?" Tony decided to ask, though he knew bringing up a recently murdered friend to this odd grouping of women might not be the wisest thing to do. But he could not think of a wiser question, and the sudden turn in topic might surprise some honesty into the answer.

"Marissa loved Professor Teuma," Nancy insisted. "It was Professor Teuma who got her so into St. Teresa and her true teachings in the first place. But Veronica Teuma is dogmatic, like the church itself, so Marissa did get frustrated. But why does any of that matter now?"

The way Nancy asked her question, stepping toward Tony as she did so, though under the guise of picking up Teresa's wine glass to refill it, made him feel she suspected he thought he could find answers, or at least their beginnings, to Marissa's murder in his present line of questioning. But her tone of voice, her whole green-eyed demeanor, warned him to be careful about admitting his suspicions too openly. And he was reluctant to share with these college students his awareness that Marissa's murder had to be linked to those of a priest and nun, even though he himself suspected these classmates might already be aware of that connection.

"I guess it doesn't. I just know how sad Veronica is that she doesn't have a chance to work things out with one of her most promising students. It's such a tragedy, after all. I know it has to have affected you all tremendously. I didn't mean to remind you of your grief."

"We'll never forget Marissa or her pain," Teresa declared, in what now seemed like her habitually odd tone.

The overall darkness of the room, the weird intensity of these young women, who were involved in such serious and dubious study, made Tony decide he did not need to remain much longer. He drew the conversation back to St. Teresa, to his own beliefs about the Holy Spirit's feminine nature, his past advocacy for women priests and married Catholic clergy, but also on his own continued emphasis on the injunction to "Love thy neighbor as thyself."

Nancy's politeness was absent in her response. "See, Angela, he's not in sympathy with us, after all. 'Love thy neighbor.' Teresa of Avila did so the only really meaningful way possible, by teaching each of us how to unite with the divine. This can never be done by groping around with the rest of the unenlightened, but only by giving oneself up to a higher law, by realizing the best way to serve others is to not serve them at all."

"Oh, so St. Teresa was a Republican," Tony joked, and he saw Angela smile, but the others, as he expected, seemed insulted, though Nancy feigned amusement.

"If you take any great person out of context, they might seem so. Thoreau has been accused of the same thing, just for being suspicious of philanthropists."

"Now you're sounding like my girlfriend, Faith. Do you know Faith Covington, by the way?"

Angela smiled and seemed about to respond, but Nancy quickly intervened, "No, is she an English professor at Smith too?"

"No, Art. But a big fan of Thoreau nonetheless." Tony let it drop, learning more than Nancy seemed to want him to know.

When he was saying his goodbyes, both Angela and Teresa did not hesitate to offer an embrace, instead of the curt handshake of the rest of the troupe. "Divide and conquer," came to Tony's mind. Maybe he needed to figure out a way to meet with these two fans without Nancy's judging presence. But that would be for a different evening. Tony was happy to say his goodbyes and head back to his car.

Once there, the cold steering wheel reminded him that he had forgotten to bring his gloves back out of the house. They were a fairly expensive and comfortable pair, soft black leather, with rabbit's fur lining, so he needed to retrieve them. Still, he hesitated, wondering if he should leave them as an excuse for another visit. He decided to make the walk back up the driveway, but looked at the house's bay window before he got to the door, only to see, dimly, by an antique candelabra's light, Shanti and Sally with their hands interlocked and their eyes closed, a hand-holding that reminded him of his post-Thanksgiving encounter with Faith.

Tony considered drawing closer to the window to better observe their behavior, to locate the other women and see what they were up to, but then he saw that he too was being watched. Nancy, from the opposite side of the room at the far right edge of the window, was observing him closely and, somehow, like a cat's, her green eyes were glowing at him through the darkness. It was only then Tony remembered he hadn't worn his gloves out at all that evening, after which he turned quickly on his heel and headed for the safety of his automobile.

Chapter 11

Paying over a thousand dollars for five nights in Manhattan did not seem unreasonable to Tony, but when he could have been staying back in Queens for free, at Christmas time, with all the wonderful holiday foods his mother and sisters were preparing, less fancy but to him far preferable to the cheapest $38 "prix-fixe" menu option for three meager courses at the Washington Square Hotel's North Square Restaurant, he could not help but feel uncomfortable.

Though Tony could well afford the expense, and though he loved the hotel's location in Greenwich Village, he was too much his parents' child ever to enjoy an unnecessary expense. But Faith was just not a good match for five days with his family and only partly because she would have insisted on sharing a room with him, something his inveterately Catholic parents weren't going to go for. So it was Greenwich Village instead of South Ozone Park, cab rides instead of the subway, and, overall, as Faith Covington-ish a holiday as she could manage outside of New England.

Tony was unsure himself how much his acquiescence to Faith's preferences was motivated by his lingering affection for her, and how much by his desire to continue to uncover what she might know about the alumbradas. A part of him still hoped his suspicions were unfounded, though another part was taking him closer to a belief that his brother Mike had been right. Even if Faith was not mixed up in any killings, she really was not the right mate for him.

Every time he noted the confidence in her gold-green eyes, he thought of how unaware she was of his own secret agenda, though he wasn't discounting the continuing power of that confidence or of those amazing eyes.

Their relationship had gotten weirder and weirder during the last few weeks of the semester. Though this weirdness made him even more suspicious, he felt he had nothing to fear from her so long as she was convinced of his loyalty. Tony was careful then not to balk as Faith more and more overtly sought to exercise a kind of control over him and showed herself less and less tolerant of his former ways. Tony had had to play along, wondering where it would lead. Mostly it had led to a lot of intense hand holding and shared silence. Upon arriving in New York, Tony, who had made no progress in figuring Faith out, shifted his strategy. It began with his announcing to Faith his temporary break from trying to keep with her vegan preferences.

Not only would he refuse to abstain from his family's traditional Christmas Eve seafood dinner or their Christmas day lasagna and turkey courses, but he also wasn't going to pass up the filet mignon au poivre or the pan seared Alaskan halibut while he was being overcharged at the Washington Square Hotel. He was hoping to test the level of Faith's patience and also maybe to get her angry enough to reveal some of what she might know

about the alumbradas. With each bite of steak or fish,
pasta or pastry, he would be getting the double benefit of
his gustatory pleasure and her possible loss of patience.
Meanwhile, though, he was wondering how he could explain Faith to his parents.

A few hours before leaving the hotel for Christmas
Eve dinner, Tony took one more shot at preparing Faith
for what it would be like at his family's home on the most
traditional night of their year.

"I've already explained vegan to them, so just have
some spaghetti al aglio, maybe a zeppola, some olives, a
Christmas cookie or two and you'll be fine, right?"

"Yes, that sounds like more than enough food. If only I could get you to agree to the same terms."

The cab ride to Queens on the evening of December
twenty-fourth was quiet, but not serene. Faith and Tony
had gotten into an argument over the length of Faith's
dress, a navy blue mini that was too mini not to make his
mother think of Tony's newest love interest as "just another *puttana.*" That she was an exceptionally well-
educated and intelligent woman from a high-class background wouldn't make her any less *puttana* to Mrs. Cupelli, who already was not happy with the idea of her
former monsignor son bringing home a girlfriend of any
sort. This mini would knock over the stacked deck and
send the cards splattering onto the old hardwood floors.
But Faith would not relent or wear pants, so they jour-
neyed to Queens in icy silence, in spite of unseasonably
warm temperatures in the forties and a light drizzle outside.

When the cab turned off the Van Wyck Expressway
and into the neighborhood of Tony's parents, he was certain he noted a suddenly wary eye and wondered if Faith
had ever in her life been in a working-class neighborhood. Of course, Faith was far too politically exact to ev-

er admit to being afraid of either relative poverty or various shades of brown skin, so Tony didn't bother to call her on her apparent uneasiness. There would be plenty of that coming up when they did get inside the one house on the block with white people in it.

Mike opened the door for them into the Cupelli home.

"Hey, nice to see you again," he greeted Faith. "You too, I guess," he smirked at his brother.

The initial introductions seemed to go well, as Faith met the Cupelli parents and his two sisters Rose Anne and Beatrice.

"It's nice to finally meet you," Rose Anne, Tony's oldest sister said without sarcasm.

But then Faith, who was wearing a knee length, dark red cloth coat, took it off and handed it over to Mike.

"*Really* nice to see you." He winked, at both Faith and Tony.

No one else said a word, but no one else needed to. Tony got Faith seated on the living room couch, but then went after Mike, who was taking the coats to an upstairs bed, with the excuse that he had left something in his own overcoat.

"Hurry up you two," Rosa yelled, as she fled, on unsteady legs, back into the kitchen. "We'll be eating in five minutes."

"What's with that dame?" Mike chortled. "Didn't you tell her what Mom is like?"

"I think that's why she did it. She just bought that excuse for a dress yesterday."

"Is she plain rude or just a little nutty?" Mike wondered, as he laid the two coats on his parents' bed.

"I'm still not sure. Well, by your standards, certainly, she's a little nutty, but you'd probably feel like that about any vegan eco-feminist."

"Yeah, silly me."

"No, listen, I'm not kidding," Tony assured him, as he grabbed his brother by the arm. "I'm really wondering if she could be mixed up in the murders. She swears, for example, that she's never met any of the last victim Marissa's friends, but Veronica tells me she's almost certain that more than one of them mentioned Faith by name and when I mentioned her name to them, one of them was about ready to say she knew her before their leader shut her up. So I think Faith's lying to me."

"Or maybe it's Veronica that's lying. How come you don't want to look at that angle?" Mike looked at Tony with a look Tony refused to accept as knowing.

"In any case, I'm wondering how I can get Faith to really open up to me. But so far I'm just making a big mess of it."

"Maybe I'll take a crack at her."

"I don't know if that's such a—"

Tony was interrupted mid-sentence by his dad's booming baritone. "What the hell are you two doing up there? Let's go—time to eat."

"Don't do anything crazy," Tony insisted, before finally letting go of his brother's arm.

"Who me?" Mike laughed. "You bring in a girl about half your age with a third of a dress to a mother who still isn't a quarter over all your past screw-ups and you're worried about me acting crazy?"

Conversation around the dining room table was neither as painful nor as nonexistent as Tony had alternately worried.

Faith, though she was willing to shock Tony's parents via the length of her dress, could not, once sitting down with them, be anything but polite to her hosts, if perhaps just a bit patronizingly so.

"I'm amazed how flavorful this spaghetti al aglio is,"

she said. "Just a little garlic and olive oil can do so much."

Mike nodded. "Yeah, you can't beat Ma or my sisters as cooks. Here, try one of these," he advised, as he passed the smaller of two bowls filled with zeppole.

"Also prepared in olive oil, right?" She waited for assurance of the fried dough's vegan friendliness.

"Nothing but," Mike promised, with a smile too angelic not to be phony.

But Faith didn't seem to notice, or else she took Mike's smile for just another nod to how attractive he was finding her to be, as they reprised their flirtations from the last time they'd had dinner together.

The meal might have gone on more smoothly than anyone had imagined possible, mostly because the Cupellis could not be rude in their role as hosts, and because, though she wouldn't touch a bit of the fried flounder, the baccalá, the whiting, the baked clams or the other assorted flesh of the sea, Faith did show a good appetite for what she could touch. Once someone had "broken bread" with the Cupellis and shown an appreciation for that food they were offered, she or he was forever on another plain of relationship, was at least a little bit a part of the family. But Mike was not willing to let things go quite that way.

"You've hardly touched your zeppola," he noted, ten minutes or so after she had first received it from him. '*Mangia, mangia,*' like my mother says. Bite into it."

Faith obliged, but then said mostly for Mike's ears: "You know, it's very good, but just a little saltier than I thought it would be. Tony told me he used to like to put powdered sugar on his."

"Yeah, you can do that with the ones without *alice*," Mike told her, with a nod to the larger bowlful of zeppole.

Faith tried to repeat the foreign word Mike had ended his sentence with. "*Ah lee che?*"

"You didn't give her the ones with *alice?*" Rose Anne fretted. "You knew she was a vegan, Mike, no?"

Mike smiled. "Oh, geez, for a minute I forgot. Well, really, it's just a really small fish—like an anchovy—just enough for flavor, you know? Dad loves 'em like that and Tony too."

Faith, knowing she had the remnants of a small, dead fish in her, seemed torn somewhere between annoyance and an insistence on maintaining decorum.

"You seem upset?" Mike actually patted her on her shoulder. "I guess this isn't the time then to tell you that the spaghetti has some butter in it too."

"Mike!" Tony protested, not because he hadn't already known that fact, but because he had been confident it could stay a secret.

"What? Weren't you telling me yourself you wished she didn't have to miss all this good food?"

"I, well I, uh—"

Faith smiled, while she pointedly patted his shoulder herself. "It isn't something I could suppose your brother could understand."

"Yeah, I mean, I guess you gotta be a lot smarter than I am to figure on why a little bit of fish or butter is so much worse than all the eggs that were aborted for that zabaglione you devoured last time I saw ya."

Faith's face registered a quick "touché," but her voice made no reply. She instead pointedly took another bite of her zeppola, chewed it with something close to voluptuousness, and then announced, "I guess there are worse things than a little fishy tang, right Michael?"

Mike laughed. "Now you're talking."

"Mike, you're impossible," Beatrice scolded, but with a smile, seeing that their guest did not seem too upset.

Rosa looked as if she might say something, but when she did it was only, "Could someone please pass the baccalá?"

Tony expected an earful on the cab ride back to the hotel, but Faith did not berate him a bit, which made him certain she was saving it all for when they would not be within earshot of a cabbie. But after a mostly silent ride, Faith still did not seem angry or even needful of venting over the way Mike had tricked her. Tony felt restless and put on the TV, even though it was another item of contemporary culture for which Faith had little approval. He thought he heard her talking briefly on the telephone and wondered what it could be about. After about twenty minutes had passed there was a knock on the door.

Tony asked a little nervously, "Who's there?" only to be answered with "Room service, sir."

Having seen more than one TV show where that lie had gained a killer entrance into his victim's room, Tony answered back with conviction, "I didn't order any room service," but then he heard Faith call out from the bedroom.

"Oh, I did. Please let him in, Tony."

Still not certain it was beyond the realm of possibility that Faith had called up the ultimate revenge, and that Tony was to be the next victim of the crimes of the alumbradas, he still hesitated. But, feeling embarrassed by his fear, he opened the door, upon which a polite and efficient hotel employee brought in trays with the food Faith had apparently ordered—some kind of fish dish, and some sort of chocolate dessert. Tony tipped the man and wondered what Faith was up to. He didn't wait long to find out.

Faith emerged from the bedroom of their suite in only a bra and panties, in matching hunter green, Tony's favorite shade of his favorite color.

She smiled. "I see the food has arrived."

"What's this all about? You know I ate plenty back home."

"Yes, but I didn't, and I realize you think your brother ruined my evening, so I wanted to be certain to distance you from that misperception."

Since her tone was anything but amorous, Tony quipped, "Let me distance you from pneumonia. Here, put on this hotel robe before you get a serious chill."

"I'm fine, Tony, and I want you to know how fine."

Faith sat at the small table where the food had been deposited, quickly cut up a piece of fish, sole apparently, and ate it with obvious enjoyment.

"What are you trying to prove?" he asked his scantily clad, fish-eating girlfriend.

Faith continued to eat the fish, and some asparagus within a buttery sauce, but, in between bites she explained. "I know you're a Borges fan, so you'll remember 'The Writing of the God.'"

"I'm still not following." Tony tried to turn away and pretend to be looking at Sports Center, but even he knew that was a feeble dodge.

"The Aztec priest, once he uncovers the handwriting of God, in the pattern of the jaguar's spots, has the key to all things in the universe, and so merges with God, and has no care for any of the trivial matters of his former life, even to the extent of no longer needing to escape his imprisonment."

Tony laughed, sat in the other chair near the table, even thought he might try some of the chocolate dessert, which he guessed now was mousse. "So, by eating an anchovy, you've found the key to flesh eating and can now enjoy a filet of sole? So, this night wasn't a total loss after all, right?"

"I've been keeping this from you, Tony, waiting for

you to catch up, but I know now it's hopeless. Once you've reached union with the divine, there isn't any more sin, there isn't any right or wrong, you no longer think in right or wrong—whatever you do is holy, since you yourself are encased in holiness."

Faith grabbed the mousse away from the table, took a big spoonful straight from the bowl, and began to eat it hungrily. "Your brother was right. Zabaglione, fish, butter, raw red meat if I so choose—what does it matter? That part of me that saw those things as impediments to holiness—which they really still are for you—to me, have become without meaning. To the goddess there is no sin. Whatever I should like to do, I can do. And even though you aren't worthy, tonight I'm going to show you all you'll be missing for the rest of your life without me, without this divine truth."

Faith got up, pulled Tony's chair out enough so she could sit on his lap. Alternately she fed herself and Tony fish and mousse and intruded her sense of divinity upon him like an assault. Tony did not know how to respond, worried—now that Faith had essentially admitted herself to be an alumbrada—whether it was safe to remain with her. As she began to unbutton his shirt, he wondered if the food had been poisoned, but she was eating right along with him and seemed way too smug to be suicidal. He wondered whether the knife used to cut the fish was sharp enough and long enough to kill him, but she'd have to catch him unawares and he was very aware. Was he to be offered as a sacrifice, his heart cut out in celebration of this crazy alumbrada's divorce from all worry about good and evil? He also keenly felt how wrong it would be to stay bound to this woman who was expressing something much closer to contempt than love, even as she sat nearly naked on his lap. Every bit of sense he still owned told him to get out and take a cab or even the subway back to the safety of his family in Queens. But Faith had never come near to approaching this passion or sensuality before, and he found he had room for the chocolate mousse, the sole was lighter than any of the fish he had had at his mother's, and even—what serendipity—asparagus was his favorite vegetable.

Chapter 12

Christmas was about over. Presents had been opened, church had been attended, a huge dinner had been consumed. Mike and Tony retreated to the basement of the Cupelli home in Queens in order to be alone in their discussions, their ready excuse that they had no desire to watch *It's A Wonderful Life*, yet again, a late blooming tradition for Christmas night their two sisters had cooked up about ten years before. Their father might have joined them, if it had been a bit less chilly in the basement and if the big blue couch in the living room had been a bit less comfortable.

As soon as they were alone, Tony began insistently. "It makes me sad to say this, but I'm also certain Faith is an alumbrada. And I doubt she can be one without being involved somehow in this mess. If you can get to her, I bet the case will be practically solved."

"Listen, Ton', it ain't as simple as that. I mean, yes, it's good, it's progress even, maybe, but we're still a long way from done here."

"What's left?"

"Are you serious? Even if we think we 'know' now that your girlfriend is in some kind of cult, so what? It doesn't prove they had anything to do with these murders and certainly doesn't prove she had anything to do with them. Hell, she was with you when the second one happened. I mean, we don't have any real evidence. This is just the start and, now that she knows that you know, well, you ain't getting nothing else from her anytime soon, right?"

"Right. Yeah, we didn't leave on good terms."

"Okay, it probably couldn't have been helped. But, hey, it's time to start getting really serious. You've got how much time before you gotta teach again?"

"The new semester doesn't start for another two weeks."

"Good. There's some things you can do with me here in New York, and then I want you back up there, checking some other stuff out."

"Okay, whatever you say."

Mike chuckled. "I think you really mean that, ace. You know, you haven't said one thing to annoy me the whole day. It's gotta be some kind of a record."

Tony had neglected to explain all the circumstances leading up to his confidence about Faith's leanings. Not only had he left out the sex, but also the scary way Faith had insisted on her having access to the rapture that never ends. Tony had felt immediate regret after making "love" to Faith, without even the pretense of any kind of affection between them, and now was more convinced than ever that something potentially very dangerous was brewing among the women ready to identify themselves as alumbradas.

He was certain they were taking all of their ideas from a misreading of St. Teresa, since in *The Interior Castle,* the final rapture was a permanent state, one that could easily be mistaken for what the alumbradas sought. Tony himself knew he would have to study the saint's writings far more carefully to find out how, if at all, the ideas really did differ and whether any such difference might matter in solving the crimes.

Meanwhile, he settled for telling his brother, "You can joke all you want. I just want to stop these people before they kill someone else."

"I believe you, Ton'. Meanwhile, now Faith knows you ain't planning on playing for their team, you have to be more careful. You could be the next person on their list."

"You'd hate for that to happen, right?" Tony said, with a flippant tone, but also an understated wish for a positive, unequivocal response.

"You know I would, so you be careful," Mike responded with conviction, though he somehow could not keep himself from adding, "The folks would be plenty pissed if I let you get killed helping me on one of my cases."

The next day Tony spent rereading *The Interior Castle,* a book he could read, sitting in his parents' living room, without criticism, aside from Rosa's lament, "If only you had stuck with the saints, your whole life would have come out different."

"God forgives, Ma, even if you don't," Tony reminded her.

"Don't be a wise guy. You know what I mean." His mother was not a bit shamed. "But I'm still glad you're reading our own parish saint's book. She suffered a lot, but she turned her pain into something good."

"Yeah, but Mom, that's because she thought pain was good. You know, because the more we suffered the more we had a chance to emulate Christ. But the thing is, a lot of people misunderstand that and—"

"But you don't, right?" Rosa interrupted.

"No, no, not me," Tony assured his mother, even as he tried to assure himself.

He couldn't get Mike to explain why he needed him at the precinct, later that same afternoon, but once he entered the gray hallways of the 107th Precinct in Flushing, where Mike had worked for the past two years, and was escorted to his brother's desk, he didn't have long to wonder.

"Come in here with me. You need to see this," Mike stated as he walked Tony over to a room closed off from the open area he had first entered. "This just gets weirder by the minute."

Mike pushed a few buttons on a DVD player and noted, "We just got this in the mail today with no return address. Take a look."

Mike had not prepared his brother for the shocking nature of the video. It lasted less than ten minutes but in that amount of time the two brothers witnessed four women praying together, two of them at kneelers, with their hands tied behind their backs, each with a woman standing over her, choking her with some kind of brown, beaded chord. The kneeling women wore long, dark gowns, but their heads were bare, while the standing women wore similarly dark garments, but with their heads and faces shrouded by cowls. The tighter the pressure each woman applied to her partner, the more fervently the women prayed, with particularly eerie and ironic emphasis each time on the end of the prayer, which Tony recognized as the Ave Maria, "*nunc et in hora mortis nostrae*." After a number of Ave Marias, Tony understood the Latin of the Glory Be and then some weird variation of the Our Father, which had now become, essentially, the "Our Mother," *mater* having been not so seamlessly substituted for *pater*. It was with horror then that he realized the women were praying their version of the Rosary, while being strangled by Rosary beads.

"Oh, my God, no." Tony was close to tears.

"You can say that again, man. Yeah, those are Rosary beads all right. We already had this all blown up before you got here. Guess what their hands are tied with."

"Their hands? By scapulars, brown ones, right?"

"Yeah, how'd you know that?" Mike asked, though not with much surprise in his voice.

Tony shuddered. "This is so sick."

"Aren't you even curious who these women are?"

"I can't make out at all the two who are standing up, their faces are covered and the camera never seems to focus on them, but, for that matter, I don't recognize either of the ones we can see. They aren't any of the last victim's friends are they?"

"I don't know about that. But the first vic, Sister Maria Dolores, that's her on the left, kneeling."

"But, but how is that possible? She was a nun, a discalced Carmelite nun."

"Where do you think this little bit of porno was filmed?

"Don't tell me."

"Yeah, I'm sorry, Ton', I've been there, remember— it's the convent in Brooklyn."

"But this means—"

"This means our poor little nun must have been an alumbrada, had second thoughts, and now she's a poor dead nun. And it also means you're in more danger than ever."

"What are you talking about? This is the New York part of the crime. What's it got to do with me?"

"I told you there was no return address. But the postmark—you didn't ask about the postmark."

Tony was pretty sure he didn't want to know, but

some things are impossible to avoid, like the clear, round, gray ink postmark on the manila envelope his brother put in front of his face, distinctly stating Worcester, MA, just as distinct as the words the nuns continued to utter in a nightmare he knew also could not be denied. "*Ora pro nobis peccatoribus, nunc et in hora mortis nostrae, Amen.*"

Chapter 13

Mike had advised Tony to stay home for New Year's Eve, a quiet night with the folks, watching the ball come down from the friendly confines of an old house in Queens, beside his father's snoring, his sisters' and mother's trustworthy chatter. But Isabel Goya had paid a fortune for the tickets—$195 per, he'd looked it up on line—and so how could he turn down a night of dining and dancing in the "legendary Grand Ballroom" of the Garden City Hotel? And now that he was certain he and Faith were through, why not consider a possible relationship with Isabel?

Though he promised himself to take it slowly, he now could admit his attraction to her more openly. He also knew she was about as far from the world of vegans, militant feminists, and especially alumbradas, as any woman he knew.

Besides, it wasn't like he was going to join all the crazy revelers in Times Square—he was going to an affluent Long Island neighborhood to celebrate the ringing in the new with other couples who could afford four hun-

dred dollars for one night's festivities. There was nothing
he could do by way of investigation that night anyway, so
why not spend the evening with a beautiful young woman
who was also a trusted friend?

Isabel wore an elegant long, black dress with the
classic sexy slit, revealing her long legs, legs that insisted
on spending more time on the dance floor than Tony
would have chosen. Tony always found it difficult to say
no to a beautiful woman, so he faked his way through an
evening mostly on his feet.

It helped that Isabel seemed totally charmed by him,
no matter the ineptness of his dance steps. He had insisted on meeting Isabel at the party and he fully planned to
drive back to his parents' place, shortly after the party
ended at two in the morning, so he knew not to do more
than maybe sip a bit of champagne. He was happy with
sparkling water to wash down all the food he felt free to
consume.

Isabel didn't seem to mind that choice either and her
lack of criticism of his decisions was a welcome relief
from Faith's various indictments. Tony's enjoyment of
this contrast prompted him to share with Isabel his certainty that he and Faith were no longer a couple.

"Really? For certain? I mean, this isn't just a temporary break-up you'll patch together once you both have
nothing better to do in that little town, is it?" Isabel wondered, even as she held him closer still for one of the
evening's slow songs, "Unchained Melody."

"No, we're definitely through. I don't see how it
could be any more definite."

"Well, that's wonderful news. I mean, this really is
getting the New Year off to a good start." Isabel embraced that forthcoming newness by inserting one of her
legs just below Tony's crotch. On the crowded dance
floor of hundreds headed toward drunkenness, if not al-

ready there, no one seemed to notice the overt tone of Isabel's movements.

"I can't wait for midnight, Tony. I've been waiting too long as it is," she assured him, as she gave him a long lasting kiss, and then another, a reverie only interrupted by the shift of music to a fast-paced song.

At first Tony was elated to know Isabel wanted him in every sense of the verb. And for the next half hour, as they sat holding hands, sharing food, and looking longingly into each other's dark eyes, Tony felt an odd mix of excitement and relief in being with a woman every bit as attractive to him as Faith, but with none of her demands or recently exposed dangers. But then Isabel excused herself to use the ladies' room. And in those minutes she was away, Tony had time to look at his surroundings, time to think about where he really was.

Ironically, it was the preponderance of people dressed in black, particularly one man whose white undershirt was peeking out from under his black shirt and suit jacket, that first took Tony some place he was not expecting to go. Though he hadn't had more than a few sips of alcohol, his mind raced dizzily away from the party and back to his former priestly garb and the reasons he had worn it proudly for many years. Though he had not lived up to his vows, among his sins had never been a desire for material things. Yet now he was centered in a mad celebration of too much drink and food and misplaced passion, and he was suddenly ashamed. And once his mind took the beginning of that path, there was plenty of room for further travel.

A priest, a nun, and a college student had been the murder victims. In his role as either priest or professor, he felt related to all of them, and also as if he had let all of them down. How could he be at a crazy, wasteful party, how could he be open so soon to another sexual relationship, how could he think of his own urges only, when their killer was still loose, free to murder more?

And then the woman he was with was not only too young, but too enamored of him because of his history as her father's childhood friend and her aunt's illicit lover, an aunt she knew she resembled too much. Tony guessed that at least part of what Isabel wanted was to shock her parents, while becoming the new obsession of Tony's life. Tony's priestly devotion had been waylaid by his mistaken passion for Maggie Rosario, a woman whose controlling nature allowed him to feel seduced rather than responsible for his sins. He had just escaped a controlling, unhealthy relationship with Faith, and now, not a week later, was poised to begin another. Never one to worry about New Year's resolutions, he decided in that brief moment away from Isabel, it was time to start worrying. It was time to recognize his responsibility for his path in life, time to say no to the ridiculous idea that seduction left him no choice.

As he saw Isabel walk back toward their table, he still was uncertain what he might say, if anything. As she got closer, he realized he could hardly distinguish her from the Maggie Rosario of twenty years before. When closer still, he thought he noted the same almost predatory look to her eyes and her smiling lips.

"Did you miss me?" she asked then smiled again as she touched his cheek with her hand before returning to her seat.

Tony shuddered at Isabel's touch. "Your hands are cold," he explained.

"You'll have to warm them for me, then," she countered with a smile.

Tony decided to do nothing drastic, not try to cut the evening short of its witching hour, just stick with the plan of heading back after the party, sober in every sense, to his parents' home in Queens. But after another close dance, during which Isabel might have sensed something had changed, she made that plan inoperable.

"Listen, *mi amor*, it's driving me crazy too."

"What is?"

"Don't be coy now. I know what you want, what we both want, but you're always such a gentleman, plus you know how much I spent on this evening, so you're thinking we shouldn't cut it short at not even ten o 'clock."

"Well, no, Isabel, that isn't it exactly, I'm—"

"But you don't have to worry," Isabel assured Tony with another gentle brushing of his face with her hand. "I checked before we arrived and there are some rooms right here, still unreserved. They're discounting them in fact, not that that matters. We can leave right now. I've got what I wanted. I can have you in a king sized bed and start our New Year's together with a lot more than a kiss in a crowded room of drunks."

Tony had never believed in celibacy and had, for years, convinced himself it was not a sin to go against an untenable vow. Still, when he had entered the priesthood, he had been the virgin his religion wanted him to be, mostly because of a combination of inept shyness around women and his inability to be with the one woman he had always almost worshipped, Maggie Rosario. When she had come back into his life years later, he had reveled in his ability finally to attract her and had since found himself always happily surprised when any woman wanted to be with him.

But some strange thing had begun to blossom in him, something like regret, but not as wholly negative. Somehow the thought of letting Isabel take the blame for his own carnal desires made him feel sad and even nauseated.

His Catholic faith, the faith that he was, only now,

willing to concede had rightly dismissed him from the priesthood, insisted he employ his free will.

"Listen, Izzy, I don't know how to explain this, but I'm not really ready to rush into something new, especially not this fast. I'm sorry."

Tony had never been more sincere. He knew Isabel was too smart not to note that in his voice, his demeanor, the way he could look her in the eye without his normal mix of flirtation, desire, and feigned reluctance.

"Where is this coming from? It's like you're not the same person I left when I went away for ten minutes. Did you just get a call from Faith saying all is forgiven? How can that much change in ten minutes?"

"It has nothing to do with Faith. It's a New Year coming and maybe that's it. Or maybe I like you too much to settle for you being just my next seductress."

"That's crazy, Tony. I know who you are and there's nothing wrong with liking to be seduced. People don't change. You'd still be a priest if they could."

But Isabel made no move to touch Tony on the face or anywhere else. One more look in his eyes was enough.

"There's no point extending any of this. You look sober enough to make it back to your mother by yourself, right?"

"Yes, right, by myself," Tony agreed.

He resisted saying anything more. Isabel turned heel on him quickly and was soon a memory only of what had been about to be.

Not being a bit inebriated, Tony had no trouble finding his car and making his way onto the Southern State Parkway, back toward Queens. He felt oddly exhilarated by the prospect of actually making it back to South Ozone Park in time to see the ball drop down with his two lonely sisters and his so elderly parents. He felt cleansed and thought of how this one change to his life might help in his solving of the case with his brother. He remembered how his own involvement in the "sign of the cross" killings of three years before had been muddled by his sexual involvement. He had escaped a repeating of that history by ending his time with Faith and, though he knew Isabel had nothing to do with the case, he felt confident that staying away from his old patterns could only enhance his chances of really helping this time.

Perhaps it was because of his focus on what lie ahead, that he did not notice at first what threatened from behind. Though he was in the second right lane of four headed south, and could easily be passed from the left, he discovered a large car following him much too closely. Aware of how drinking made some people aggressive, he took his first opportunity to get over to the next lane to the right, to allow the madman to pass. But his pursuer switched lanes with him and drove all the more aggressively, getting so close that Tony was expecting to feel the jolt of contact any second.

He felt helpless. He instinctively drove faster, but his little Toyota could not possibly out gun the bigger car in pursuit. He felt himself beginning to sweat and soon after he was praying, mouthing the words of a "Glory Be" out loud. The only response was from the car behind, which finally did bump his car, once and then again even harder, hard enough to send his Corolla into a skid, which he was barely able to correct.

Tony tried to use his mirrors to look at who was behind him, but it was impossible to see a face, and he had all he could do to stay on the road. He saw a sign indicating that only a half mile remained to the next exit and so he decided he would try to lose his antagonist that way, perhaps search for some open establishment, gas station or otherwise, for safety's sake. But before he could reach the exit the car behind hit him harder, hard enough to make Tony lose control of his car. He fought with the steering wheel and the brake at once, trying to slow down, to stay on the highway. He did decrease his speed enough so that when the vehicle careened toward the shoulder, banging into the guard rail was enough to bring him to a dead stop.

Having his seat belt on and no air bag in his old blue Corolla, Tony was seriously jarred but had nothing broken or bloody, with only his left knee in some pain. He looked frantically, fearfully for his pursuer, but the dark car had disappeared. Tony tried to calm himself, but he could not get his heart to stop racing, nor quiet himself even enough to locate his cell phone. After a few minutes had passed, he heard the sure, though somewhat distant, sound of a police siren and then saw flashing red and blue lights speeding toward the scene. A moment later the state trooper was at Tony's side, and Tony hurried out as well as he was able, which caused the officer not to rush to his aid, but to draw his weapon and instruct Tony to put his hands on his battered car.

"What in the world are you doing? I thought you came to help me."

"I'll help you plenty buddy, as soon as I'm sure you're not carrying. I guess maybe you've had too much celebrating to realize you never come rushing out of a car when an officer approaches."

"Yeah, okay, sorry, but I'm telling you I had nothing to drink, maybe a half a glass of champagne all night. Some nut just ran me off the road. A big sedan, maybe black. That's who you should be getting after."

"One nut at a time, okay?" the trooper advised Tony, as he patted him down and then let him get back to a fully upright position. "You won't mind taking a breathalyzer test just to show me how little you really had, buddy, right?"

"For you, anything, 'buddy.' And I guess I don't care whether you believe me or not, since I'm actually very glad to see you."

Chapter 14

Someone had tried to injure or maybe kill Tony and the police, though more willing than the first officer on the scene to take his account seriously, had made zero progress in locating his assailant.

"Let's try to be logical about this," Mike suggested, as the brothers sat together New Year's night in Mike's own home, a fairly modest two story in Astoria, which he had kept after the divorce once his ex-wife had decided to move herself and their youngest daughter nearer to her new job in Bridgeport. "I mean, who would want to harass you and why?"

"It must have something to do with the case, right?" Tony responded, with some impatience.

"Well, sure, that's what anyone would guess first, but it isn't like you haven't made yourself some other enemies over the years."

"I thought we were on the same team now, finally, Mike. Why do you have to continue to reference my 'checkered past'? I'm sure it was one of these alumbrada nuts and—"

"But you admitted to me before, you can't even say for sure it was a woman."

"Okay, then, who do you think it was?"

"Well, here's something. How do I know it just wasn't Fernando in that black car? I checked and found out he's driving a Town Car these days, though we haven't had it checked for dents or anything yet."

"Fernando? Fernando Goya? Only one of my oldest friends?" Tony made the opening move toward getting up, but his brother gently pushed him back into his seat on the brown leather couch.

"Shut up and listen, all right? I don't really think it's Fernando either, but, hey, we know he wasn't a bit happy about you dating his daughter, plus, he's one of the few people I could guess would know where you were going to be that night."

"That's right, but Fernando? Fernando was going to kill me? Please."

"For all I know he was a little tight himself, wasn't even thinking he'd knock you off the road, panicked and drove off once he realized he had. The guy always did have a temper." Tony was about to protest further, but Mike talked through it. "All I'm saying is if you really want to help, and, damn, if you really want to stay alive, you can't rule anything out."

"Listen, Mike, I know you're mostly right, but this Fernando thing—maybe I should tell you he was at a fancy party with his wife and some friends in Manhattan all last night, and any number of eye witnesses could attest to that I'm sure."

Mike smiled. "I know. Izzy already told me and I've already had it confirmed. I'm just talking hypotheticals here and approach."

"Can we talk real suspects now?" Tony wondered.

"Do we have any?" Mike wondered back.

"Well, Faith comes to mind."

"Ah, c'mon, she must drive some little hybrid, not a big, bad black car."

"Okay, not her own car—she wouldn't be that stupid, anyway. And maybe not even her driving it, but her group all the same."

"So the alumbradas really are out to get you. I know I warned you myself to be careful, but now, in the light of day, we have to ask why."

"Because we're trying to stop them. They killed Heamey because he was trying to expose them. And that's also why they got the nun. And maybe the student too."

"But that doesn't really make any sense, does it?"

"Why doesn't it?"

"We think we know there's this new group of alumbradas. But they're a pretty secret bunch, right?"

"Well, of course they're secret, I mean, they're killing people, after all."

"No, you've got something backward there," Mike argued. "Back in the day when they had a good reason to be secretive, they apparently weren't sneaky enough not to have their asses hauled up before the Inquisition. But—news flash—there ain't no freakin' Inquisition no more. In New York there's every fringe group you can think of, even some you'd never think of, and they've got the web sites and the blogs and the conventions to prove it. So why do they have to be secretive about what they're up to at all? And why do they have to kill people to keep their secrets?"

The questions Mike asked were simple. The answers, Tony figured, had to be even more horrifying than he had at first considered.

"Well, they must be...I don't know...enacting revenge for what the Inquisition did to them all those years back. They must be serial killers, and there's no telling how many more victims might be ahead. We don't even have any clues to pattern or principle."

"You read too much, or worse yet, you watch too much *CSI* or *Bones*, though I will say that *Bones* girl is a looker."

"Yeah, you will say that." Tony shook his head again. "So you don't think they're serial killers?"

"I think everything and nothing just now. But let's say, for argument, they aren't. What are they trying to protect? Are there maybe a lot of religious mixed up in this? We already have several nuns, for sure, involved."

"That's right? Have you identified the other nuns in that video? Have they been brought in for questioning? I forgot all about that with this New Year's Eve mess."

"Well, two of them, as you know, can't be viewed well enough to identify, but the other one, the one we could see, is right from the same convent as our vic, and, no, we haven't talked to her yet. We're doing that tomorrow, in fact."

"We, meaning you and a few of the other detectives assigned to the case?"

"No, we, as in you and me, your former monsignorness."

"What? You're kidding? What for?"

"I want her to know she can't smoke screen me—that I've got a religious expert with me, and maybe even one that's sympathetic to her crazy ideas a little. It couldn't hurt. You get to be the 'good cop.'"

"But are you sure this is kosher? I mean, shouldn't this be strictly police business now? I mean, I shouldn't be interrogating suspects, should I?"

"Listen, I've cleared your participation now with my CO. So long as I don't get you involved with anything dangerous, so long as we always make clear to whoever we're talking to that you're not a cop, so long as I don't give you a gun, he's fine with it, okay?"

"I guess. I just hope I don't screw things up."

Mike got up to get himself another beer, brought one also for his brother, though Tony's first Beck's was only half finished. He then continued. "We don't want it to seem like an interrogation at all. You being with me, that makes it seem all the less so. But we'll be upfront with her and she'll know you're not a cop. But we're gonna find out what this nun knows. We especially want to see if we can figure out how many nuns might be involved and whether it's local, national, international, intergalactic, whatever. Maybe then we'll have a better idea."

"But they're not all nuns, not if Faith is involved."

"If, yeah, that's right, if."

"You think she isn't?"

"No, man, I'm with you. I think 'if.' Remember, she could be one of these alumbradas and still not be a killer. I mean, they could have a whaddaya call it, a 'lunatic fringe,' right?"

"How can you tell them apart without a scorecard?" Tony was surprised he could make even that feeble of a joke.

"The ones who poison or strangle people or try to run them off the road—those are your extremists, I guess."

"But let's not forget this secret writing of St. Teresa stuff. That's got to be key. Do you at least agree with me there?"

"I don't know. We'll see what the sister spills tomorrow. Meanwhile, I want you to stay here with me tonight. I've got your little Toyota in the body shop on a rush job to get repaired—it pays to know people—and I've already told Ma not to expect you."

"Do you really think that's necessary?"

"I don't know, but if someone's tailing you, I want them to know you're not at the folks', so they'll be safe. And here with me, you'll be plenty safe, frater."

"Latin, from you?"

"Hey, I wanna be ready for that nun, okay?"

"Yes, certainly, that's okay with me frater meus."

"Always gotta one-up, don'tcha?"

"Old habits. But what am I going to do for clothes? My suitcase is back with the folks."

"It's not for nothing we're practically twins. *Mi ropa es tu ropa.* Except maybe for my black leather—but you've already got a coat with you."

"Okay, hands off the leather." Tony laughed before finishing off his beer and grabbing the second. "And I will feel safer, thanks."

He sipped his beer and wondered what he would say to that nun the next day. He also wondered how safe he would feel once he had to head back to Smith for the new semester. But for now, he felt a little lift, from the Beck's perhaps, or maybe from working with his almost mirror image and, for the first time in years, not having that image smirking or snarling back at him, not even a little.

Chapter 15

The discalced Carmelites' convent in Brooklyn was just across the Queens border, a little past Ridgewood, off Highland Boulevard. Rows of elegant, spacious Victorian houses, sometimes referred to as "mansions," by the uninformed, lined the boulevard leading up to the Carmelite buildings on Roberts Place.

Mike and Tony drove together in Mike's black Mustang, arriving a little before the scheduled ten o'clock meeting. It had taken some doing to get all the people with a vote to allow them to talk with Sister Anna Teresa alone, with the Prioress, Sister Perpetua, being especially reluctant, but she'd had to acquiesce to her superiors.

Mike reminded Tony of how careful they had to be in how they questioned this nun, in case they needed some of what she might reveal to be admissible later in a court of law.

Sister Anna Teresa had been the other of the two nuns who were at the receiving end of the choking rosary. She met them in the small room reserved for the occasional visits allowed to the sisters, a room freshly painted in an off-white shade with sturdy, simple pine chairs stained a dark brown and a large, oak crucifix on the wall facing where Mike and Tony sat. She was fully habited in the traditional Carmelite attire, which would not allow a bit of leg nor a wisp of hair to be exposed, but even so, it was not difficult to see she was attractive. She was almost as tall as the Cupellis, with a figure that somehow announced itself in spite of the habit, a fair, rosy complexion dotted with a few freckles and bright blue-green eyes.

"Hello, sister, you remember me, Mike Cupelli?"

"Yes, Lieutenant Cupelli, I do. And I'm told this is your brother, Mons—Professor Antonio Cupelli. I very much enjoyed your book on the Holy Spirit, Professor."

Sister Anna seemed composed. Her voice was assured and almost soothing. It was the brothers' best guess that she knew nothing about their awareness of her connection to Sister Maria Dolores. In her first interview with the police, she had only expressed sorrow and surprise over the sister's passing.

"It's very gracious of you to say so," Tony said to her compliment of his work. "I was afraid my exit from the clergy, my disgrace, would have made you hesitant to even agree to speak with me."

"Our God is a God of love, and forgiveness. Our place is not to judge any man."

"Yes, that's all well and good," Mike agreed, "but sometimes we all have to make judgments. If Tony here has a student who writes a rotten essay, no matter how forgiving he might be by nature, he's got to give the girl a low grade, and me, for me it's even worse. No matter how much I might like or at least understand some criminal, if I think she might be guilty, I've got to book her, though of course, I leave the ultimate judging to a higher authority."

"To God, you mean?" sister asked with a voice full of approving innocence.

"Nah, Sister," Mike smirked. "I mean to a judge and jury."

Sister Anna smiled, seeming to appreciate the rough playfulness of Mike's tone.

Though as a discalced Carmelite she spent the largest part of each of her days in silence, she did not seem to mind talking at all.

Small talk prevailed for another ten minutes or so. The brothers learned that Sister Anna had grown up in Philadelphia, had come to the religious life after an undergraduate degree at Temple in theater and English and a year of graduate school in creative writing at NYU. She found the contemplative life challenging at times, against her nature as an outgoing, engaged person, but she took consolation in St. Teresa herself having been of a similar personality and having still found her way as a Carmelite. Finally, though, the purpose of their visit had to be gotten to, and Mike started things off.

"Back to what we were saying earlier about judging or not judging. It sure isn't my first inclination to question what you sisters do to get closer to God, but something has come to our attention, involving both you and Sister Maria, that I could use some help figuring out."

Sister Anna's demeanor seemed to take a subtle turn toward worry, but if she had let that emotion surface at all, it was gone again in a flash, as she assured the brothers, "Of course I'm anxious to explain whatever I can that might be of help."

"Sister." Tony took over, mindful of using an as "seeming-sincere-good-cop" voice as he could muster. "I don't know if you were even aware you were being videotaped, or by whom, but the police have been sent, anonymously, a video of you and three other women, in the chapel here, saying the Rosary in a most unorthodox way."

Sister Anna did not gasp and only hesitated a few seconds before focusing her blue-green eyes on Tony. "I'm certain you're familiar with St. Teresa's writings. You mention them more than once in your book."

"Yes, but I'm not sure I see the connection."

Sister Anna sat up straighter in her chair, and leaned toward Tony as she added, "I've also read you have a devotion to Saint Pio of Petrelcina, a saint from your grandmother's own village in Italy."

Tony began to feel as if he were the one being interrogated, though Sister Anna's tone and demeanor could not have been taken by anyone as threatening. Mike noticed too and grew impatient.

"What's Padre Pio or Tony's books got to do with two nuns being tortured while praying by two other women? I especially want to know, since the other of the two who was tied up and choked is now dead," Mike said, with more edge than he perhaps wanted to.

Anna remained calm. "As your brother can tell you, Padre Pio, recently made a saint, was known to lash himself severely and to find other means of self-torture. He also is famous for having received the gift of the stigmata, given to him as a special blessing by God, though many were skeptical and accused him of self-inflicted wounds. And Saint Pio is only one of many saints who have chosen to mortify the flesh, so, you see, what you might have considered as something perverse, is clearly within the Catholic tradition."

"That may be so," Tony agreed. "But St. Teresa herself was not in favor of self-mortification and argued against it when it was suggested to her as a means toward greater humility and piety."

"Yes, you know her well. So you know she didn't

need outside help since her life was filled with exquisite pain."

"Odd adjective," Mike noted.

"Not at all, Detective. St. Teresa says to her 'spouse,' the Lord Jesus, 'I wish to suffer Lord, because you suffered.' And the pain she feels when in the Lord's embrace is her very means to the 'rapture' that she wishes never to end." Sister Anna's voice was close to rhapsodic itself as she continued. "She hopes the 'hurt will never cease.' In her autobiography, she goes so far as to say she would 'gladly have myself cut to pieces, body and soul, to show the joy I felt in that pain.' So, you see, what we were doing was just a first small step toward trying to suffer as Christ suffered for us and as our founder, St. Teresa of Avila, would have us do."

"So this is all just run of the mill stuff for around here, right?" Mike questioned. "So if I told your mother superior or whoever about it, she'd just give you an 'atta girl' and ask you to teach a seminar on proper rosary choking methodology, right, Sister?"

If Sister Anna felt insulted by Mike's shift in tone, she did not show it as she calmly replied, "No, I might agree that our particular prioress might take exception to what we were doing, and, overall, we aren't overtly encouraged any longer toward such endeavors, but that doesn't mean we did anything wrong."

"Disobeying a superior not wrong? What catechism are you working off?"

In response, Sister Anna leaned her body toward Mike, a bit more aggressively than she had with Tony. "Even the Baltimore catechism you were probably asked to memorize says a sin is a conscious decision to knowingly do wrong, but my conscience is clear on what you witnessed. Though I will tell you, I was not aware anyone was taping us, and that part is disturbing. I can't imagine who would have done that or why."

"You're a pretty cool customer, I'll give you that. But let's get all our cards out. Sister Maria Dolores was killed, we think, because of something having to do with some secret writings of Saint Teresa. You sure you didn't get this rosary choke from something you read there?"

"I know of no such writings. Your brother can tell you that all I just quoted from St. Teresa is hardly a secret, coming from one of our greatest Catholic mystic writers."

Maybe Tony noticed a subtle shift in tone now that metaphoric cards were on the table. The young nun seemed maybe to be enjoying how Mike was not getting the better of her, like an actress might enjoy playing a villain convincingly.

"And you're not, then, an alumbrada yourself?" Tony asked in a gentle tone, implying a quest for information over any accusations.

"That's a term I'm only vaguely familiar with. St. Teresa had a few close calls, I think, when some tried to label her one, but she was vindicated as a true believer, not a heretic."

"Okay, so I guess you won't mind telling me who the other two women are in the video tape. We'd like to talk to them, see if they can maybe help us," Mike pressed.

Anna shook her head and leaned back in her chair. "My conscience tells me now I must refuse."

"Oh it does, does it?"

"Yes, Lieutenant, I can tell you mean no good toward these women. I know they would prefer to remain out of the spotlight, and I am confident they know nothing that could help you with your investigation."

"So you refuse to cooperate with the police in finding out who killed an innocent Carmelite nun?" Mike's tone ignored his surroundings.

"I don't believe she was killed. Though it's tragic, I believe she committed suicide," Sister Anna responded.

"But if she was murdered, don't you want us to seek justice for her?" Tony injected.

"I trust in a justice that never fails, Monsignor Cupelli."

"And you're not afraid of a potential charge of hindering an investigation?" Mike countered.

"I know you'll do whatever you think is right, as I am also choosing to do," Sister Anna Teresa informed both brothers as she rose from her chair, preparatory to an exit. She pointed to the crucifix behind her and smiled benevolently at them both. "St. Teresa tells us to welcome any opportunity for suffering. She tells us, 'Do not fear the cross.' Go with God, gentlemen."

"In other words, Tony—" Mike almost laughed after Sister Anna had left. "—she's telling us to 'bring it on.' We'll see if she's still smiling when I get through with her that witch, I'll—"

"Calm down, Mike, we're still in a convent, remember?"

"Hell," Mike muttered, as he got up to leave. "I never did like nuns, but I'll tell you I prefer the ones who used to whack me for almost no reason to that smiling character."

"Yes, she was more than a little scary," Tony agreed.

"'Go with God,' she says." Mike chuckled. "She might as well have said, 'Go to Hell,' 'cause that's sure enough closer to what she really meant."

Chapter 16

Three days later Tony was visiting with his parents and sisters, though planning to return to Massachusetts after lunch. His brother had had no luck in uncovering who the other two women were in the video. All the other nuns adamantly denied any involvement and the prioress assured them that the garments worn by the women in the video were not Carmelite issue. Sister Anna Teresa would have been asked to leave the convent if it had been up to her superiors alone, but Mike had prompted them to discipline her only, since he had no idea where she might go if she were kicked out of the convent.

Lunch was bounteous but Tony, though he still ate a fair-sized hero sandwich, skipped dessert, and, overall, did not relish the food as much as usual. He thought he might be experiencing the beginnings of regret for his too frequent flirtations with gluttony, even as he had surprised himself by resisting Isabel several nights before. He found it ironic that since breaking up with Faith, who had pushed him, minus one late, last notable exception, to be less carnal and less an addict to his appetites, that he was now finding himself seeking self-control far more than when she had been coaching him. It was as if all the deadly sins were calling him out and challenging him to do better. He decided it wasn't too late to get his New Year's resolutions started and declined his mother's offer to take some pastry home with him.

About ten minutes before he might have left he received a call from his brother on his cell phone.

"There's been another murder," Mike told him point blank.

"Oh my God," Tony blurted. "Who was it this time?"

"Another priest. Listen, you don't have school for a couple days still, right?

"No, not until Monday, but I was just about to leave and—"

"Forget about leaving for now. You need to meet me over at the crime scene right away."

"Crime scene? Are you sure you have clearance to have me at an actual fresh crime scene?"

"Yeah, why not? My CO is back to trusting me. Can you get here quick?"

"Where is here?"

"I'm not fifteen minutes from where you're at—Sacred Heart parish, in Glendale. You know how to find it?"

"Yeah, I think so. I've been there a few times for meetings when I was a parish priest." Tony cringed. "Are you totally sure this is necessary?"

"It would help. You gotta trust me, Ton'."

"Okay, then, I'm on my way."

Tony promised his folks he would stop in again before he actually left Queens, explaining he needed to stay in town another day or so at Mike's place, since there was something important Mike wanted to share with him.

"It's good to see you two getting along again." Angelo nodded his approval, while Rosa shook her head suspiciously. "There's something you're not telling us," she divined, but Tony just kissed her quickly and went on his way.

When he arrived at the church, it was swarming with police ready to deny access to the average citizen, but Mike soon came and brought Tony in. "The vic's in here. I wanted you to see something, see if you can make any sense out of it, before we get him out of here."

What Mike led Tony to could hardly have been more disturbing. This was especially true because the dead man was no stranger to the former Monsignor Cupelli.

"Oh, God, that's Dave Sweeney!" he realized. "What did they do to him?"

Father David Sweeney, pastor of Sacred Heart parish, was in a wooden arm chair, upholstered in red cloth, facing the large crucifix affixed to the wall behind the tabernacle. Sweeney had his hands tied behind his back with a large, brown scapular, while around his neck were rosary beads and the ligatures they had caused when he was strangled by them.

Tony had to suppress a strong desire to vomit. He was able to compose himself only enough to say, "Why, Mike? Why did I have to come?" There were tears in Tony's eyes. "You see he's been killed the same way they were torturing those nuns. You know the Carmelite convent isn't more than five minutes from here. Why did I need to see this poor man killed this way?"

"I'm sorry, Ton' I really am. I had no way of knowing you knew the man, but there's more and you're gonna have to get closer."

Father Sweeney was bald, entirely. On his head had been neatly placed with brown paint the letters NTMDLC, with a brown cross just above the letters.

"What do these letters mean? What's the killer telling us?"

"How am I supposed to know?" Tony could not, at first, compose himself. He took a few deep breaths and continued. "It's not like it's INRI—these letters have nothing to do with the cross as far as I can tell."

"INRI? What's that stand for again?"

"You know, the inscription on the cross, 'Jesus of Nazareth, King of the Jews,' but what NTM DLC is, I mean, unless, unless it's also the first letters of some other Latin inscription, I don't know. It's certainly not anything I'd know about any more that you would. Couldn't you have just told me the letters over the phone?"

"Well, I wasn't sure, but that maybe the arrangement of the body or some other little thing on the scene here might have been something you'd think mattered."

"No, nothing like that," Tony insisted, as he wiped his tears with a tissue.

"I'm all the sorrier I brought you here, then. But, on the other hand, you knew this guy, so maybe that can help us?"

"I doubt it." Tony shook his head. "Like I said, it's Dave Sweeney. He was two years ahead of me at Cathedral Prep. I hate to say this now, but the truth is he was kind of a jerk to us underclassmen, I remember. He would have been pretty happy being head of the hazing committee in a fraternity. Since he's been a priest I haven't heard too much from him. He hasn't been one to make waves or show any particular interest in anything, as far as I know."

"Yeah, but if he was basically a conservative sort, maybe he somehow got wind of these nuts and was doing his own looking into it and they offed him," Mike hypothesized.

"I guess. It just seems like more than a coincidence,

though, that a few days after we talk to Sister Anna that this should happen this way. I mean, it's not like the others. None of the others had their hands tied behind their backs. And, to tell you the truth, I don't think Sweeney was the kind of guy really to want to get mixed up in any investigations. I mean this was a man who prided himself on keeping his homilies under ten minutes always and who loved Easter season mostly because he got to splash people with water all the way to Pentecost."

"Well, what are you saying, he's a random victim? These nuts are just going to start killing priests?"

"How do I know? What do I know? You're the professional, not me," Tony protested before adding, "Can't I please get outta here? And can't you please untie the poor man?"

"Yeah, sure, sorry, Ton', of course. Okay, guys, we're good here. Do what you need to do."

But suddenly Tony shouted, "Wait, hold on," as he went over again to where his former fellow student sat. He looked carefully again at the letters painted onto his head, shuddered, and then blessed himself before turning back to join his brother.

"I remember when Dave had a full head of red hair," he sighed. "Those initials aren't Latin or English, they're Spanish, you know, the language of St. Teresa. Sister Anna's advice to us."

"Go with God?" Mike remembered.

"No, just before. NTMDLC, '*No tengan miedo de la cruz.*' Don't fear the cross."

"That *is* too big a coincidence. I guess it's time to have another conversation with that nut. Like right now."

Mike and Tony anticipated no trouble in getting in to see Sister Anna Teresa again, so it was with some surprise that they heard the prioress herself tell them it would be impossible.

"I don't understand, Sister," Tony said in a tone at once pleading and annoyed. "I thought you were on our side in this."

"Yes, well I'm afraid you don't understand, either of you." Sister Perpetua shook her head. "You can't see Sister Anna because she isn't here. She disappeared some time before morning prayers."

"Disappeared? Couldn't she have just gone AWOL? Did she leave a note or anything?"

"She left no note, but I'm sure she's not coming back—she took our altar cross with her."

When Mike didn't seem to register the importance of that last remark, the nun made herself clear. "Our solid gold cross, our Sbarri and Gentili cross—it's priceless."

Mike let out a low whistle. Tony just stood dumbly, as the nun glared at them both.

Chapter 17

Sister Anna Teresa could not be found. She was now not only a suspect in the killings, but an almost certain perpetuator of a very grand larceny of a sixteenth-century gold altar cross encrusted with emeralds, whose worth easily had rested in the high six figures before the price of gold had gone crazy. Sister Anna was being actively sought for questioning by the police. Adding to the mystery was Sister Perpetua's testimony that the valuable cross was only put into use three times a year and was usually kept in a hiding place that only she and one other sister knew.

Once Tony had filled in the police on all he knew about Father Sweeney and had helped Mike in talking to the other Carmelites about their dealings with the missing nun, there was nothing else he could do but return to Smith for the new semester.

His worry about the possible motivation for the most recent murder, with Father Sweeney's apparent lack of connection to an investigation of the alumbradas or to St. Teresa or her secret writings, kept Tony up nights, wondering if a series of murders against the clergy was about to commence.

When he received an invitation from Hank Gallagher to come over either Saturday or Sunday to watch playoff football, Tony first thought to decline the invitation, but he realized the distraction of both the NFL and Hank's good company were exactly what he needed. He had been remiss in his interactions with his old friend even before the murders, since Faith and Hank were not a good match in any social setting. So Tony had that further incentive for agreeing to stop over. He chose to skip the afternoon game, but on Saturday evening he took the very short drive to Hank's home, armed with a six-pack of Sam Adams and some homemade "cheese pennies," a longtime favorite of his longtime friend.

Hank lived alone, since his most recent divorce, in a spacious Tudor, whose furnishings and toys reflected the status not only of a department chair, but also of someone who had always been at least as successful in playing the stock market as he had teaching and writing about literature. Tony found his boss in the spacious family room, its pool table, full bar, and plush carpeting just a few of the features that made it a comfortable place to spend a Saturday evening. Both men were still in mourning for the Jets, who they had rooted for since they were little children, and who had missed the playoffs again, even though they had, for a change, been favored to make them. The game showing on Hank's big screen TV between the Titans and Bills hardly mattered to them, except as an excuse to get together. And Hank was in particularly good form, not having waited for Tony to begin his beer drinking or football watching.

"Did you catch the first game?" he asked, without a trace of a slur to his speech, but with the reemergence of his old Queens accent, and his light blue eyes sparkling in the way Tony knew they only did after three beers or more. "Can you believe Romo blew it one more time? That guy chokes worse than the Boston Strangler."

Tony knew it wouldn't be worth pointing out that the Strangler had been the one who choked people, not the one who choked the way Hank was claiming Tony Romo had. Once Hank had some beer or whiskey in him, he did not like to be corrected, not that it was a favorite pastime of his even when he was sober.

Tony also knew enough to forget about trying to get some sympathy or insight from his friend and current boss over his own troubles. Beer, football, and a lot of boisterous yelling at the television were about all he could expect from the evening.

He was surprised, then, when, near halftime of a game that was neither close nor compelling, Hank introduced the topic himself.

"So what the hell is going on with you, Tony?" he blurted, as he handed Tony another beer, long before Tony needed one. "This isn't what we agreed to when you first came here looking for an escape."

Tony was taken by surprise so his response was not immediate.

"And don't pretend you don't know what I'm talking about," Hank continued, blue eyes now close to blazing, with a finger wag that almost hit Tony in the nose as Hank lurched back onto the sectional sofa. "You came here three years ago, totally devastated by all that church crap and those crazy murders. And who saved your butt? Me, your old friend from Cathedral, and everything's great until you get yourself mixed up with all this crazy stuff your brother's investigating. I mean, I can tell you're as tense as a virgin on her wedding night. You've got to let the cops do all the investigating. Just stay out of it if you know what's good for you, right?"

"Hank, man, I don't know where this is all coming from. I—"

"Oh, don't bullshit me. I called your mother's place to see when you were getting back here and your mother, knowing it was me, your old friend, she told me about the car on New Year's Eve and all the other baloney you've been going through. *She* tells me, but not word one from you to me on any of it. And you know why?" Hank leaned toward Tony, his Wild Turkey breath cluing Tony in that more than beer was responsible for Hank's mood and its decibel level.

"No, why?"

"Because you're ashamed. Because you know you should leave all this nonsense to the cops and that it's bad for you to be mixed up in any of this again, but you can't help wanting to show off how smart you are, and your brother's too stupid to keep you off the case."

"I don't know where this is all coming from Hank, I really don't. I appreciate all you've done for me here, but this case now, it has nothing to do with me personally. I'm just helping Mike with the religious angles on some of it, I—"

"You're getting run off the highway by maniacs, you are, but there's nothing personal about that, right? What do you take me for? I'm tellin' ya, you need to steer clear of all of it, just teach your classes, do your committee work, and live the good life here. I didn't go out on a limb to rescue your ass just to have you climb up an even bigger fucking tree."

Hank's tone was angry, but Tony could also hear concern in it, and he was touched by his old friend's level of worry about his welfare. He did his best to assure Hank he would try to follow his advice as well as he was able, and Hank took the conciliatory tone well. Before Tony knew it, Hank was back to remembrances from their time on the baseball and basketball teams together, the teachers they had both despised, and the few they had thought were good guys, even though they were priests.

"No offense or nothing, Tony." Hank laughed. "I mean, you never were a priest like those guys were anyway, bunch a Puritans or fags or both, that's why you never could stand it. Best thing you ever did, get away from that bunch of morons."

His second day back in Northampton, the Sunday before the start of the new term, Tony received a call from Faith. She invited him to come over and pick up his books, a sweater, a tooth brush, and other reminders of his former presence.

Tony really did not want to see Faith at all, but he had been encouraged by his brother to find a way to probe at what she might know at least one more time, before the police officially got involved in trying to round up alumbradas and question them as possible murder suspects. He was at her door within an hour of her call.

Faith was dressed casually, blue jeans and a light tan sweater that helped to draw out the gold in her gold-green eyes. Tony worried that she would just hand him all of his belongings in a box and expect him immediately to leave, but she invited him in and even invited him to sit. He took the invitation, taking off his blue down coat and laying it beside him on the scarlet divan. Faith picked up the coat, hung it up in the nearby closet, and sat herself in its place.

"I don't think there's any reason for hostility, Tony. Now that I've had time to think, it was foolish of me to ever hope we could be compatible. I misread who you really were from reading your books. You just aren't the kind of person ready to go on the kind of life journey I'm involved in."

Tony had the feeling that Faith had almost practiced

this speech, maybe even had help with it. She aimed toward dissolving the final remnants of their connection without discussion or controversy. But Tony could not let that happen. He knew he was looking at a last opportunity to find out the truth about her.

He turned more directly to be absolutely face to face with her as he began. "Yeah, I'm ready to be done too. But before I get up and go gently into this cold night here, I have to tell you, the reason I can't travel with you on your 'life journey' is not because I don't measure up, but because it's a bad trip, kid. The alumbradas were wrong-headed 500 years ago and it's still a screwy way to live today." Tony made sure he stayed latched onto Faith's eyes as he said the word alumbradas, thinking it crucial to look for clues in her reaction to its uncovering. And he was certain he had hit home, so he didn't hesitate to keep up the pursuit, in spite of the feigned innocence of her "alumbradas?" "Don't worry about blowing your cover, kid—it's blown already," he said as he shook his head.

"What cover? And will you please stop calling me 'kid'?"

"Why? That's what you are, to me at least, no matter how seriously superior you think you might be. And it sure wasn't very mature to get mixed up in the mess you're in now."

Faith's face now registered shock and then anger. She got up but then sat back down. "I was trying to be polite, civilized, and now you have the nerve to insult me when it was I who had to endure your antics the whole time? But you're just trying to upset me, I can see, especially with this nonsense about, alumprados or whatever."

"You're a lousy actress. If alumbrada were a new term to you, you'd have pronounced it just now, that's how you are, a quick study. I'm just hoping you're not all the way involved. You don't seem like a killer to me, though I've been wrong about that before. I—"

"Are you insane?" Faith asked by way of interruption, but Tony continued as if she hadn't spoken.

"—I think I've learned better how to judge since, and I'm telling you, if there's anything you know that could help us stop these killings, you'd better come clean and soon. The cops are only a day or two away from your door here."

"Now I know you're insane. What would the police want with me? You're not making any sense."

"Have you read the secret writings of St. Teresa?" Tony switched tracks just enough to try to keep his ex off balance.

"Saint Teresa? I read the autobiography many years ago, but I have no interest in your Catholic saints and I certainly don't know about any secret writings."

Faith stood up again, this time walking toward the closet that held Tony's coat. She quickly retrieved it for him, came close to throwing it at him, as she strongly insisted that it was time for him to leave.

Tony rose from the uncomfortable sofa, but instead of putting on his parka, he threw it across the room, where it landed on a matching scarlet armchair. He was shouting at Faith now and felt happy to do it. "Believe it or not, I'm trying to help you. We're up to four murders now, two priests, a nun, and a coed, and we know you alumbradas are mixed up in it. It's just a matter of time before the few of you we know about for sure are hauled in for at least questioning. Help me now and you'll not only save yourself a lot of trouble, but you'll, more importantly, maybe save somebody's life." He grabbed Faith by the wrists, looked directly in her eyes again and added, "I want to believe that matters to you. I want to believe I know you well enough at least to think you've had nothing to do with any killing. Let me leave here at least knowing you're not part of all that."

Faith did not try to release herself from Tony's grip, though he knew she was well able to defend herself. She looked, instead, as if she maybe were about to reveal something to him. But as quickly as that possibility seemed to assert itself it left her visage again and she instead said, coldly, "Please let go of me now and leave immediately and I won't have the police you're so fond of come here to pick you up instead."

Tony looked again into his former lover's eyes, took a deep breath, and let go of her. He retrieved his coat from the chair, grabbed his box of belongings, and headed for the door.

He turned to Faith and got in his last word. "These local cops are just as onto you as my brother and his NYPD pals are. Go ahead and call them and see if you enjoy the visit. Meanwhile, whoever's in charge of the poison and strangling department of your girls' club might be keeping a close eye on you, especially if you start getting visits from the men in blue. I'd be careful who I drank my herbal tea with in the days ahead."

Tony left the door open as he exited. He only missed guessing by one beat the number of steps it would take before hearing it slam from behind. That resounding noise made him hope all the more that he had gotten through to Faith. It vindicated him at least a little, as he drove off into a late Sunday winter's night.

Chapter 18

There was nothing unusual about the first week of classes at Smith except for Tony's level of distraction. Normally, he loved a new semester—new students, new opportunities to both teach and learn. And Tony was not skilled at hiding when something was troubling him. Students who were expecting the jokey, supportive presence of the most controversial professor on campus were surprised by his subdued demeanor in class and in his office. Yet Hank, with whom he almost always had lunch on Tuesdays and Thursdays during the school term, would not accept no as an answer when Tony tried to bypass that bit of his normal campus behavior.

"I hope you're not still upset over what happened Saturday. You know how I can come on too strong sometimes," Hank offered.

"No, that's okay. It was nice to see you cared."

"I'm glad you feel that way, since I'm still worried about you. You've seemed more than a little put out, since the new semester started, maybe even a little morose," Hank said as he worked his way through the last of his club sandwich. "I didn't think much of it, at first, but this is the second consecutive time you've passed on dessert here and, as you know, we mostly come to the Yellow Sofa because you swear by their desserts."

Hank did not seem to mind the maybe seven pounds he had put on over the holidays, so Tony knew he was not going to believe for a moment that his comparatively slender friend was trying to watch his weight.

"What's gotten into you? It isn't just this detective crap, is it?" Hank continued. "Faith hasn't finally converted you to the no-fun diet has she?"

"Faith and I aren't seeing each other anymore, Hank. Hadn't I told you?"

Tony knew he hadn't, but understood that normally it would be the kind of thing you would share with a good friend. Hank was easily his best friend at Smith, something Tony was in no danger of forgetting, since Hank was always ready to remind him. Still, in spite of their closeness, the circumstances of Tony's break-up with Faith had made it easier just to try to avoid the subject.

"So that's what's got you down then? Girl troubles?" Hank laughed a good ol' boy sort of laugh, though he had been raised just a few parishes over from Tony's St Teresa of Avila at Holy Child. They had been classmates and teammates at Cathedral Prep in Elmhurst, and thereby products of Catholic education from first grade through twelfth. Though Hank and Tony had not remained close once they took their separate paths to becoming Ph.D.s— Tony by first entering the seminary at Douglaston and Hank by the more direct path of scholarship student at Harvard—since their time together at Smith, Hank had taken on the role of a kind of older brother, and clearly he was still counting on Tony to appreciate the continued attention he paid to his often troubled friend.

Tony had no desire to get to the core of his real trou-

bles over lunch, so he jumped on Hank's misplaced suspicion. "Yeah, sure, that's it, Hank," he claimed. "It's
depressing enough that we're in the middle of another
New England winter, with all the holiday cheer behind
us, and now I've got to be alone, too? It kind of sucks,
you know?"

"You'll only be alone as long as you want to be.
You're about the most eligible bachelor I know. Especially if you'd act your age and stop trying to be someone
you're not just to get a young thing to tolerate you."

Tony grimaced. "Was it that obvious, Hank?"

"Let's face it," Hank went on. "Faith's a full-fledged
feminist and a vegan to boot. How in the world you two
lasted as long as you did is the thing I can't figure. If this
hot Latina back in New York you've been telling me
about wasn't so young, I'd say that'd be your next move
right there, but those younger girls are nothing but trouble, believe me."

"But, wait, Lisa was what, maybe ten years younger
than you and—"

"Never mind Lisa. I'm telling you they're nothing
but trouble. Hell, you don't have to take my word for it,
you know now yourself firsthand. No matter what your
next move is, you're well rid of Ms. Covington."

"Well, I mean she wasn't as bad as all that—"

"Bullshit, man, she was worse. Only someone des-
perate would put up with all she probably put you
through. I mean, listen, you're well off, well known, and
not a total zero looks wise either. What available—or
even unavailable, for that matter—woman, say in the thir-
ty-five to fifty range, wouldn't go for that? I mean, take it
from someone who knows, it won't take you long to find
someone better than Faith Covington."

Hank's advice, coming as it was from a man who
had been divorced twice, both times with acrimony and

alimony, could be taken for what little it might be worth. But since Tony was only pretending to need it, it was all the easier to accept.

"Yeah, I'll be fine, man, you're right. And, what the hell, why should I pass up that great lemon tart they have here? I mean, I'd like to drop a few pounds, sure, but nobody likes a fanatic, right?"

"That's the Tony Cupelli we know and love." Hank laughed. "Hell, I'll have one too, just so you won't be lonely."

Tony got through the week without any major incidents. He didn't even once happen to run into Faith, on our off campus. His focus remained elsewhere, though, and, as soon as the week was over Friday evening, he headed to Worcester. He had a date, a kind of a date, anyway, with Veronica Teuma.

As Tony drove to Veronica's house, on a bitterly cold, but clear night, he remembered the advice his brother had given him to rule no one out as a suspect. And yet Tony had not only an attraction to Veronica physically, but also spiritually. He could not believe she could be involved with the alumbradas and the whys and wherefores of his faith in her seemed to him something like his slowly renewing faith in God, something that could not be proven but just the same was real. Still, he promised himself not to reveal anything to Veronica that could be of aid to a possible murderer, even as he prayed that he would not hear anything from Veronica's lips that only the killer could possibly know.

Veronica offered to make dinner, but Tony insisted on taking her to a restaurant. She suggested The Sole Proprietor and her reason rang true to Tony's growing impression of her. "It's been rated one of the top ten seafood restaurants in the country and, being Maltese, I love seafood. But, to be honest, I almost always have seafood

on Friday, whether it's Lent or not. I just love the old traditions. I think if I had my choice, the Mass might still be
in Latin, if I thought most people wouldn't be put off by
that, at least."

It was a very pleasant restaurant, neither stuffy nor
overly expensive. Tony enjoyed both the swordfish and
the authentic key lime pie that followed—he hated graham cracker crust over real pie crust or fake whipped
topping over meringue. Veronica seemed equally happy
with her stuffed flounder and her Boston cream pie. Seeing someone enjoy the rich food the waiter put before
them as much as he was enjoying it himself made Tony
feel more at ease than he had ever managed to be with
Faith. The two chatted about the holidays, their new semesters, and almost seamlessly about what connection
the murder of a priest in Queens might have with what
had happened to Veronica's own student and two other
victims.

"More and more it seems to me that these women
have found something in St. Teresa that makes them feel
justified in doing all manner of horrible things. And I'm
afraid much of it is tied to these secret writings, which, of
course, we've yet to uncover."

Veronica sipped her coffee, put the pretty white cup
down to her right, and shook her head almost sadly.
"Surely you know that if there are any secret writings,
they could not be anything but consistent with what St.
Teresa says in her published writings, none of which
could inspire anything but holiness in all but the most
misled minds."

"Yes, but who's misleading them? The more I reread
her work, the more I see Teresa proclaiming a love of
suffering, almost for its own sake. She prays that her pain
will never go away; she proclaims if she had to stop suffering, she'd rather die; she calls her pain exquisite and

prays for it to remain, just the opposite of what most people might do. You don't have to be a nut or a fanatic to think she might have been a bit of a masochist."

Veronica's face flushed with surprise. "You can't really believe that. I can't be wrong about you—you can't really believe what you're saying."

"Help me not to, Veronica. I'm just having a hard time seeing the beauty in grievous pain. And maybe even more importantly, it's not beyond reason for me to think that a woman so devoted to mystical union and so willing to establish nuns as cloistered as the discalced Carmelites were and are, maybe, just maybe, could have been more of an alumbrada at heart than she knew it would be safe to admit."

Tony said these words with an expression that was far from his usual, aggressive style and demeanor when arguing. He knew he was saying something Veronica would not want to hear, and it was paining him to have to be the one to say it to her. She seemed to understand and appreciate those feelings, though not the content of what Tony was suggesting.

Her tone was once again calm and absolutely convicted. "You know I'm a secular Carmelite myself. You know I try to pray in the way St. Teresa has directed us. I can tell you that it's a beautiful and powerful thing, but also one tied to God, to holiness, and, thereby, to love."

"Besides giving our heart and soul to God, the other great commandment is to love our neighbors as ourselves. How can we do that or even care about that when we're seeking union only with God?"

"How can we not?" Veronica answered and her eyes seemed as sincere as any the former Monsignor Cupelli had ever looked into. "We're made in his image and likeness. If we achieve a lasting, ecstatic union with the Godhead by praying the way Teresa has taught us to pray, it only all the more brings us to the inevitability of a commitment to charity for all. That is the only acceptable way to approach meditative prayer, and that's what Teresa preached and wrote about. There's nothing in it that could lead to sin, much less murder."

Their voices were intense but not loud, so as not to draw attention within the crowded restaurant.

"But you'll admit, there is room for misunderstanding, in the very least."

"Anyone who reads her work carefully will understand it, unless they are willfully trying not to understand it. She constantly warns us against the devil and against false visions, and by those she meant any that exalt the self and forget others. God lets us suffer, but he doesn't lead us astray."

Veronica seemed close to tears. Tony had an instinct to take her hand, to assure her he understood. But, even as he had the thought, he thought too of his brother, Michael, and his warnings. If Veronica were somehow mixed up with all the alumbradas, she was certainly convincing enough to fool anyone, since he totally wanted to believe in what she was saying.

He resisted the urge to get closer and, instead, kept voicing his doubts. "But some of your own students have misunderstood, apparently. So what are they, what am I, missing? And why am I missing it? To me, Teresa is too interested in glorying in pain. To me, though she pays lips service to all the orthodox things, it's the divine contact she craves. The rest really could have been just self-protection from the blood-thirst of the Inquisition. And if there really are secret writings that make this even more explicit, I don't know what you could say to that."

"No such writings can exist. I won't believe it possible. Or if they exist, they too have been misinterpreted by women who have given themselves over to the devil."

Veronica rose from her seat, seemed ready to abandon Tony at the table, though they had come in one car. But he halted her, with his eyes mostly, and gave her a further challenge.

"I think I know how to find out if they exist or not. I think the answer may be right here, in Worcester, right here at Holy Cross. Help me find those writings and we'll see what they say. Will you help me?"

Veronica looked deeply into Tony's eyes, every bit as dark and Mediterranean as her own. She seemed to be seeking a proper response to him in those eyes, somehow, took a moment, sat down again. "I believe you are seeking the truth. I believe you are trying to help to save lives, and maybe even souls. So I will help you uncover and undo these lies. But only if you'll do one thing for me."

"If I can, I certainly will."

"Study the saint, study her with an open heart and mind, study her with me and pray with me. Pray for the grace she can share with you, through the intercession of our Lord Jesus Christ."

Veronica's intensity somehow transported them out of the restaurant, took them away from contact with anyone else, was almost too much to fathom, much less bear. It resembled what he had experienced with Faith, when she held his hand until he felt it almost on fire. This similarity frightened Tony, argued with him of the proof of Veronica, Faith's friend and former teacher, being of a similar bent, an alumbrada bent. But something about it was just a little distinct, importantly distinct, he hoped, and purer, since he responded.

"Yes, I'll pray with you, Veronica. I want to learn, really, how to pray like that."

Chapter 19

Veronica first helped Tony by looking up the phone number and address from her college's data base for Teresa and Angela Sargento, the two sisters who had been most on Tony's side when he had visited Marissa Hitzel's friends before Christmas. Tony had not known their last name, but had remembered them with description enough to jog Veronica's own memory. Teresa had never been her student, but Angela had, though she had dropped the class a few weeks before Marissa's murder. The two sisters shared an apartment just blocks away from the Holy Cross campus.

Tony decided not to have Veronica call, but rather subcontracted her to be a kind of spy for his own sleuthing, asking her to let him know when she felt confident she could say something about their routines. Veronica did not like the idea of spying, but she had promised to help, and Tony assured her what he was asking her to do could be invaluable to discovering the truth.

Less than two weeks after his own dinner with Veronica, Tony drove back to Worcester, picked up Veronica, and headed for the young women's apartment. Veronica had been able to ascertain that the two had no Thursday evening classes or any extracurriculars those nights. Of course, she couldn't know with total confidence that they would be home, but Tony decided he could not wait for certainty. He needed to see the sisters, by surprise, and without Nancy Temple and her roommates to influence what they might say or not say. Veronica, at first, refused to accompany him, but Tony once again persuaded her away from her first instincts.

The sisters' apartment was a modest one bedroom, the renovated lower floor of an old two story house in a lower middle class neighborhood. When Tony knocked, he expected it wouldn't take long for a response, but it was several minutes and more knocks before Angela came to the door, in blue jeans and a baby blue sweater. Her hair had been cut short, which only made her eyes seem even larger and darker.

Her demeanor seemed open and pleasant, maybe even pleased, as she noted, "Professor Teuma and Professor Cupelli. What a surprise. What in the world brings you here?"

"Sorry I didn't call to forewarn you, Angela," Tony began. "Ever since our first meeting, I've been wanting to follow up on our earlier conversation. I happened to be in town today, visiting with Professor Teuma on a research project, so, I thought, why not see if you and Teresa might be in? You don't have anywhere to run off to, do you?"

"Well, no, not at all." Angela smiled. "I'm a little embarrassed to admit our big plans for the evening are to watch this week's results night on 'American Idol.' But we'd much rather talk to you. Come on in. Sorry, though, the place is a mess," she sighed as her guests entered. "We went into attack mode on some of the clutter when we heard the door, but there's only so much you can do in five minutes."

"Oh, we're sorry to intrude, I told Professor Cupelli we should at least try to call first, but he preferred to just pop in like this. Besides, everything looks fine."

Veronica wasn't just being polite. The apartment was clean. The furniture, though clearly second hand, was arranged with flair with colorful throws to offset wear on the couches and a fresh coat of light blue paint to cheer up the old walls. Tony had expected something gloomier, but even the other sister, Teresa, who had reminded him of Morticia Addams, seemed this time more like a typical college student. Her hair was still long, but it was tied back in a ponytail, and she was, like her sister, bedecked simply in blue jeans, and, in her case, a mint green cardigan over a white turtleneck.

"Hi, Professors. I hope you like Cheez-Its and chocolate-covered almonds, because that's all I could scare up on such short notice," Teresa apologized.

Tony was almost put off by how less lugubrious Teresa sounded. He began to wonder if she was even the same person he had met just a month before. Not wanting to give away his doubts, he answered. "Chocolate covered anything sounds great to me, and I love Cheez-Its. Plus, look, I brought a coffee ring from the bakery. You girls are Italian, right? We never come empty-handed, am I right?"

Angela smiled. "Actually, we're Spanish, or at least our grandparents were, from around Segovia, I think. But that's how we were raised too."

"Yes, the Maltese are that way too. The Italians don't have a monopoly on being good guests," Veronica added with feigned anger.

"Sorry, I didn't mean to say otherwise." Tony raised the pastry box up, as if to use it as a shield. "Besides, the coffee ring is innocent, in any case."

Angela laughed. "And I bet it's delicious, and we do have coffee. It's starting to sound like a party."

Only with that laugh did Tony note maybe a bit of overplay. Maybe these girls were just good actresses and knew now that they had to *act normal* in order to fend off whatever these two professors might have come to deliver besides pastry. Or maybe something had changed and the reason for that change would be something well worth uncovering, if they would let their covers slip.

The two sisters and their guests sat around a second hand, red, Formica kitchen table with four red and white chairs, two of which were a little wobbly—the sisters were careful to choose those. As Teresa put the pot on for coffee, Tony munched on some Cheez-Its, which he really did love, and tried to seem as casual as possible in his introduction of the evening's topic.

"Segovia, eh? So it's '*Sar hen tow*,' then, not '*Sar jen tow*,' eh?"

"Well, that's right, but we never correct people. We aren't even really that fluent in Spanish or anything ourselves," Angela explained.

"Segovia," Veronica broke in. "If I'm remembering correctly, that's not far from Avila, is it?"

"Not very far, I don't think. But we've only ever visited Spain once, though I'd love to go back," Teresa responded.

Though they weren't twins, Tony still noticed how similar the sisters looked and acted, in spite of the different hair lengths. Now that Teresa was acting more extroverted, as the four talked casually about their Christmases, their new semesters, the weather, he even noticed the similar timbre of Teresa's and Angela's voices. He thought of his own sibling, one year older, strikingly similar in looks, but so essentially different in personality.

He wondered if these two sisters might also be more distinct from each other than they presently appeared. Which, if either of them, he wondered, could be the more readily coaxed into revealing what he needed to know?

"Listen, I don't want to take up all of your evening. 'American Idol' isn't on for another hour, right? So, what I'd really like to do is pick up on our conversation from last time, where, you'll forgive me if I'm wrong, but it felt as though you were both being held back by Nancy and the others from saying what was on your minds."

"Oh, no, that wasn't so. I don't always agree with Nancy, or especially Shanti, but we're one in our devotion to Saint Teresa," Teresa assured Tony, with a very innocent-looking smile.

Tony didn't expect a lot of help from Veronica. He had her there mostly so the two young women would be less worried about opening up to a man, and a former priest at that, so he was surprised when she jumped in.

"Girls, I worry about that devotion. Angela, you dropped my class, even though you were doing well grade wise, and I can't help but think it was because of how I criticized Marissa and you for your misreadings of the saint's writings."

"You call them misreadings," Teresa blurted, a little more harshly than she might have meant to.

"I'm also wondering, Angela, why you just misrepresented to Professor Cupelli your fluency in Spanish. I saw you with a copy of *The Autobiography* in the original language and you quoted from it directly in your last paper."

"Maybe she was just being modest, Veronica," Tony jumped in to be the good cop. "We didn't come here to accuse them of lying."

"But you did come to accuse us?" Teresa asked, with the smile no longer apparent on her face.

"I'm worried about you both," Veronica said, but more like a police woman than a mother. "You're good Catholic girls, or you were, but you are willfully misreading one of our greatest saints, making her into some kind of selfish savant, who delivers herself to a God who doesn't care about Christian charity and advises us all to be just as selfish. This has to stop, and you both have to help us stop it!" Veronica's voice was raised and her fervor for her favorite saint was fully awakened.

"Well, you see, Professor, this unwillingness to see an alternate point of view is just the reason I had to drop your course," Angela noted, calmly.

Tony saw that Angela wasn't going to be drawn into any revealing conversations, but he knew there were two Sargento sisters in the room.

"*Cúidate, muchacha, debes tener más respeto, verdad?*" Tony advised with asperity.

"*Es usted que debe tener cuidado, Profesor Cupelli. Puede ser peligro en qualquier rincón.*"

Teresa's response seemed to shock everyone, but Tony. Angela looked at her sister with alarm, as if she could not believe she could be so readily drawn into Tony's trap. In one sentence she had proved her fluency in Spanish and also had threatened him with the danger that could be lurking in any corner.

"So, now you're threatening me? Maybe you were right, Veronica, maybe we should just leave them to the police."

"Oh, well my sister just likes to be dramatic, but just because she is doesn't mean you have to follow suit, Professor. Now it's a crime to think differently from your professors? I thought that went out long ago."

"Like, with the Inquisition?" Tony baited. And Teresa took the bait.

"Yes, those monsters silenced many of our sisters.

But they couldn't silence Teresa of Avila. She fooled them all and left for us all that we needed—all that you'll never understand."

Teresa was practically hissing now, but Veronica's own anger was also coming to the forefront.

"You two children think you understand more than we do? You've been taken over by Satan himself, and you're too ignorant to realize it."

Teresa seemed all the more incensed at being dismissed as a child. "My namesake has warned us of just your type, one who is falsely devoted to a corrupt church tradition. Teresa knew your kind and your foolish allegiance to the Church, but as she tells us, '*Los sacerdotes no saben nada de Dios, ni de los pasos verdaderos a la gloria eterna.*'"

"No!" Angela shouted and took two steps toward her sister, as if meaning physically to silence her, though she had to know it was too late. All four people in the small kitchen knew Spanish well enough to understand what Teresa had said, "Priests know nothing about God or the true steps to eternal glory."

"My first introduction to the secret writings of St. Teresa of Avila? Surely, you won't deny me access to more. Maybe there would be hope for me yet, if only I could learn the 'true steps to eternal glory.'"

Tony looked alternately at both sisters and then at Veronica. All three women wore looks of chagrin. Tony felt Veronica's pain. What she held most dear was being threatened by this strange young woman, and this pain was his motivation to be all the sterner with the two college students who now stood together holding hands.

"You're going to give us a look at these secret writings, and you're going to tell us everything you know about the people who have been killed."

Teresa turned angrily toward Tony.

"And to think I imagined you'd understand. The church expelled you, but you still do their bidding. As soon as I saw you accompanied by this fascist here, I knew it was hopeless. But we're not compelled to share any secrets with you, and we know nothing of any killings, except, in Marissa's case, to suspect the church's involvement in silencing voices of protest, as they have always done. I'm going to ask you both to leave."

"What have you to fear in letting us see these writings? Why wouldn't you want the whole world to know the truth?" Tony prodded.

"The writings have always been secret and will remain so," Teresa answered then quickly added, "We'll deny anything you claim to have learned here. We know nothing of any murders. Now get out. Please get out."

"Yeah, enjoy 'American Idol,' girls." Tony laughed as he put on his coat and helped Veronica with hers. "I wonder if they have television in prison these days. I'll have to ask my brother. Or you ask him yourself since you'll be seeing him soon enough, along with some of Worcester's finest too, I'm guessing."

"But Shanti said we had nothing to worry about," Teresa said, with some panic, to her sister.

"Will you be quiet? Haven't you said enough? Just keep quiet now, Teresa, please!"

"Enjoy the pastry ring. I doubt you'll get anything that good where you'll be going."

Teresa scanned the room with a suddenly terrified look, before grabbing Tony from behind as he approached the door to leave.

"No, stay, please. I swear, we don't know anything about any killing. We'll show you the writings. You're right—it's time the whole world knew. Once you read them, you'll see, we have nothing to do with killing. Only the glory. *Solamente la gloria!*"

Angela made a move as if to stop her sister from talking further, but then stayed still. Veronica also looked very disturbed by what Teresa had said, but made no response.

Tony felt a desire to say something more to Angela, but restrained himself as he saw her collapse on the old green sofa, cover herself with the multi-colored throw, and begin to cry.

Chapter 20

Teresa did not have her own personal copy of *Directives Toward the True Path of Glory*, in fact, she only had a little more than a page of quotations, in her own handwriting, which she claimed to have copied from the larger document. Her handwritten pages were in English, but she further claimed to have seen the document in its original Spanish. The alumbradas who were not fully initiated were not allowed to own a copy in either language, as the security risks were too great. She was not even supposed to have copied the passages she had, but they were her favorites, and she used them constantly for inspiration. It was with a sense of pride that Teresa shared the quotations with Tony and Veronica.

Angela continued to protest, then begged her sister not to retrieve the pages, but with Teresa firmly committed to the revelation, Tony did not let Angela bully her sister away from what he needed to see.

Since Teresa's handwriting was unusually tiny, with letters precisely formed, but practically in need of a magnifying glass to see clearly, she volunteered to read from the pages out loud. Now that she had committed herself to this exposé, she seemed strangely calm, but one paragraph in particular had anything but a calming effect on Veronica.

"'God made each, woman and man, in his own likeness, though only women, prayerful women, are meant to be the brides of our Lord, Jesus Christ. Almost all the priests who are supposed to represent Christ on earth are not worthy of the office, but those who openly challenge their power suffer the dire consequences of such folly. For this reason I have established this order of discalced Carmelites, so we can dedicate ourselves to this way of perfection, with the least possible scrutiny or judgment from those who claim to know all, but know nothing of this true way to union, the joyful pain that never ceases, the Lord's own pain, which we gladly take on for a lifetime, a lifetime sequestered from the foolish ways of man.'"

The rest of Teresa's quotations were about as disturbing, as the writer explained how the very life laid out for the discalced Carmelites, with its limited interaction with the outside world, with many hours each day without direct scrutiny by anyone, including other clergy, male or female, was the perfect way to avoid detection in their true calling to the kind of meditative prayer that would lead to a direct connection with divinity. Of course, after Teresa finished reading, Veronica and Tony were both anxious to question her.

"She doesn't have to tell you anything. You aren't police officers, and, even if you were, we haven't done anything wrong. Could you please just leave now?" Angela asked, with a kind of desperation that made her seem even more like her younger sister.

"And if we don't, what are you going to do? Call the local police? I'll be happy to see them. I met a lot of them when I was here back when Marissa was murdered," Tony reminded Angela and she decided not to protest further.

"Angela, don't worry. They can't stop us. I want them to know the truth. Keeping it a secret was necessary in Teresa's time, but men don't rule the world anymore. I want them to know the truth."

"If you think I'm going to believe a few pages in your own handwriting, and almost certainly of your own invention, are the truth, you're crazier than I imagined," Veronica said, more scornfully than Tony might have guessed her capable of.

But Tony did not side with her. Instead he seemed to take Teresa as seriously as she clearly took herself. "So when and how did you first get to read this secret writing of the saint?"

"All initiates hear passages from it early on in their novitiate. Only some are allowed to actually see a copy. I've had the honor of seeing it also in Spanish. In fact, there's been talk of me getting to be one of the people to work on a new translation into English."

"That's not going to happen now," Angela cautioned her sister.

"Angela, whatever happens can't possibly affect what matters most. I know the way, and that can't be taken from me. And St. Teresa's words—I have them practically memorized. I already am carrying them with me always. Professor Cupelli." Teresa turned back to him with a smile. "What else would you like to know?"

Veronica, with a kind of controlled rage, spoke before Tony could ask his next question. "Would you have us believe, that since the time of St. Teresa through to-day, there has existed a secret writing that goes against all of what normal Catholics believe the saint was about? Are you suggesting that all these years the discalced Carmelites have been secret alumbradas and not Catholics at all? How do you expect anyone to believe that they could have kept their heresy a secret from all the Church?"

"I agree, that would have been impossible, Professor. And that's what the sisters themselves must have decided, maybe after a few generations. None of us are quite certain. The truth is the little book was lost for centuries, some few copies of it were only rediscovered ten years ago, in a hidden chamber of an old convent in Burgos. And it's only since then that the secret has been shared, by a generation of women more ready to hear it and act upon it."

"Both nuns and secular women?" Tony wondered.

"I will respect the privacy of our numbers, though you must have guessed by now who some of us are, and you know, I'm sure, that Sister Maria Dolores also believed so that answers your question, does it not?"

Teresa's voice had once again taken on the eerie and almost other worldly tone Tony had heard upon first meeting her.

"But doesn't it trouble you that Sister Maria was murdered and that another of your members, Marissa, was also killed?" Tony pressed. "And the monsignor who was murdered at Smith, would it surprise you at all to know that he had been in correspondence with Sister Maria Dolores, and that they were close to uncovering the secret writings?"

"You have that all wrong, I'm afraid," Teresa answered placidly. "Sister Maria killed herself, your own police say so. Perhaps it was because she felt she had betrayed us all by consorting with that priest, though she might have also been troubled by her unworthiness to lead a life of prayer toward perfection. As for Monsignor Heamey, I'm sure he had made plenty of enemies. I'm told you yourself humiliated him in a debate just before he died, and I know you were a murder suspect yourself only a few years ago."

Tony ignored the insult and continued. "And Marissa?"

"Yes, exactly, Marissa," Teresa almost seemed to be enjoying herself, even as Sister Anna Teresa had. "If you think one of us killed Maria Dolores for her disloyalty, then how do you explain Marissa's murder, when she was the one who recruited us in the first place? She never had any second thoughts, either. Angela can tell you that."

"I think you've told quite enough already," Angela said.

"Why are you worried?" She turned to her sister and tried to take her hand, but Angela refused. "I'm just letting these two misguided people know that we have nothing to do with killing. We have no interest in others, only support for those who wish to be truly enlightened. We have nothing to hide."

"What about these Carmelites who are living a lie, then?" Veronica wanted to know. "They are pretending to be Catholics while they are really heretics."

"They were drawn to the order because Teresa was its founder and because most of what she teaches, her published teachings, have the same essential message as her secret writing." Teresa was speaking not condescendingly, but with a tone of a professor with a few students she thought might be able to grasp what she was sharing if they would only concentrate. *The Way of Perfection, The Interior Castle*, what you have devoted your life to, Professor Teuma, is all bona fide. Even you, if you read those texts carefully enough, would see Teresa has no real need of men, no real need of performing acts of charity; all that she cares about and shares with others, is the way to union with Christ. And, of course, a few methods on how to work together in prayer to achieve that union that she could not share with priests."

"Like choking a Sister with a Rosary?" Tony asked.

"Out of context, none of it will make any sense to you. Especially if you're not really trying," Teresa chided.

"Do you know what I think?" Veronica asked. "I think you're crazy. I think that you and maybe some other misguided girls made all this secret writing up, and that you're more than capable of having killed anyone who didn't quite see it your way. I think the police should come up and arrest you before the night is over. That's what I think."

Tony looked at his friend with some surprise, read the mounting anger in her eyes, but said nothing.

"You have no evidence, Professor Teuma," Teresa responded. "You have nothing but your own misogynistic alliance with a church that your companion here has admitted in writing has always been against women and the sacred feminine. No one is going to be arrested."

"Completely insane," Veronica simply muttered.

"I'm not going to be discounted as some sort of maniac," Teresa insisted, with a sudden shift in voice and tone that belied her attempts to stay calm. "If you want to see the entire book, it can be arranged. In fact, Professor-Former-Monsignor Cupelli," Teresa mocked, "there's at least one copy I know of right back in Northampton."

"And I could take a look at it?" Tony nodded.

"Shut up, Teresa, are you crazy after all?" Angela shrieked and this time she did try to restrain her sister, but Tony grabbed her from behind and held her, though she continued to kick and yell for her sister to be quiet.

"Apparently there's only one way to prove I'm not. Go, Professor, if you hurry maybe you can even see it tonight."

"You're lying," Veronica challenged.

"Am I? Or are you two both too afraid to hear the truth?"

"Please, no!" Angela screamed.

"Go ahead," Tony encouraged while struggling not to hurt Angela or be injured himself.

"It's your own former student, Veronica, and your former lover, Tony, who has a copy. Our mentor, our guide to the only truth that matters."

"Faith Covington?" Tony and Veronica each asked at once.

"She might deny it at first, since you're nonbelievers, but tell her Teresa sent you—she'll know which one." Teresa laughed again, while her sister, unsuccessful in escaping Tony's grasp, once again began to cry.

Chapter 21

After Veronica invited Faith to a small dinner party at her house on a Friday evening, she expressed no qualms to Tony about "setting up" her friend and former student. As she explained to both the Cupelli brothers, the greater good now was to stop a mass murderer and to clear the name of one of Catholicism's greatest saints. Which of her motivations was stronger hardly mattered to the Cupelli brothers, so long as she was willing to help.

When Faith arrived, both Tony and Mike were waiting for her. The dinner party part was no fabrication, and a fine dinner it was, with roasted salmon with cranberry-mustard sauce and cheese-less eggplant parmigiana—tofu subbing for mozzarella—so that both Veronica's preference for Friday fish and Faith's dietary restrictions could be honored.

Faith might have been initially surprised by the company Veronica was keeping, but if she was, she did not show it. Instead, she presented for the first hour a complacency that belied what the other three suspected she had to be feeling. Though she did not take the other extreme and act as though the four of them were in the midst of a double date, Faith did seem to want to make it clear that she was not intimidated.

Once dinner itself had actually begun, she seemed happy to be the first one to try to prod them away from small talk.

"I know you've had plenty of time with your brother lately," Faith smirked as she received the salad bowl from Mike. "You must have come all this way now especially to see me or Veronica, Lieutenant. Which one of us is it?"

"Oh, don't ask me to choose, Faith." Mike smiled. "Though, long term, I think she's got you beat in the kitchen, at least. I don't see a big future for me and any vegetable person."

"But I bet this eggplant parmesan is going to be delicious."

"No doubt." Mike nodded. "As a side dish."

It wasn't until a little after the homemade marble cheesecake and espresso that the inevitable discussion of the alumbradas began to take place.

Veronica, after moving her guests to the greater comfort of her living room, began. "Faith, you studied mysticism with me, and though I know we've gone our separate ways in how we apply its purpose as part of God's plan, I trust that you can't have strayed as far as these two gentlemen have suggested is possible."

Faith kept smiling. "And what are these 'gentlemen' saying about me, then?"

"I'm afraid it isn't just them. We're hearing from my own students that you are mixed up in something that really is surprising and disappointing to me."

"Veronica, it's not my place to judge, but, really, I'm the one who has more reason to be concerned about you.

I've been hearing, in fact, that you'll soon be up on charges of harassment, for intruding on students' privacy and letting these two and their friends threaten students' very sense of religious freedom."

Tony was not surprised by Faith's aggressive tactic. He had foreseen, in fact, that a case could be made that Teresa and the others were perfectly free to believe in anything they wanted to, and, secret writings or no, had not been connected yet to any crime, much less multiple murders. But he thought he knew Faith fairly well, and hoped that knowledge would find a way to get past her usual cool command.

"It's funny you should know about any of that. You told me you didn't even know any of the students in question, and yet, here you know about their business with us, not to mention that Teresa Sargento insists you're the go to gal for a look at St. Teresa's little booklet, 'Secret Confessions of a Closet Alumbrada.'"

"I'm glad you think harassing students is a joke. Of course, with your history with women, I guess I can't be surprised. Your turn, Lieutenant. What snide remark have you been waiting to drop?" Faith, who was sitting closest to Mike, on the dark gray couch, while Veronica and Tony sat across from them on a matching love seat, touched him lightly on the hand as she questioned him.

"I'll leave it to you Ph.D.s to try to out-clever each other. I'm worried about solving murders, maybe saving a few lives. We're here, as you know, I guess, because we want to find out if these secret writings are a figment of Teresa Sargento's imagination or if they really exist. And the only reason I give a damn one way or the other is because it might help us stop a killer or killers. And if you haven't got anything to do with any of these crimes, I don't see why you wouldn't want to help us, right?"

Faith said nothing, looked from one person to the other.

Mike persisted. "Am I right?"

"Are you? Your brother didn't share all aspects of your investigation with me, so I really don't know where any of this is headed. On the face of it, I see no reason why you think some young women positing that a certain saint might have been a closet feminist and free thinker, or, if you prefer, alumbrada, makes them murder suspects. How is it any different from when the ex-monsignor here argued that the Catholic Church had wrongfully suppressed the idea of a feminine Holy Spirit? Of course, he ended up being accused of murder too, but like the women in question now, I'm told he was innocent of all charges."

"So are you admitting there aren't really any secret writings?" Veronica asked.

"What did I just say that could have sounded like any kind of an admission?" Faith seemed more put off by Veronica than by the two men in the room.

"So you're saying there are secret writings?" Tony sought to conclude.

"I'm not saying anything beyond that I'm pretty sure it's none of your business and if you don't apologize to these young women, I'm going to encourage them to follow through on plans to have you both charged with harassment."

Faith looked pretty comfortable, as if the only inner debate she was having was whether or not to try a slender slice of cheesecake.

"Of course, I don't have to worry about harassment charges, not having okayed anything these two have been up to," Mike declared, "at least not so's you could prove it, right, honey?"

"Yes, I guess that's true, *babe*," Faith replied.

"Listen to me, if I could convince you that even if these girls are innocent, even if I believe you're totally innocent, which, between you and me, I do believe, but if I could convince you that someone on your team is knocking people off, including your own members, well, would you want to cooperate then?"

"I doubt I can believe anything you say, but since you drove all the way from New York to chat, you can go ahead and say anything you'd like. But I do have to be going soon. There was a fifty percent chance of snow for the late night, so I want to be back home before then."

"I'm gonna level with you, Professor." Mike tried to seem more serious still by putting his plate with the merest remnant of cheesecake down on the oval, blue glass coffee table between the two couches. "You can believe it if you want. I can't control that. We've got four dead people. The first two knew each other and seem to have been working together to expose your outfit. Even though it looks like the first vic, Sister Maria Dolores, was in with your gang for a while since we've got video on that. Then, this Marissa who knew these other girls, she's dead and strangled, just like Heamey and the other priest. Speaking of him, Father Sweeney, I frankly don't know how he fits in, except his body had been left in a way to suggest there must be some relation among all these crimes. I don't know if this secret book stuff is true or not and I don't know what we're even hoping to find, if we can get our hands on it, but I'm telling you, it would help us a whole lot if you'd just choose—choose, I'm say-ing—to cooperate."

Faith seemed a little surprised by this approach and looked at Mike keenly, but said nothing, so he continued.

"I don't pretend to get all this stuff about these alumbradas or the church. I mean, I'm with you, there's a lot screwed up with the Catholic Church, no argument there, but I'm pretty sure, if I read you right, that while you might be into feeling superior to most of us poor dopes, you aren't looking to kill anyone, no matter how stupid. And as weird as Teresa Sargento and her sister are, I don't see them as killers either. Now Sister Anna Teresa, who scared me a little bit, has skipped the convent after we interviewed her. Then, a few days after she split there's another dead priest, but, whether she's the killer of one of them or not, someone on your team isn't really playing by team rules. Hell, remember, two of the people dead are women, young women just like the ones you say we're harassing, but we haven't laid a finger on any of them. Still, let me tell you, you can't get any more harassed then being murdered, I'm thinking, and, in our own way, I think you can even see that we're in the business of not letting anyone get killed, whether we agree with their religion or politics or not. Do you see what I'm saying, Professor?"

Mike's tone had begun matter of fact, but grew more earnest by the line. By the end of his speech it would have been difficult for anyone to question his sincerity, in spite of or maybe because of, his long windedness.

"You certainly make more sense than your brother ever did. But I'm really not convinced. There's no one I know on our 'team' as you call us that I would even vaguely suspect of being capable of murder."

"Do you know all the players?" Tony asked.

"Well, actually, I guess not."

"Well, then. Listen to me, Professor. What's the harm in helping us rule people out?" Mike followed through. "What's the harm in trying to see if someone somehow on the periphery of what you're all about is the nut behind all this? Like Teresa Sargento said, it's the twenty first century, why does the organization have to be secret anymore? Now that she's exposed the writings and you haven't denied them, we're going to go off in our typical cop ways and keep digging until we find that book. Why not spare us and whoever else we might harass the trouble? Why not work with us and tell us what you know?"

Faith shook her head and glanced, with some obvious distaste, across to Tony and Veronica. "It just seems impossible that it could be a good thing."

"Are you afraid if these lies are exposed to an expert's eye that your group will be undone?" Veronica challenged

"I'm also worried about your personal safety," Tony added. "Now that your name has been put out there, you'd be a lot safer with the police than with whoever has been trying so hard to keep this all a secret."

Mike gave his brother and Veronica a searing look that seemed to say, "As close as I'm getting you two have to screw it all up now?"

But Faith again surprised him.

"Tony, there's a lot you just don't understand and probably never will. The peace I've found through holy meditation and sisterhood has made me totally unafraid to die. And yet, Veronica, as much as it might pain you, I can't keep from you any longer the authentic words of the woman you claim expertise on. In fact, once you've read these pages, you'll be a great source for us in further authentication, since, unlike Tony, I know you value truth more than anything else, even though your loyalty to the church has obscured your vision of it for so long. Let an alumbrada like me, an illuminated one, bring you just the light you need."

"So you're going to help to retrieve those papers for us?" Mike concluded.

Faith smiled, almost seductively, her gold-green eyes bright with power. "No need for retrieval, Lieutenant."

"What are you saying?" Tony wanted to be sure.

"They're right here." Faith pointed to her oversized, dark blue handbag. "I never travel anywhere without them."

Chapter 22

What Faith produced from her handbag was clearly a contemporarily published document. It had the look of a poetry chapbook from a mediocre press, with a plain, pink paper cover and staples for binding, and was about as many pages, thirty-one.

Seeing the doubting looks on her otherwise rapt audience's faces, Faith hastened to explain. "Oh, this of course is a contemporary translation and a recently printed one. There are, I've been told, only four copies of the original left, and three of those are still in Europe. But I've seen the one that's here in the U.S., and the translation came right from that original."

Veronica seemed immediately ready to argue, but Mike and Tony were more interested in what the pamphlet actually contained.

"Are you going to allow us to take this with us and get a chance to read it carefully?" Tony wondered.

"I am, actually. I've got more of these. I can spare one for now so you can see for yourselves that there's nothing sinister in any of this, no murder directives or messages from Satan here. Keep it as long as you like, but I think I'll get going now."

"Oh, please, Professor, would you hang with us just a little longer? It's not snowing right now and I'd really like to ask you a few more questions," Mike insisted without being too insistent.

Faith seemed unsure of whether to stay or go, but Veronica, who had been greedily reading the pages of the pamphlet even as the other three conversed, brought her eyes up from a particular passage and spoke in a harsh tone.

"I'll give you credit, the prose here sounds very much like a good contemporary translation of Teresa. But anyone who has read her books carefully could mimic her style. This proves nothing, absolutely nothing."

"Here I am sharing this information with you, in most ways against my better judgment, and you're already calling me a liar?" Faith made as if to leave after all.

"I hope not a liar, only one deluded to believe what she so wants to believe. Why this passage I'm reading now, it almost seems lifted from a passage in *The Way of Perfection,* except for being so much colder and unloving than the real saint."

"Which passage are you looking at?" Faith was curious. She actually went over to where Veronica was seated in order to look over her shoulder at the offending words.

"'Any nun who actually enjoys visits from her relatives and the gossip and talk of the everyday that goes with it, has absolutely no business to be with us. It is insufferable enough to have to put up with the priests we are in no position absolutely to avoid, but to also have to abide the many mediocre minds who would harm us by their orthodoxy and inability to see beyond dogma, not to mention their very embracing of the world we flee from, should be more than any true sister wants to tolerate. An absolute rejection of all such visits is impractical, but should be the ideal we fervently would wish for. Those who are unable to do without the ways of this world should have no part in our sisterhood.'"

"Yeah, that sounds pretty harsh," Mike agreed.

Veronica frowned. "Really, in some ways it isn't much harsher than what is in *The Way of Perfection,* chapters eight and nine, where Teresa actually advises her sisters to 'shun' their relatives and says that no real good can come from frequent interactions with them. She even says they take us away from our 'obligations to God,' but—"

"Exactly, Veronica," Faith agreed, "even in her standard writings, for anyone really paying attention, Teresa is endorsing our way, our rejection of the ordinary world and the way it keeps us from union with the divine. In many ways she reminds me of Thoreau, who was no feminist, certainly, but who also stressed how trivial connections and associations only took us away from our divine natures."

Veronica seemed anxious to respond, but Mike spoke first.

"Listen, you're letting us keep this, so we'll have a good chance to read it all through later. I don't want to keep you here all night, so now's not the time for debate about philosophy or theology or whatever you want to call it. There's other things I really need to know sooner than that."

Faith had stood up to be next to Veronica. Mike

pointed her back toward the sofa and Faith decided to accept the less than gracious invitation.

"What else can I help you with, Lieutenant?"

"For starters, do you know Sister Anna Teresa and where we could find her? Who's got this authentic original copy of the secret writings you say you've seen? About how many alumbradas are there? Is this a national group, international, just local? And why would anyone think it was necessary to kill someone, more than one someone, over any of this?"

"Last question first. The Catholic Church has seen fit, over the centuries, to kill many, many thousands of people over just such things as this." Faith looked more at Veronica than Mike as she made that assertion.

"Yeah, but not recently, right?" Mike countered, "and, plus, why would they be killing off their own, especially a defender of theirs like Heamey?"

"I'm not saying the Catholic Church is responsible, I'm just reminding you of the contexts that can't be ignored."

"Thanks for that," Mike said. "Now tell me about the alumbradas and how you all interact. Do you have a leader?" he prompted.

"Well of course." Faith smiled, "St. Teresa of Avila."

Veronica seemed to be suppressing a scream. Mike ignored her and pressed on. "I mean someone running the show for her these days," he clarified.

"I know Tony used to like to read mysteries, but I thought you were the sensible one," Faith chided. "There's no big secret organization here. What happened was that a Spanish scholar uncovered these books in an old abandoned abbey, fairly recently, I think. We're still trying to piece together why they were lost for so long, though, of course I can guess that the Carmelites for whom Teresa was writing just were too afraid to go on with her true work once her charismatic presence wasn't there to prod them on. The original scholar, predictably enough, as a Spaniard, was Catholic and tried to keep the writings secret, but he shared his incredible find with a few others, and one of them broke his confidence enough so that word of the writings got out, though, again, with secrecy. But as more people became aware of these writings, they've passed them on to others who might be interested. As for the continued secrecy, I guess, ironically, it's been out of respect for the Catholic Church, not to come out with this book just to upset the church when it has more than enough to worry about. If this came out, there would certainly be one less saint in the Catholic firmament and since Teresa was the first female doctor, that would be a big loss."

"But how is it then that the book is back at work in at least one Carmelite convent in Brooklyn?" Tony could not help asking.

"Unlike you, Tony, I've never pretended to have all the answers. I guess it was inevitable, though, just common sense, that some discalced Carmelites would eventually find out about the book's existence and would want to see what their founder really had to say to them all those years ago, though even now, sadly, within their church, her message, however true, would not be any better accepted. You can see, then, why those sisters would want to keep things secret."

"Why don't they just leave the convent and the order, and the church, for that matter?" Veronica asked angrily. "There is freedom of religion. They can practice whatever they choose. If they want to be fools and believe this nonsense is from St. Teresa, surely they can do so outside of the convent without repercussion."

"I can see the problem, though." Tony turned to Veronica. "If they really believe that St. Teresa wanted them, as discalced Carmelites, to follow what is in these secret writings, then they would be tempted to follow her example, of seeming compliance hiding behind true revolution."

"That's right, Tony," Faith said with enthusiasm, though she seemed to temper it quickly, given with whom she was agreeing. More calmly she added, "Yes, this truth was starting to make its way among some of the nuns. I don't know, though, how widespread it has been, but I can see why Monsignor Heamey would be alarmed."

"Shocked and horrified, rather," Veronica countered.

"Yeah, but still, this explains why the church might be upset enough to want to rub this out, but not why two priests who we'd guess were against it, one civilian who was for it, and one nun who was both for and against it are all dead now. That's the part that needs attention, people. So, Professor Covington, do you know Sister Anna Teresa and can you tell us where we can find her?" Mike asked.

"If she doesn't want to be found, why should I go against her wishes?"

"Are you aware of the video we have of her, with the corpse-to-be nun, involved in some sort of weird sadomasochism that was supposed to be sanctioned by St. Teresa? Does this booklet here go over how that works? Were they crossing some lines that Sister Maria Dolores thought were too much, maybe, and then that's why they had to shut her up?"

"Why are you asking me these questions? They seem very far-fetched, but I can't know any of what happened, can I?"

"Can't you?" Tony wondered.

"No, I can't," she answered with particular asperity.

"No, but maybe Sister Anna can. Do you deny knowing her?" Mike asked.

"No, I have no reason to deny it. She hasn't done anything wrong."

"Well, actually, this is still being kept quiet, but she stole a very expensive cross from the convent," Mike corrected.

"You have proof of that?"

"Direct proof? No, but—"

"I didn't think so," Faith smugly interrupted.

"Okay, fair enough, but how can you be so certain she's innocent of all we suspect?"

"The same way I'm certain that these really are the words of St. Teresa of Avila. Anna is the one who has been entrusted to guard the book, to share it with the other nuns, at first in Brooklyn. She would never be involved in anything violent. She's totally involved in saving St. Teresa, in making her real truths be known."

"I can't take this anymore," Veronica growled. "It's all a horrible farce. These words are no more St. Teresa's than they are mine. I can't let you continue to blaspheme like this, I can't."

She seemed ready to attack Faith, but instead she tried to tear the book in half. It was just thick enough to make the move impossible on a first, rushed try, and Tony wrestled the booklet away from her before she could continue.

"Oh, leave her alone, Tony," Faith suggested. "We don't need that copy to prove St. Teresa was and is the leader of the alumbradas. I've seen the original. Anna showed it to me herself and even left it with me to seek authentication."

"With you? How could you authenticate it?"

"I couldn't, but she knew of my hesitation to share the writings with others unless I knew they were real. She knew at a university I was in a perfect position to find someone who could vouch for its realness."

"Why didn't you ever show it to me then?" Veronica challenged.

"And give you a chance to do with the original what you just tried doing with a modern translation? Besides, we had someone right at Smith who I knew could help more objectively."

"Someone I know?" Tony questioned.

"That's an understatement."

"You can't mean?" Tony knew the answer that he somehow did not want to hear.

"Yes, I can, Tony, you're boss, your pal, your friendly local Renaissance scholar, Hank Gallagher."

"That's impossible. I mean, if he, I mean I'd know about, a—" Tony stammered.

"Could he authenticate it?" Mike wanted to know.

"Well, he's something of a manuscript expert, but he'd have no specific expertise on a Spanish document from that time period," Tony noted.

"That's right, but he knows more than one scholar with that expertise. The nearest one is at Harvard, Ernesto Villareal, and he was delighted to take a look for us, Hank tells me."

"And?" Mike prodded.

"And all that your brother's drinking buddy wanted to know after he brought it back to us was whether I realized how much it was worth. I told him I did, but he's too much like you, Tony. He didn't have a clue I wasn't talking about money."

Veronica looked now more terrified than angry. Tony looked to comfort her, but she only turned from him, as if in disgust. Only Mike seemed unemotional.

"So where can I find this Sister Anna?" he calmly asked again.

Chapter 23

I just can't believe you didn't tell me about any of this," Tony scolded Hank as they sat together in Hank's spacious office after hours.

"But, Tony, I don't know what you're so upset about. Why would I think you'd even be interested? It wasn't like I was keeping it from you on purpose."

Hank seemed most upset that his old friend was so suddenly angry at him. His own tone seemed more hurt than defensive.

Tony had tried to remember how much, if anything, he had told Hank about the case. Of course, the murder of Monsignor Heamey had happened virtually on their campus, but Tony recognized he hadn't really indicated to Hank any special interest in things related to St. Teresa. In spite of their closeness, Tony had had to keep most of the details of the investigation quiet. Still, he somehow could not keep himself from some anger.

"But you knew I was dating Faith, so why didn't it at least come up in conversation that she had come to you with what she thought was a sixteenth century manuscript?"

"Well, actually, she asked me to keep quiet about it. She said the owner wasn't certain what he was going to do with or about it once its authenticity was confirmed, but they didn't want any publicity yet. So, you know, that's why I kept quiet. You know it goes against my nature, but she insisted, so I said okay."

Hank was dressed in jeans and a dark gray wool sweater, having changed out of his work day suit, and only reluctantly agreed to meet in his office, which he usually liked to be out of for the day at five o'clock sharp. He fiddled with a copy of Shakespeare's sonnets, a thin, red leather bound book that he always kept on his desk, as he waited for Tony to calm down.

"Okay, Hank, I'm sorry, but, listen, are you sure the book's the real thing?"

"Like I told Faith, I don't claim to be the world's greatest expert. But it certainly had the feel and look of sixteenth-century books I've seen. But I knew Villareal was an expert, so I arranged for him to get a look. That's all there was to it from my end, Ton'."

"But weren't you suspicious? Wouldn't it just be common sense to be a little doubtful? We're New Yorkers, after all."

"What, that they found some more writings from St. Teresa? I mean, the woman wrote a ton, right? Especially for a woman of that time period, right? So they found a few more manuscript pages. I mean, it's worth a lot of money, but it isn't all that startling, is it? And if it was bogus, you couldn't slip it by Villareal."

"And Faith didn't tell you what the pages were supposed to be about? And you didn't try to find out?"

"You know Spanish isn't one of my languages. I mean, I've got Latin and French, so I can make out a few words, but, as far as I knew, there was nothing controversial in any of this. I may make it look too easy, but being chair of this department is a pretty full time job, without me looking into any Catholic lunacy."

"But Professor Villareal, surely he told you something?"

"Well, first of all, when I told him what I thought we had, he was willing to drive down here from Cambridge. Faith sure didn't want to send the thing UPS, and I didn't feel like schlepping up to Boston, but, luckily, a manuscript nut like Ernie Villareal, he couldn't get here quick enough. So he came and examined it and he told me it was all bona fide, in terms of the paper, the ink, etc. He asked me if I knew what it was all about and I told him I didn't, but he didn't volunteer anything else. He seemed pretty interested, though. Said he'd like to have a chance to bid on it if it was ever up for sale. That's when he told me about how much he thought it might be worth, especially to the church, he said."

"And you didn't ask him what he meant by that?"

"Come off it, Tony. What's this third degree bull-shit? Why would I ask him what he meant? I thought I knew. Of course, it would be worth a fortune to the church to have some uncovered writings by one of their big saints. And they've got the swag to outbid anyone, right?" Hank had picked up and then again let go of the Shakespeare book. His own anger had finally risen, and so he let it back down with a thump.

"Hey, sorry, man, I'm just kind of in a state of shock, you know," Tony apologized.

"No, I don't know. You still haven't told me what all this is about. Are you telling me it's got something to do with Heamey's death? I don't get the connection."

"It's just as well. I really can't talk about it. I wish I had told you long before, though, so you could have gotten all this information to me a lot sooner. I sure would like to get a look at the book myself."

"Faith hasn't got it still, I suppose. But she knows who does, right?"

"We think we know who has it, but we can't find her just now. Of course, she can be found. I don't know why it matters though, really. If Villareal says it's the real thing, who am I to doubt it? The main thing now will be to make some sense out of it and see if it can help us with these crimes."

"Listen, Tony, more and more I'm seeing what all this investigation crap is doing to you. I mean, isn't that better left to the professionals? The last time you thought you could solve a series of crimes it all blew up in your face big time, didn't it?"

Tony wondered why his friend felt the need to re-mind him of how badly he had failed three years before in figuring out the "sign of the cross" killings, where the killer had outsmarted him at every turn. He decided to ignore the shot and proceed as if he hadn't heard it.

"So, really, I guess we should at least talk to your Harvard man. You have his phone number handy?"

Hank paused a few beats, as if trying to decide whether to call Tony on having ignored his advice. "Yeah, sure," he said. "But I'll tell you, he's kind of a dinosaur, doesn't even own a cell phone. Still, I'll give you his home and office phone numbers, if you want to talk about it with the expert. Just tell him I gave you the numbers."

"I'll do that, Hank. And sorry about all this. It's nothing you did. I just wish I had known about all this sooner."

"Yeah, no problem, Ton'. You want to go get a beer, so the night won't have been a total downer?"

"I can't. I'm meeting someone else in a few minutes. Rain check."

"Yeah, absolutely," Hank agreed, finally putting his

Shakespeare back in its place on his desk, at the left end of a set of smiling gargoyle bookends. Tony shook his hand firmly before exiting the room.

Tony had been in no mood to go out drinking, something Hank was always a little more enthusiastic about than Tony to begin with. He hadn't lied to get out of it since he really was due to meet someone. He was meeting his brother, Michael, who had remained in Massachusetts and was staying with him. As soon as Tony walked through the door, Mike was ready with questions.

"So, how'd it go? Did he confirm what Faith said? Is this thing on the level?"

"He not only confirmed it, he gave me the Harvard guy's phone numbers so we can talk to him ourselves. From all indications, there really were secret writings. And, you know, I've already read the thing in English, cover to cover twice, and it seems just like what these alumbradas are claiming it is, an admission on St. Teresa's part that she was just gaming the Catholic Church to keep from getting roasted. And that she really believed you didn't need good works to get to Heaven, but just a good way to meditate, pray, and suffer your way into a union with God."

Mike who was sitting in a dark green recliner, his favorite place to sit in Tony's living room, scratched his head and laughed a tired little laugh. "So these nuts haven't just been making all this up. Fine. And it's clear why no good Catholic would want this stuff to come out. Fine again. But then why is it we have casualties on both sides? Could it be like I thought at the beginning, that one killing was a kind of way of avenging an earlier one? That we really may have two sets of killers?"

Tony who was ill at ease on a blue, red, and gray plaid couch, absently munching on some almond biscotti, was no less puzzled.

"It could be, I suppose. At least we know now that there's something solid behind what these women believe."

"I'm still not sure I see how that helps us."

"I think you do see, but just aren't looking."

"Clue me in, then," Mike advised, as he stood up, leaned over the coffee table between them, and grabbed one of Tony's cookies.

"If there really were no secret writings, then it would be more likely we were dealing with nuts, people fabricating a world so it could turn out the way they wanted it to. And people like that could be harmless, mostly, but you could see where they also might kill without what you'd call real provocation. But since all this is real, well, it makes things way more threatening to the church. It makes what Heamey was up to more urgent, explains why the Jesuits in Chicago haven't been too forthcoming in trying to help us solve Heamey's murder, makes me question whether they'll fully cooperate still, and makes it possible that a fanatic on that side of the scale could be involved with at least part of this. What we've really got to do is find Sister Anna or those other two, who were in the video, that maybe weren't even nuns. And we've got to maybe come down on those other girls we know about—maybe one of them will crack. Though, since we haven't got a damn bit of evidence against anybody, I don't know how we're going to be able to do that, unless..."

Mike gave Tony an odd look, grabbed another cookie, Tony's last, and said, "As a cop I can't bring any of these people in, except Sister Anna, and we can't find her. But you, I mean, you've got the track record. Maybe you could convince them, now that you've seen the book, convince them you're a believer, and maybe you could get in with them and see if any of them knows anything."

"How good an actor do you think I am? And isn't this all just a women's group anyway? When your husband is Christ, no substitute will do, right?"

"Yeah, for the pure of heart, I'm sure that's enough. But, hey, at least one of these chicks must want to settle for a flesh and blood substitute once in a while. I mean, isn't that what Faith was trying with you all along? Seeing if you could come along for the ride? Seeing if a man could understand. I doubt she'll give you a second chance, but maybe one of these other nuts will give you a first."

"I just don't think I can pull that off. I'm an English professor, not an undercover cop or a professional actor."

"Don't take this wrong, Ton', but for years you had people fooled about you and Maggie, and you sure were convincing then about there being nothing between you two. I think if you reach real hard, you might be able to manage this."

This was just the sort of remark that, in the past, would have made Tony cringe, then get angry, and then have him lashing back with something equally hurtful at his irreverent, inconsiderate, impossible brother. But Tony really was starting to feel a change. At the core of that change was his honesty with himself. He knew, essentially, that Mike was right. He had spent most of his career as a priest lying in one way or another, hiding his affair with Maggie, constantly trying to convince himself that the church was at fault rather than him. And though he had done many charitable things as a cleric and had cared a lot for and about most of his parishioners, he had spent most of his years with them pretending to be someone other than who he was. His brother was just honestly assessing what he was capable of doing.

"Yeah, I guess I could manage it at that. I'm not sure it will accomplish anything, but at least I'll be trying."

"That's the spirit. I'll leave it to you to figure out which mark to play and how to play it. Meanwhile, you think it would be worth it to give this Harvard professor a call? Maybe there's something about the original that would help us out some?"

"I was thinking the same thing. It's only five after nine. I hear he's an old grouch, but you think he'd still be up?"

"Yeah, the older you get the less sleep you need, plus the more likely you're home too, I bet."

Mike could only clearly hear one end of Tony's phone conversation, but he felt confident it did not include any discussion of sixteenth-century Spanish printing.

"What's the matter? Didn't you get him in?"

"He wasn't home."

"You talk to his wife or something?"

"No, I talked to one of his graduate students who's house sitting for him. Professor Villareal is on sabbatical this semester. He's off somewhere in Spain."

"Well, can't we reach him there? If you want, the department will pick up the tab."

"No, you don't understand. He's traveling all over. He can't be reached. He doesn't want to be reached. We can't ask him a damn thing until maybe August."

Mike gave his brother one more tired laugh. "I hope you have better luck getting into the alumbrada club. Someone's got to give us something we need, and soon."

Chapter 24

Two weeks passed and no progress was made in the case. Tony could barely concentrate on his school work, actually taking a full week to get students a set of papers back, when he'd always prided himself on getting work back the very next class. It was difficult for him to focus on the allegories in Hawthorne or how best to advise revision of yet another set of memoir essays, when he was far more intent on concocting a persona who could convince the alumbradas of his true conversion experience. Though Teresa Sargento seemed like the best possible "in," her sister Angela was keeping her closeted away, and Teresa saw Tony's working with the police force as absolute proof of his lack of trustworthiness. He next considered Nancy Temple, though he did not expect her to be sympathetic.

When she did not respond to his first few emails, he sent yet another, each time with more evidence of his close and enthused reading of the secret text. Meanwhile, Veronica, though still on speaking terms, was adamantly against the idea of him trying to pretend to be an alumbrado, warned him against trusting any of those "crazy students," and stubbornly refused to admit the authenticity of the evidence against the St. Teresa she cherished.

To Tony, though, these new pages where Teresa linked predominating pain as the path to an ecstatic union not requiring a mortal husband—"For the way of the cross is a journey rich with pain. The only way to be worthy of union with our spouse is to accept suffering joyously, to never be without it, to embrace it for an eternity of commitment to Christ"—was perfectly consistent with the Teresa he had encountered in her mainstream writings, a glorying in pain as a way to glory, "let me suffer or let me die." Veronica only shook her head sadly and refused to continue the conversation.

On a Tuesday afternoon, a little before Tony was about to head out of his office, he received a call from Nancy.

"Professor, I was thinking that philosophical discussion and email are somehow antithetical. So, if it isn't too short of notice, I was wondering if you'd like to attend another of our meetings."

Tony had been hoping to just see one alumbrada at a time, to focus on one who might be willing to help him find Sister Anna, or offer some insight into possible motives for the killings. But he didn't feel he could turn down this offer, the first contact they had allowed him since before Christmas.

"Yes, certainly, I'm free. Thanks for asking."

Once again, he drove up to the secluded house in the woods outside of Worcester a little before eight o'clock, on a spectacularly clear, only moderately cold night, with stars all ablaze, alongside a large and yellow crescent moon. Again the electric lights were out but he could see the candle light, illuminating the house through the bay window, and he easily found his way to the door and knocked. This time Shanti Patel answered the door, dressed in a long black robe, like a nun, minus the veil and wimple. When she wordlessly let him inside, he saw that Nancy and Sally McGuire were seated on opposite ends of the couch, similarly clothed. He noticed too that each young woman wore the brown scapular of the Carmelites around her neck.

"Thanks for inviting me," Tony said to Nancy, but she said nothing at first, and seemed lost in a kind of reverie, as did Sally. He decided to wait a few awkward moments, not even taking off his coat or presuming to sit himself.

Finally, Nancy seemed to notice him for the first time. "Hello, Professor. Won't you sit down?"

Nancy pointed not to a spot on either facing couch, but to one of two dining room chairs about two feet apart from each other off to the left of the two couches. Being in no position to question his hostess so soon, he sat on one of the wooden chairs. A moment later Sally got up and sat down on the chair next to him, though she did not say a word.

"You'll pardon our lack of small talk, Professor. We hope to share something very special with you this evening, and all but the most necessary words will be left unspoken."

Nancy's tone seemed welcoming, though Tony was not sure if it was the overall atmosphere or the unusual seating arrangements that made him hear something sinister in it as well.

"I've spoken with my sisters, spoken of how difficult it is to believe a man could understand St. Teresa, the real St. Teresa, and respect what she really means to us all."

"Well, I—" Tony began, but he was hushed by Sally, who actually put a hand to his mouth, and Nancy continued.

"Because your book on the female nature of the Holy Spirit was one of our early inspirations, and since you have never taken back what you wisely wrote in that book, we had hoped you might be an exception, particularly since you also left the misogyny of the Catholic priesthood. Our disappointment was great when you looked to accuse us of evil doing. Now you come to us, penitent and claiming to share in our vision of the Saint. And so we are ready to share with you the first way to the union that she taught us to search for, the all-encompassing union with the divine."

At a soundless signal from Nancy, Shanti took the scapular from off of Sally's neck and used it to bind her hands behind her. Nancy also arose, took the scapular off her own neck and moved toward Tony. What she planned to do was clear. Also clear was the similar set up and number of people as in the video of Sisters Anna and Maria and two unidentified others. At least one of those people, Sister Maria Dolores, was now dead. Though his brother knew he was at Nancy's house, Tony had not conveyed that information to any of the three women, so it would be a meager consolation to know his death might be avenged. Still, he had witnessed what was on that video, and no one had died on screen. He decided he had to take the chance.

Nancy first had him remove his coat and sweater and then tied his hands securely behind him. As she did, she said, "St. Teresa teaches us how to pray, teaches us that there are many difficult and painful steps to walk the way of the cross. Jesus was one of the few redeeming men ever, God in the form of a man. He shows us that it is possible even for a man to be one with the Holy Spirit. But only the way of the cross will take us to a painful and real enough way to bring us to union. And so we begin to pray and to understand the pain needed through this exercise in prayer that mimics his suffering on the cross. The novice understands, of course, the need for absolute compliance and abandonment to this redeeming pain."

Nancy and Shanti waited for the two who were bound to register their accord with what was about to happen.

Sally said, in a clear and proud voice, "I understand," and so Tony, with an attempt at sounding as convinced, said the same.

"We'll begin with a reading from the Gospel according to Matthew," Shanti announced, much to Tony's surprise, though he immediately understood the reason behind the passage selected, the middle portion of the famous passage concerning the man who sowed seeds on various kinds of ground.

"'The disciples approached him and said, "Why do you speak to them in parables?" He said to them in reply: "Because knowledge of the mysteries of the kingdom of heaven has been granted to you, but to them it has not been granted. To anyone who has, more will be given and he will grow rich; from anyone who has not, even what he has will be taken away. This is why I speak to them in parables, because they look but do not see and hear but do not listen or understand. Isaiah's prophecy is fulfilled in them, which says: '*You shall indeed hear but not understand, you shall indeed look but never see. Gross is the heart of this people, they will hardly hear with their ears, they have closed their eyes, lest they see with their eyes and hear with their ears and understand with their hearts and be converted, and I heal them.*' But blessed are your eyes, because they see, and your ears, be-

cause they hear. Amen, I say to you, many
prophets and righteous people longed to see
what you see but did not see it, and to hear what
you hear, but did not hear it.'"

Shanti's look toward Tony and Sally seemed to him
contemptuous rather than nurturing. "Take, novices, the
opportunity to 'grow rich.' Blessed be your eyes because
they see and your ears because they hear. Leave the parables for the fools who will lose what little they have.
Take what is offered only to the truest disciples."

Shanti and Nancy placed upon Sally's and Tony's
laps each a rosary of brown, sturdy-looking beads. Shanti
then came behind Sally and wrapped a larger pair of
brown beads around her neck, in a choking position.
Nancy did the same for Tony.

"Since you have only read the truth recently revealed
to you of our saint in English translation, you may not be
immediately familiar with the opening phrase, we say, in
her honor, in Spanish. '*Dulce es el dolor, el dolor que me
ofrece mi marido, mi salvador*, Jesus.' We have just recently substituted these words for the 'Our Mother' prayer."

The saying of the Rosary, then, was not entirely un-
conventional. There were still the decades of Hail Marys
and the ending of each decade with the "Glory Be," but in
place of the Our Fathers that should have started each
decade, there were now the words which in English read,
"Sweet is the pain, the pain that my spouse offers me, my
savior, Jesus."

And so they began the prayer session, with the rosary
beads wrapped around the necks of Sally and Tony. The
choking was real and consistent, though far from life
threatening, however, it was most enthusiastic during the
added brief prayer: "Sweet is the pain…"

Each time that phrase brought on an added force to the choking, a force that made it difficult even to say the words. And as they got farther into the decades, Nancy got more and more enthusiastic. Tony could feel the added difficulty in breathing, the tighter strain on his Adam's apple, the greater danger to himself. He tried to reassure himself that he was safe, that this was something these strange women did periodically and lived through. But he also knew he was in a room full of murder suspects, and that they might be using his own desire to figure them out or incriminate them as a perfect way to have him participate in his own demise. And so he prayed, in earnest, but whenever he would try to feel the meaning of the Hail Marys, the strength of the choking and the hot breath and strain of the young woman who was choking him, took him somewhere else, some place close to where they wanted him to be, a place nowhere close to the divine.

Through his peripheral vision he could see that Sally was in a sort of rapture, with tears streaming down her face and eyes pointed heavenward. Her Spanish accent was weak, so her saying of the pain prayer seemed all the more otherworldly, not like any language at all. When what he counted as the final decade was over and he had survived, he wondered how much they now trusted him and how he could use it to his advantage. But this was not the rosary his mother had taught him as a young boy.

Nancy and Shanti each adjusted the beads so that the brown wooden crucifix, with its representation of the dying savior, would be right up against the throats of their penitents. Each woman then put great strain into pressing the Christ side of the crosses into their victims' throats as they said, solemnly, "Repita." Sally knew what to repeat and Tony guessed correctly:

"*Dulce es el dolor, el dolor que me ofrece, mi marido, mi salvador*, Jesus."

"Repita," the two women intoned, this time with all the more force. Each time, each repetition, they pressed the choking crucifix more tightly, making the pain stronger, sharper, more all-encompassing. Tony thought to resist, but Nancy applied a firm hand to push him down whenever he tried to rise up, mimicking Christ's inability, after a time, to use his legs enough to keep from suffocation at Calvary. Tony felt certain he was about to die, but still they expected him to repeat the words.

"*Dulce es el dolor, dulce es el dolor, dulce es el dolor*" was hammering in his brain, even as he saw only burning candles, and darkness all around him. It was a total giving over to that darkness that finally seemed to stop the searing, powerful strain. His heart raced, his neck was burning, but he could feel that the rosary had left his neck, or rather it had been left around his neck, without any pressure. When he dared to open his eyes, he saw Shanti and Nancy, together and standing in front of him, holding hands. They stayed there silently for what had to be at least ten minutes more, though Tony felt as if time had in most senses stopped for him.

Finally, Shanti spoke. "You have honored the true memory of the Saint. Though you have much still to learn, we hope now you will be ready to take the next steps toward divine union and abandon the foolish notions that our sisterhood is interested in anything but bringing rapture to those worthy of its divine power."

Tony doubted he could even speak, but Nancy brought him a glass of water and helped him to drink it, not offering yet to untie his hands.

She then kissed him lightly on both cheeks, even as Shanti did the same for Sally. "Now that you've experienced exactly what you witnessed on that video tape, can you see how Sister Anna was seeking grace and not anything evil? Will you stop trying to find her to allow the police to harass her?" Was this a question she asked to a true convert or a threat offered by a woman who still held him captive? Either way, Tony, raspy and in pain, knew how to respond.

"I'm humbled that you allowed me this grace. I'm done seeking clues to murders here, but rather clues to finding a spirituality I thought I'd lost forever. But there are still murders to be solved and I'm hoping you'll work with me to protect your sisters and the others who are threatened."

Shanti looked with a sort of disdain at Tony, and he wondered if she would next request a prolonged chance at choking him herself. But Nancy did not seem to take his persistence in the same way.

"We have no idea who killed the two priests, though we're glad you realize that we would have had nothing to do with them in any way. We believe Sister Maria Dolores really did kill herself, perhaps out of shame for having lost the courage to pursue the divine truth." Nancy seemed ready to say more, but hesitated.

"Tell him, tell him," Sally encouraged, with a voice so raspy it frightened Tony anew.

"I can offer you only one suspect, Professor, but you won't like what I have to say. Still, I'm hopeful the truth you've found this evening will help you realize what you have to do."

"Of course, please, honor me further with your trust."

"I'm still amazed," Shanti said, in a tone that at least hinted she was more incredulous than genuinely surprised. "Amazed that you had such a different reaction to the secret writings than Veronica Teuma did."

"How are you aware of how Professor Teuma reacted? I didn't say anything about it in my emails, did I?"

"You didn't have to," Nancy explained.

"Veronica Teuma saw the secret writings long before you did," Shanti claimed.

"What!"

"Marissa showed them to her," Nancy continued. "Marissa was so certain that Veronica would become a believer with us. Instead, she totally rejected the truth, totally rejected Marissa, even threatened her if she didn't forsake the evidence she had put in her mentor's hands."

"What? How can this be? Teresa and Angela said nothing about this. And Faith didn't act surprised when Veronica was so upset that night in the Sargentos' apartment."

"They didn't know," Sally told him. "Marissa told only Shanti and Nancy. And when we saw that we were all suspects, rather than Professor Teuma, and instead, you had her helping you, we didn't see any reason to share our suspicions with you."

"But the wait was worth it." Nancy smiled, as she untied Tony's hands, even as Shanti did the same for Sally. "Now you know that the writings are authentic, not the 'blasphemous lies' Veronica claimed them to be. Now you know that she is the liar, absolutely in denial about the life of the woman she claims expertise on. And Marissa, her prized student is dead, murdered, and who with a better motive of crazy revenge against the trusted person who brought such bad news to her?"

Nancy put the scapular over Tony's neck. "You're one of us now. Protect us from our enemies. Let your brother know what you know. Veronica Teuma killed our sister. She just could not accept the truth."

Tony, rubbed his hands to bring back the circulation, looked around the room at his new sisters, thought of Veronica, and felt the suspicious pain that is never ending, but in no way rapturous or redeeming.

Chapter 25

Tony knew he needed to report his findings to Mike. He also knew that this accusation about Veronica's prior knowledge of the contents of St. Teresa's secret writings not only made her a suspect in at least the death of Marissa Hitzel, but also made her potentially unreliable all together, since she had certainly acted as if the writings were new to her when Faith revealed them at Veronica's dinner party.

Tony was torn between wanting to continue to believe in Veronica, and at least give her the opportunity to explain herself before giving the information over to a police lieutenant, and being angry even at the possibility that he had once again been fooled by a woman he trusted. The truth was he had never fully committed to even admitting his attraction, but it was futile to keep lying to himself about what he had felt, and, sadly, was still feeling, about Veronica. He had once been so confident of a woman's long term friendship and later intimate affection that he had entirely missed even the possibility that she had killed two people. In spite of that experience, he had still felt that this time he could not be wrong, that Veronica was a wholly good person incapable of any real evil. But this perhaps unwarranted trust was why, he realized now, he had refused to suspect her of lying, though his brother had warned him to never rule out any person during an investigation. And this was why he still wanted to hold out hope that it was Nancy and Shanti who were lying.

So he called Veronica first. She didn't answer either at home or in her office. He left a message on her voice mail at work, a message that did not hint at what he needed to talk to her about. She had no answering machine at home. Veronica did not own a cell phone and was not on Facebook. These facts, which had seemed innocent instances of an "old-fashioned girl," now seemed more potentially sinister. She was a woman who resisted change; preferred the Mass in Latin; came from the "most Catholic country in the world; refused to believe clear, authenticated evidence that went against what she wanted to believe; and even refused to admit she had had a chance to see it long before Tony himself had. This was a person who might be capable of snapping. Though he was unable absolutely to give up on her, he knew what had to be done. He called his brother.

"So how did it go with the nutty students? I guess you survived your encounter, since you're calling, unless you're a disembodied spirit calling me with heavenly, I hope heavenly, insight into this mystery," Mike said, playing his normal role, though Tony thought he could hear an edge of relief mixed with the sarcasm.

"Yeah, I'm alive, but not well. That sicko thing with the choking rosaries—I got a dose of that. Thought I was gone for a moment there, but now it looks like I'm 'in' with their bunch, though I'm not sure what good that will do us."

"Wow, they really are nuts then, huh? I'm glad you're okay. What'd you find out?"

"Well, they're a pretty extreme bunch, but I still don't see any clear motive."

"How not?"

"It looks like they'll go on with their little cult whether it's been discovered or not, so I don't think they would have killed to keep it a secret. I mean, you might want to look into them more, of course, but I'm not sure what more I'm going to find out by sticking with them. But I don't think my life would be in danger either, at least not with criminal intent."

"Yeah, well if they kill you by accident are you going to feel any less dead?" Mike asked, again with a tone that spoke both the usual sarcasm and the unusually overt concern.

"I'll try to be careful. Meanwhile, I did find out one thing, not about them, but about someone else that does concern me."

"Who?"

Tony hesitated, but realized it was pointless, since he had already half revealed the message. "Veronica. According to the girls, she knew about the secret writings. Marissa showed them to her months ago. That was the real reason for their total falling out, and, you know, Veronica never even hinted she had actually seen the pages."

Mike paused a few beats. "Damn, that's a surprise. I mean, you had me almost convinced she was legit. So there's proof that this went down this way?"

"Proof? All of them swore by it. The three that knew, anyway. And why would they lie?"

"Are you really serious? So's they could get you off their cases and onto hers? Does that seem like a possibility? Let's at least hear what Veronica has to say for herself before we go taking the word of some nuts, okay? I mean, we know they're nuts, but the jury's still out on Teuma, right?"

That Mike was more fair-minded and objective about Veronica's possible guilt than Tony himself was further proof of the kind of volatile feelings he was having about the St. Teresa expert. When he volunteered to find out for himself what Veronica would say, he was only a little surprised that Mike agreed to that too, especially when Tony explained that the reason she wasn't returning his calls might simply have to do with her continued anger over his believing in the authenticity of the secret writings.

Tony decided he could not let this wait for a phone call that might never be answered. He only had one class on Wednesday, in the early afternoon, and it was a small-group rough draft workshop, where he'd hardly be directly involved in what the students were doing. Surely, he could leave instructions to have them hold the class without him.

He needed to drive up to Worcester on Wednesday and confront Veronica before any more time passed or any other person died. If he skipped his class he could be in Worcester in time to be waiting outside Veronica's classroom. So the next morning he called his department office, and was surprised to get Hank himself on the line.

"Both secretaries are late coming back from a breakfast meeting. They're planning a surprise fiftieth birthday party for one of their own over in Music. Far be it from me to try to stand in the way of a gaggle of secretaries."

Though in no mood to joke, Tony, from long standing practice with his high school classmate, felt prompted to say, "You'd better make sure one of them isn't bugging the line or they might find out what you're really like."

"Little chance of that, Tony, me-boy. What can I do you for, anyway?"

"Really, I was just going to let one of them know I have to miss class this afternoon, and wanted them to just pop in before the start to let the students know to go on with the planned workshop without me."

"That's the great thing about abandoning the lecture route, eh? You don't really need to be there most of the time, especially with these workshops. Are you sure you still should be drawing a paycheck, with all this amateur sleuthing you're doing instead?"

The tone was still jokey, but with a clear edge to it. "Sorry about all of this, Hank. I'm out of my league, I know, but my brother thought I could help with some of this, and, well, really, I don't think I'll have to take any more time away, I—"

"Hey, forget it. I gave you my advice about this crap more than once and you ignored it, so it's washing my hands time, I guess. We're still on for lunch Thursday, right?" Hank's tone for that last question felt to Tony almost like an accusation somehow.

"Yeah, sure, of course. I wouldn't miss it."

"That will remain to be seen. Where are you headed, anyway?"

"Back to Worcester."

"You're not seeing that Maltese dish again are you?" Hank asked, with a voice suggesting the leer his eyes must be registering.

"It's pretty complicated, actually, Hank, I'd, I'd rather not say."

"When are you going to leave the fanatics alone? You just escaped one type and now you're headed the other way? Have you no shame, boy? Or no brains, better?"

Tony laughed, glad that Hank seemed to be back to

his jokey tone. Ten minutes later he was on his way to the Holy Cross campus.

About ten minutes before his arrival there, Tony received a call on his cell phone. Though not one who normally liked to talk and drive, seeing that the call was from his brother, he answered.

"What's up, Mike? I'm on the road, on my way right now to find Veronica. I'll call you back when I find something out, no?"

"Sorry, Tony, no. This can't wait," Mike said, in a tone enough unlike any Tony had ever heard from his wise guy brother to frighten him.

"What is it?" Tony asked, his own tone having shifted considerably.

"It's Dad. He's had a heart attack, a pretty bad one. He's in intensive care over at Jamaica."

"Oh, oh, God, no," Tony said, stunned. Why he should be stunned that an almost ninety-year-old with consistently-too-high blood sugar and a more and more sedentary lifestyle should have had a heart attack would be beyond reason, except for most children who have very elderly parents they have unconsciously willed to be immortal. He knew this was one more thing he now shared in sympathy with his brother.

"W—when did this happen?" Tony stammered.

"Just a few hours or so ago, I think. I just took the call from Rose Anne myself."

"So I should get home then, huh, Mike?"

"I think it would be the best idea, if you can swing it, brother."

"I'll see you later, then."

"Okay, man, drive safe."

Tony's level of distraction already ruled out the idea of totally safe driving. His first decision to make was whether to head immediately to Queens or else first take care of the errand that had him on the road. Since he was only minutes away from campus and since he really was hopeful that somehow Veronica would have a good explanation that would free him of suspicion, he kept his Toyota aimed toward Worcester.

Tony was familiar with the layout of the campus including the location of Veronica's classroom building, from both previous visits to Holy Cross and from having looked up her schedule on the Holy Cross web site. He got to Veronica's "Comparative Catholicisms" course with twenty minutes to spare and waited patiently outside the classroom. However, instead of Veronica, he saw, as he looked in the now-opened door, a younger male professor chatting with a few students, preparatory to exiting the room. Students heading in for the next class jostled Tony a bit as he tried to figure out if he had somehow waited outside the wrong door. He double checked his information, found no discrepancy, and had no recourse but to question the young man in his early thirties; tall; thin; with sandy brown hair, trimmed neatly; round, wire-rimmed glasses; and the same gray tweed jacket with patches he'd probably seen professors wear in old movies when he was a child.

"Excuse me, Professor," Tony said when the last of the students had left the man to collect his materials before heading out himself.

"Yes, how can I help you?" the man asked, politely, but not enthusiastically.

"I was led to believe Professor Teuma was teaching this section. Have I gotten bad information?"

"Well, no, not at all. I'm subbing for Dr. Teuma."

"May I ask why? She's not sick, is she?"

"Might I know who's asking?"

"Oh, sure, I'm Tony Cupelli. I teach English at Smith."

"Oh, Tony Cupelli. Yes, I know who you are," the man responded, as if the knowledge did not make him at all inclined to be more cooperative.

"Well, that makes two of us, then," Tony responded with a similar stridence, annoyed that he even had to talk with this unfriendly teacher, wishing he had decided to head straight for Queens after all. Still, he had come too far to leave with just more mystery to unravel. Tony actually placed himself in the Professor's path. "Where is Professor Teuma, please?"

"I'm not really at liberty to say. If they feel differently at the department office, well, that's up to them, not me. Will you excuse me?"

Tony very much wanted to grab the man, shake him, and maybe worse, but since he knew the department office was only one floor down, he left the junior faculty member without any further exchange. He went immediately up to the department secretary, a woman about his own age, with ruffled gray hair in a loose perm and neutral blue-gray eyes.

"Can I help you?" she also asked, but with more of an implied admission that such help was part of her normal job description, for which she had no objections per se.

"Yes, please. I went to find Professor Teuma and discovered she wasn't in today, but I really need to talk to her. I've driven all the way over from Smith in fact, as there's something we're working on together and if I don't get with her soon, we're going to miss an important publisher's deadline."

What he lied sounded credible enough to him, so he hoped it made sense enough to pass inspection. But the department secretary, Sherry Olmstead, according to her desk placard, was not at all as guarded about Veronica's whereabouts as the substitute teacher had been. Maybe it had helped Tony's cause not to mention who he was at a Catholic college's Religious Studies Department.

"Dr. Teuma had to take an unplanned leave of absence."

"Can you tell me why, or how long she'll be gone?"

"I think it was some kind of family emergency. You'd have to ask our chair, and he's out for the day. I do know she went to Europe, and I know she's originally from Malta, so that's why I'm guessing that. I think I overheard her telling Dr. Santore she might need as long as two weeks, but we don't have any definite guarantee on a return date yet. She had some sick leave coming, so we're covering for her as best we can."

So Veronica had fled, just when suspicion might be directed her way, even as Sister Anna Teresa had done under similar circumstances. This explained to Tony why she had been so against him spending time with Nancy and her roommates—she had anticipated them giving away her own secret concerning the secret writings. And Europe, where she had family, was a long ways away from either Massachusetts or New York. Even as Tony had a new tinge of grief, thinking about his father in a hospital bed in Jamaica, Queens, he felt the added pain of someone he had trusted, once again proving how foolish he was to trust anyone.

"Two weeks, huh? I guess I can beg for an extension. Thanks for your help."

"Help" was what Tony needed—for himself, for his father, and for the victims of the killer he had done nothing to defeat. "Help" he requested, futilely, to no one present, as he drove alone back to Queens.

Chapter 26

Jamaica Hospital was familiar to Tony, too familiar, since his mother had been in and out of it several times for ailments ranging from urinary tract infections to a broken ankle. But to see his father in a hospital bed, with tubes up his nose and in his veins, was somehow even worse. The first sight of it brought quick tears to Tony's eyes. His sadness, though, was soon mitigated by Angelo's own take on his hospital stay. Living up to the stubborn strain his ancestors from Calabria were famous for, he refused to believe he had even had a heart attack.

"Whaddaya kiddin' me? I'm fine. It was probably just some bad gas. I shouldn't eat veal and peppers anymore," he informed his sons. "You drove all the way here to come see me, Tony?" his father demanded, close to bristling, though perhaps with a little bit of appreciation included in for good measure.

"What, Dad? You're not glad to see me?" Tony tried to joke.

"Sure, always glad, but it's the middle of the week.

Ain't you got a job? You could have at least waited till the weekend. I woulda been back home by then."

Mike had told Tony it was a heart attack, serious, intensive-care. But their father, in spite of being decorated with the various mandatory tubes of the seriously ill, was fully lucid, able to move, talk, and get as easily annoyed as usual. When his daughter, Rose Anne, a nurse at Jamaica Hospital for the past twenty years, came in to check on him, Angelo had another opportunity to show his children how normal he felt.

"Here's the one. I tell her my chest is hurting some and, pow! She's got the ambulance there so fast I can't say no. I guess she was hoping she could get rid a me for good, eh?"

Rose Anne could have easily been offended, but Tony was not a bit surprised she wasn't. Tony knew his father was really saying thank you for getting me here in time, but in a coded language in which only Tony and his siblings were fluent. Rose Anne just gave Angelo a look, took his pulse, and announced to all he was back in sinus rhythm.

"How's your mother? You didn't leave her alone did ya?" Angelo wanted to know.

"No, Dad, of course not. Bea's with her. I'll call and tell her you're already back to your old self. If you two guys are gonna stay a while, I'll go back to my floor. My shift is starting."

"Sure, go, go, who needs ya?" Angelo barked.

Before exiting, Rose Anne got her brothers a little ways away from their father's bed to fill them in on the diagnosis. "They think he has congestive heart failure, which is no surprise for his age, but they don't think it's all that advanced. He also looks like he's got some afib, but not chronic yet."

"What's that?" Mike asked.

"Atrial fibrillation. An irregular heartbeat. But as old as he is, it's still intermittent for him, so that's less dangerous and can probably be treated too. Doesn't look like this first one did a ton of damage, either. He actually could be home by the weekend. They'll give him a few new meds, get on his case about his diet a little more, and see what happens."

After a bit more chat, Mike and Tony said so long to their sister, Tony letting her know he planned to spend the night, but would be leaving early to make his 11:30 class the next morning.

"They talk about banker's hours." Angelo somehow overheard, though his hearing was supposed to be subpar. "Imagine not even having to be into work until 11:30."

"It's worse than that," Mike agreed. "That's probably the only hour he's working the whole day."

"No, actually it's a two class day, but the other one isn't until 2:30."

Tony knew this would only make his father and brother laugh harder, but he didn't mind. He was no longer defensive about what he did for a living. He now could see the odd kind of pride both men had in him for having found such a cushy job, one that took a pretty smart fellow to garner. The more he was opening himself to the possibility that his family held no grudge for his having shamed them, the more he was able to consider the possibilities of something positive in their banter and criticisms.

The two brothers stayed as long as they felt they were doing their father any good. When it got to be around nine o'clock, Angelo shooed Tony out.

"If you're staying with us overnight, get home in time not to make your mother worry. This way, you can spend an hour or so with her before she goes to bed. And you can tell her how good I'm doing too, right?"

It was a rhetorical question spoken in a voice much more like an imperative. The brothers were happy to comply, happy their father was already well enough to be bossing them around.

"Where's your car?" Tony wondered.

"I had a uniform drop me off here straight from the precinct, figuring I could catch a ride with you later. Where are you parked?"

The two men were soon in Tony's Toyota and making the five minute drive back to their childhood home. Tony gave Mike the most relevant news quickly.

"Veronica's 'fled the jurisdiction,' that's how they say it on the cop shows, right?"

"She was never in this jurisdiction to begin with, right? And she hasn't been accused of any crime or asked 'not to leave town,' so, even by cop-show standards, she's still in the clear, right?"

"But it looks pretty bad for her, doesn't it? And I can't believe you're the one trying to put a good face on this."

"Well, how'd you find out she was gone?"

"They told me at her work."

"And how did they know?"

"She told them, of course. Why does that matter?"

"How long did she say she'd be gone? And why?"

"The secretary isn't sure how long. She thinks a few weeks and the chair wasn't in to ask. She made them think it was a family thing—like maybe she went to Europe. I mean, if she really made it there, we'll probably never see her again. She got farther away than the nun that's escaped."

"You'll really going overboard, man," Mike chided. "Let's wait before deciding we're sure she's an escaped killer until she doesn't show back up in two weeks or so. I mean, we're not at the point where we can have her brought back from Malta for questioning just yet, right? Even if that's where she is and we could find her. So maybe she really did have a family crisis. Wait at least until you find that out too, no?"

"What should I do in the meanwhile?" Tony asked, impatient and frustrated both.

"I guess follow up with your new nutty friends. See if they don't let their guard down and reveal something. Meanwhile, I think we have a few leads on Sister Anna. We might have a way of getting her back soon."

"That's good, at least."

"Hey, it's been a rough day. At least Dad's way better off than it sounded like a few hours ago, eh?"

"Yeah, at least. But for how long?" Tony worried. "It's just so depressing to know neither one of them can have much longer. And there's nothing you can do about it. Good old St. Teresa would say it was a good opportunity for suffering, but then she never really cared about family anyway."

"Every day at Dad's age you're playing with house money, no?" Mike responded. "Try to find something good to take into the house now, right? Leave all the sadness and screwiness alone for a little while."

A moment later the brothers were in their family's living room, encouraging their mother beyond what Beatrice had been able to do after talking to Rose Anne about their father's condition on the telephone.

Mike acted especially upbeat. "His condition ain't none too bad, really, Ma. He'll be home in a few days, and they've got some medications they think are gonna help. He should be good."

"That's what you heard too, Tony?" Rosa asked suspiciously.

"Absolutely, Ma. If I had known how well he really was I probably wouldn't have even driven here in the middle of the week. Not that it isn't always great being here. Hey, you got anything to eat? I didn't ever really get to have dinner."

"What? Are you joking? No dinner? Sure, we've got some leftover pot roast that would make a nice sandwich. There's Italian bread, plus I just yesterday made that Bundt cake you like so much."

"The one with the chocolate and walnut topping?" Tony hoped.

"Like you don't know." Mike laughed. "C'mon, a pot roast sandwich sounds pretty good right now."

"Help yourselves," their mother encouraged as she watched them walk into the kitchen.

"Nice move." Mike patted his brother on the shoulder. "Best way to get Ma to stop worrying is to get her worrying about something else. Like her favorite son missing his supper."

"Yeah, thanks, I do what I can." Tony laughed, as he got the left over roast out of the refrigerator. He recognized how his brother was riding him, as usual, but Mike wasn't entirely kidding. If Tony seemed calm enough about his dad to quickly shift over to a request to be fed, how bad off could Angelo really be? No matter how much Tony was worried, he wasn't going to lay that worry on his mother's nervous, sickly disposition the same day her husband of over sixty-five years had had his first heart attack.

"I bet Dad really is going to be fine," Mike told him with another arm pat. "Maybe, just maybe, that professor friend of yours is sitting with her sick mom or dad right now, thinking about you and hoping you don't give up on her."

This was too much generosity all at once. Tony had to turn from his brother to mask his hand flicking off the beginnings of a tear. Mike concentrated on finding the

hot mustard in the bowels of the refrigerator long enough
not to notice.

Chapter 27

On Friday afternoon of that same week Tony got a call he wasn't expecting. It was Angela Sargento on the line.

"No, this can't wait, Professor Cupelli."

"I'm afraid it will have to. I've got a previous engagement for this evening. How about tomorrow? My morning's free."

"You're coming to see Nancy and the others here in Worcester, aren't you?"

"Well, yes, but I don't see—"

"Exactly, Professor, you don't see. I'm telling you it's exactly for that reason why this can't wait. You could say it's a matter of life and death, or maybe even lives and deaths." Angela sounded neither hysterical nor delusional.

"Well, do you want me to come by you? I can stop off at your place before I go see your classmates, and give you a chance to tell me what this is all about."

"No, that won't work. I'll come to you. Give me directions to your apartment. I can be there in a little over an hour."

Angela would not be dissuaded. She also would not even hint at what she wanted to talk about over the phone. Tony had to make a quick decision—risk alienating Nancy, Shanti, and Sally right when he finally seemed to have their trust or put off something that might be really important. But Angela was one of the core group too and it was her sister who had first revealed the secret writings.

"Is your sister coming along too?" he wondered.

"No, I'm coming alone. Please tell me how to get to your place. Please tell me you'll be there when I show up."

"Okay, I guess I can call your friends and tell them that something's come up and—"

"No! You can't tell them anything. Please?"

Tony let Angela's insistence make his decision for him. He said a quick prayer that he was making the right choice.

Angela, with her short hair and large eyes, arrived not an hour and a half later at Tony's apartment. He had been looking for her to pull up in the parking lot, and so was surprised when she appeared without her vehicle nearby.

She had taken the precaution of parking it more than a quarter mile away.

"I just had a quick supper," Tony explained. "I've got some left over if you haven't had time to eat. It's just tuna casserole, but—"

"No, Professor, I'm not a bit hungry. And I also think I'd better get out of here as soon as possible. Please, can we just sit down somewhere?"

Angela had already taken off her long, dark brown cloth coat and light green wool hat and gloves, revealing a modest white top, mostly covered by a V neck, peri-winkle sweater and darker blue jeans.

"Something to drink, then?" Tony asked, as he directed her to the plaid couch, too well drilled by his mother's sense of hospitality to have a guest, even under these odd circumstances, without offering her anything.

Angela nodded. "Some water would be nice, no ice please."

"What's this all about, Angela?" Tony asked as he handed her a green glass. "I'll tell you, after that night in your apartment, where you seemed very anxious to kick us out, I didn't expect I'd ever have you talk to me voluntarily again."

"I was hoping somehow that you would have realized what was really going on that day, that you would have detected something. But you're not a detective, after all. Maybe if your brother had been there."

Angela was not calm. Her glass of water even shook a bit in her hand when she gripped it. Neither was she angry nor attempting to be unduly mysterious.

Still, she had Tony confused. "What did I miss?"

"Do you remember how happy I was to see you and Professor Teuma when you first arrived? Why do you think that was?"

Tony leaned from his seat on his green recliner toward where Angela sat across from him on the couch. "Initially I wasn't sure, but after what happened, I figured it was a ruse on both your parts, trying to keep us in the dark about what was really going on. Are you here to tell me different?"

"Yes, yes I am."

"Go ahead, then, I'm listening. And believe me, it's not like I couldn't use some help."

"I'll ask you to recall then too that I was the one who was nicest to you the first time you visited all of us at

Nancy's house. I was the one who wanted to believe you could get what we were about and that a man could even perhaps be let into our confidence. Nancy was the one who seemed most against it, and Shanti too, remember?"

"Yes, that's why Veronica and I approached you and your sister in the first place. But instead of cooperation, we only got some information by, frankly, tricking your sister into the admission about the secret writings."

"It didn't take much trickery. Teresa, you may have noticed, is more than a little wacky. She's only gotten worse since this whole business began, and especially since Marissa was murdered."

"And you know something about that you haven't told yet? Do you know that's a criminal offense, a felony even?" Tony wanted to be certain that this time he got everything Angela had to offer before he let her leave his apartment.

"Why don't you get it?" she suddenly said with increased passion. "I'm on your side, I have been for months. But I'm afraid for my life and Teresa's too. That's why I didn't want to let her reveal anything to you yet. I wasn't sure what you'd do with it or whether we'd be safe, but now, now that you've taken up with Shanti and Nancy—"

"And Sally."

"Oh, she doesn't count. She's just in their power. She'd never hurt a fly."

"But they would?"

"I can't be sure. Let me just tell you what I know and please stop trying to guess or get something out of me. I'm here to tell you all that I know!"

Tony realized he was once again not handling a procedure properly. After all, he wasn't a detective, he wasn't even all that experienced with college students. He was mostly an ex-priest who had always thought he understood human nature a lot better than he probably ever did.

"I'm sorry. I'm listening," he assured the nervous young woman.

"You know that it was Marissa Hitzel who recruited Nancy and me for the alumbradas. And that was because we seemed like the only people in Professor Teuma's class besides Marissa who challenged the professor, who were impressed by her knowledge but sad about how she seemed so old fashioned and so forgiving of all the ways the church has been patriarchal over the centuries. It's an especially bitter thing for me and Teresa since we lost two great grandparents to Franco, the ultimate Spanish fascist and Catholic both."

"I'm so sorry, I—" Tony began but then quickly realized what he was doing and fell silent again.

Angela took another drink of water, with a steadier hand, as if this irretrievable revelation was now far enough initiated that there was no longer a reason to fear what it might bring about. "Well, some of the meetings took place at Smith, because Faith Covington was one of the sisterhood. We all thought the whole thing was great at first—the knowledge that Saint Teresa of Avila had fooled all those priests about the true nature of her feminism and her heresy, how she had brilliantly created a secret society of women right within the church, and eventually became a saint and doctor of that church. It was really exciting and we couldn't wait to learn the true path. But then I started to have some questions, and so did Marissa, and that's when things got a little more complicated."

"Go on," Tony encouraged.

"We got to see one of the original copies of the Directives, in sixteenth-century Spanish, one night at Faith's place. Sister Anna Teresa was there. She had brought the document with her, but she wouldn't tell us anything about where she had gotten it from. But she was going to leave it with Faith to have it authenticated so that none of us would have any doubts whatsoever. While she was there, she assured us that the death of Sister Maria Dolores had been a suicide, and she told us it was from remorse for having betrayed the sisterhood. She said there was nothing we could do about it now and it was nothing for us to worry about. But Marissa asked if they knew anything about Monsignor Heamey's death and Sister Anna got angry, told her not to worry about the Jesuits and all their cabals and politics. She said a true devotee of St. Teresa had no time to worry over such trivia. But that was also the night we were first introduced to the idea of self-mortification and to the choking of each other with rosaries.

"To me, the idea of self-torture seemed against all the saint had been about. She had never attempted it, except for one brief period on the advice of priests, and the choking rosary just seemed so sacrilegious, but when I said that, both Faith and Sister Anna were disappointed. Sister Anna said something like, 'A sacrilege against whom or what? You can't read these secret, holy writings and believe in them and remain a Roman Catholic. You'll have to stop your devotion to what the priests have taught you, what any man has taught you, and accept this as the true way.'"

"And so, you and Marissa were both uncomfortable with that, is that right?"

"Yes, though it wasn't until a little later that we even dared admit it to each other. And Marissa, she said she was going to find some things out, like where Sister Anna had gotten her copy of that book. For some reason, maybe because she didn't really think Sister Anna was totally trustworthy, and she knew that my sister, Faith, and

Shanti were all a little bit on the fanatical side, she really wanted affirmation that the book was for real before she would totally give up on Teresa the Catholic saint and get fully behind Teresa of the new secret book, before she could decide Professor Teuma didn't know what she was talking about."

Tony could not help but interrupt at the mention of Veronica's name.

"Professor Teuma—the last time I spoke with Nancy and her friends, they told me Veronica knew about the secret writings, that Marissa had shown them to her. Is that true?"

"If it is, I never knew it. I think Marissa would have told me. Of course, if she did do that, maybe there was something Professor Teuma saw in it all that made Marissa doubt all the more. You know, the last time I spoke to her she said she felt she was close to figuring it all out, but she thought she'd keep it quiet until she was more certain."

"And then she was killed?"

"Two days after the last time we talked. Just two days."

"But why didn't you tell anyone before this?" Tony asked.

"I was thinking about it, even though I was afraid, since maybe three people had been murdered already, each of them for being suspicious of or even too curious about the secret writings. But I didn't want to put my sister at risk either, and, since I'm telling you everything now, I wasn't sure that she wouldn't be incriminated if what I knew took the investigation that direction. No one knew I knew anything about Marissa, so I felt safe for the moment, and I didn't think anyone else was in immediate danger.

"I still don't know whether that last priest that was

killed in New York really had any connection to the rest of this."

Again Tony resisted the temptation to interrupt, but instead just urged Angela on with a nod.

"And then when we heard that Professor Gallagher had presented the Spanish document to a real expert, Professor Villareal from Harvard, and he had authenticated it, I saw that it removed any motive for Marissa being killed by someone trying to prevent her from finding out otherwise. And I was even ready to believe what the rest of the girls were certain of, that Marissa, just like Sister Maria Dolores, might have been killed by some fanatical Catholics instead."

"So why are you coming to me now?"

"Because I decided I wouldn't keep it all to myself another minute if I saw anyone else's life in danger. Nancy hates you, she always has, and so does Shanti."

"Why would I matter to them so much one way or the other?" Tony wondered.

"Don't be modest now. People all over the country have at least heard of you, but to us, religion majors, you're even more of a celebrity. But even before we had met you, when the rest of us loved your book on the female Holy Spirit, Nancy was just certain you were the worst kind of man, a hypocrite and closet hater of women. There's no way her letting you more into the group is because she's had a change of heart."

"You don't really think there was any danger they were going to kill me tonight?" Tony said, trying to discount the possibility.

"I don't even know if they have anything to do with any of the killings. I'm still praying they don't, but I'm far from sure about it and that's why I'm praying. But I know they can't have anything good planned for you— whether murder, seduction, blackmail, a framing of you somehow for a crime, or torture way beyond what you have experienced with them so far, just for their joy in your humiliation. I couldn't let you go there tonight."

"Well, well," Tony mouthed, a little stunned by Angela's certainty over how much danger she had just saved him from. "Thank you, I—"

Angela got up from her seat on the couch, crossed over to where Tony was sitting, knelt down beside him, and put one trembling hand into one of his. "You see, I've always admired you, your books, your pro-women stance in the church," she said. "I even forgave you when you got into that big mess and everyone found out what a...well, found out how many mistakes you had made. That night at Nancy's I really hoped you could convince them that a man could understand this all. I hoped that even Nancy could see we didn't have to hate men to embrace what St. Teresa was teaching. But she was furious after you left, and she hasn't changed her mind about you one bit, I know. So I had to rescue you, no matter how much danger it might put me in. For all I know, Faith will find out I've been here and then—then—"

"Again, I thank you so much for coming forward, I—"

"Don't thank me. Protect me." Angela squeezed Tony's hand and looked at him with something close to terror in her eyes. "I've just risked my own life and maybe my sister's for your sake. You've got to talk to your brother, get us away from here. You've got to protect me, you've got to."

The former Monsignor Antonio Cupelli stood up from his chair, lifting Angela from her knees as he did so. He looked into her eyes and nodded with certain assurance, saying simply, "I will, Angela. Believe me, I will."

Chapter 28

Tony called his brother while Angela was still at his place having some warmed up tuna casserole, which Tony could tell she liked better than she expected she would. He was less worried about her enjoyment of his homemade oatmeal, chocolate-chip cookies.

Mike assured Tony he would have the police in Northampton take over as soon as possible. Soon after, they arrived and promised to arrange for both Angela and her sister to be under a loose sort of "protective custody," until something more official could be worked out. Once he was certain Angela was safe, Tony called his brother back with that news.

"So what's next?" he wondered.

"Listen, Ton' we're finally making some progress. A few days ago we got a lead on some woman, way over in northern Missouri, staying at some kind of hippie-wannabes co-op or something, who they suspected might be Sister Anna. Well, they went ahead and checked it out and it was her. They've gotten through all the paper work now and are shipping her back to us. She should be here before the night is over."

"I don't suppose they found the cross on her?"

"Yeah, you don't suppose right. She claims to have no knowledge of any cross. Big surprise. But the coincidence of it going missing just when she left is too big not to at least get her sent back to us and that's all we need, so we can really grill her about all this other stuff."

"I wonder where she hid the cross. It probably wouldn't be an easy thing to sell, right?"

"I don't know. She's a pretty smooth character. But all I really want is to get her here. Whether we ever find the cross hardly matters to me right now. What did those nuns need with all that gold, anyway, right? But back to you, I guess we hold tight until we see what we can shake out of Sister Anna."

"But what about Nancy and those other two nuts? Shouldn't I do something about them?"

"What, reschedule? You got a death wish or what? Just avoid them till maybe we can pin something definite on them. This isn't Scooby Doo. We're not gonna use you for bait. Just hold tight. Oh, and Dad is getting out of the hospital tomorrow. So don't give him anything else to worry about, okay?"

Tony agreed to wait and drive up to New York for the weekend to be part of the questioning of Sister Anna. But he wasn't holding tight more than a few minutes when he realized how impossible it would be for him to just spend the night doing nothing when he could think of one person he might still have a profitable conversation with. He wondered how Faith was spending her evening.

It was surprisingly easy to find out. After striking out trying to telephone her, he simply looked her up on Facebook. He saw a note to her from a colleague reminding her of the showing of the classic Garbo rendering of *Anna*

Karenina on campus beginning at nine, saw her brief "I'll be there" response, and looked up how long that film was by going on line. He had a few minutes to spare before waiting outside for the movie goers to exit. Faith was chatting with a female friend from Anthropology, a different woman than the one who had asked her plans on Facebook, but Tony wasn't going to be deflected from talking to Faith, no matter how many friends she might be with.

"I'm so glad I was able to track you down," he said brightly, to his former girlfriend, with a friendly nod to their mutual colleague and the Facebook friend who appeared, presumably from a quick powder room visit. "I really need to talk to you."

Tony was careful not to give the impression of a jilted or angry lover, knowing Faith's friends would never abandon her to him within that possibility. Instead he tried to play the part of someone with something on his mind that somehow couldn't wait. He wasn't confident of his acting skills, but the friend from Facebook—one of the staff in the business office, if he remembered right—a short, slightly stout woman who seemed very much more at ease than she ever appeared while in the business office, did not treat him as a threat at all.

"Why don't you join us then, Professor Cupelli? We're just off to The Toasted Owl. It's a pretty cool place, if you've never been."

"Oh, well, sure, that would be okay, I guess, if you don't mind the intrusion."

"Well, actually, Sarah and Cynthia are both too polite to admit that," Faith rejoined. "Still, I think it would be better if you and I had our talk alone. Hope you don't mind, ladies?"

It was a rhetorical question, so Faith's friends went off to The Toasted Owl by themselves, only slightly puzzled by Faith's abandonment. Tony himself wondered why she had agreed so readily, but he wasn't long in finding out.

"We really do need to talk. I'm glad you were able to find me. Let's go to my place. It's closer."

"Well, I've got two witnesses that know we were 'last seen together,' though since they're both friends of yours, I'm not sure that would help me any. I guess I'll just go on my instincts—only God knows why—and I'll even trust that you'll actually show at your place, since I guess we'll take separate cars to get there."

"Actually, I walked. It's just a mile, you know. Remember, we used to walk to campus together a lot. But I'll ride with you now, Tony."

Faith looked even more beautiful to Tony than ever before as she sat next to him in his car. Her dark purple coat set off her gold-green eyes to an especially striking effect and emerald earrings glistened their approval on either side of her near perfect face. Somehow, they could not begin their discussion in earnest while they made the short drive, discussing instead Garbo and then other old movie stars and movies, until it was time to sit down together, as they had done regularly only a short time before, in Faith's tastefully decorated living room.

"I thought you should know, the police have tracked down Sister Anna Teresa and are bringing her back to New York."

With that key information delivered point blank, Tony expected a response along the lines of, "On what charges, pray tell?" so he was surprised by the slight gasp he received, followed by an "Oh, thank God."

"So you were worried about Sister Anna?"

"Yes, yes I was. I'm just so happy to know she's still alive."

"Why were you in doubt?" Tony asked, still not absolutely certain he would be getting the truth. In fact, having already received surprising revelations from one alumbrada that very evening, which he had mostly taken as gospel, he now began to suspect that he was being out-smarted once again, by women who were still in league to deceive him.

"How much do you really know? They haven't ques-tioned Sister Anna yet?"

"Why? That matters on how much you're going to spill?"

"*Spill.* You really are into this detective fantasy busi-ness pretty religiously now, aren't you? No, I just thought I'd, you know, *cut to the chase*, and not go over a bunch of things you already know."

"Just pretend I really am as ignorant, in as many senses of that word as you want, as I appear to be. What's a little redundancy among friends?"

Faith's eyes lit up with something like amusement. But they narrowed again soon and she began her narra-tive. "You know I'm a feminist and how seriously I take that role. You know too, though, that I've always been open to believing that some exceptional men might be part of the solution to gender inequity, rather than most that cause or exacerbate it."

"Yes, that much I know."

"That's why I held on for so long with you, even though it was clear that you were way more the old-fashioned man than you'd ever admit to, even though I had joined a group of women who believed in and lived a life where all things were possible without any authority or even guidance from men and with a role model who had been outsmarting men hundreds of years before any-one even knew what a feminist was."

"Yes, I can see the attraction Saint Teresa would have for you once this secret writing revealed she wasn't really bowing to men," Tony agreed, without a bit of judgment or irony in his voice.

"Yes, but I'm not naïve. How convenient it was to find these secret writings to prove that Saint Teresa was really an alumbrada all along. So at first I thought that Sister Anna, who brought the book to me after Veronica's students asked her to—"

"Why to you?"

"Well, I knew Marissa from a pottery class she took with me a few summers ago at Smith, and we hit it off quite well, especially when I found out she was Veronica's protégé, as it were, but then we really got close when she started to have trouble with Veronica's conservatism, and that's when she introduced me to all her other friends, and when I first found out about Sister Anna and some of the others."

"How many others?" Tony felt he needed to know.

"I'll get to that. Let me talk, please," Faith insisted.

As she did, Tony kept trying to figure out how one who had been fooled so often in such urgent matters, over the past three years, could even now be sure of whom was or was not telling the truth.

"This was all about a year or so ago. I was excited about the 'Directives,' but I wanted to see them authenticated. When Sister Anna was so willing to trust me with the book, it only made me a bit more suspicious still, but when Hank Gallagher was able to get such a definitive authentication from Professor Villareal, and this from two men who certainly had no stake in wanting to support a feminist undoing of the traditional St. Teresa—Villareal is a deacon of the Catholic Church, I'm told—well, I was convinced and got more and more involved." Faith's tone remained fairly calm and evinced her usual control, but Tony felt a subtle shift in urgency.

"Okay, most of this I could have figured out before,

but thanks for solidifying for me how it all came to be for you. So how did you feel when you heard Sister Maria was dead?"

"I never met Sister Maria. Only Sister Anna would sneak out of the convent. That's not something that's very easy to do for a Carmelite, but she was not your usual nun. But I just believed the story that she had felt some sort of remorse and Sister Anna told me she had always been pretty unstable, so nothing really troubled me unduly at first."

"But now?"

"Well, even after Heamey was murdered, I didn't piece anything together. I didn't know that he had anything to do with Sister Maria until I overheard one of your conversations with your brother and—"

"How did you manage that?"

"I listened in on the other line, just the one time that you actually called your brother from here."

"I didn't even know you had more than one land line in the apartment."

"Yes, I was counting on that, but even after I knew you suspected a connection, I didn't think the alumbradas could have had anything to do with it. And certainly when one of our own, Marissa, was murdered, I only suspected, like the other women, that some fanatic Catholic might be involved. I hate to admit I even suspected Veronica."

"And do you still?" Tony asked, not certain he wanted to know the answer.

"I'm not a detective and neither are you, of course, but you can share this all with your brother and the other professionals. I have no idea whether it's justified to suspect Veronica, though her having left the country, which I just found out yesterday, doesn't bode very well for her. But what I'm worried about is what Sister Anna really knows about all this that none of the rest of us do, which is why I'm so happy she's still alive. I was afraid her disappearance really meant that she was dead, as you'd say, because she *knew too much*."

"Well, they've got her now in New York. But just in case they can't get her to talk, what all is it that she knew too much of?"

"She had given me the impression that this resurrection of the alumbradas had been going on for some time, ever since the secret writings were found, both among lay people and nuns, starting in Spain, but really coming into flower in the U.S. She had given me to think that there were 'chapters' springing up everywhere, and that the fabric of the Catholic Church would be undone, finally punished for over twenty centuries of misogyny, when the time was chosen to reveal our infiltration into convents and Catholic colleges everywhere. But when I asked for some way to communicate with that sisterhood, she always put me off, saying I had to prove myself trustworthy, had to myself do a kind of novitiate."

Tony shrugged. "Did that seem unreasonable to you?"

"No, not at first, but, well, maybe I am a bit more of a detective than I give myself credit for. There was the phone call I overheard of you and your brother, and more recently a pretty thorough search on my part to try to find any evidence of a network as large as Sister Anna said existed. I haven't been able to find anything—and you know I'm a very thorough researcher."

"But it's a really secret organization, after all. The cops haven't had any better luck. Why did you suppose you'd be superior to them?" Tony asked, with just a bit of animus, as he recalled Faith's consistently superior attitude about most things.

"You're wrong about that. It's precisely because I respect the capabilities of the police that I'm suspecting the secret network more and more. After all, who was entrusted with this material? Not only a nun who was sneaking out of a cloistered convent to meet with us, but then some fairly flighty young women, including Teresa Sargento, who is unstable, and Nancy Temple, who is becoming more frightening every time I see her. I'm starting to wonder if there is any network at all. I'm starting to wonder if I have, in fact, met every single one of the existing members of this club. And if that's true, it's making me start to wonder about a whole lot of other matters as well."

"And why are you finally sharing this wonder with me?"

"So long as we were together, Tony, I was hoping not only to bring you into the light of the illuminated ones with me, but also thought I'd be safe from any possible danger. I felt confident you and your brother would find no connection with any murders to our group, but I still felt more comfortable knowing you were there, and, by implication, your brother was there too. But since I've been on my own, since we've become open adversaries, and since I've been having all these suspicions, I'll tell you I don't feel very safe at all, though at least I feel a little better knowing Sister Anna is still among the living. But only a little better, really."

Faith looked at Tony and he looked back at her, not entirely sure of what to say next. Did Faith also think she needed protective custody? Were Angela and Faith trying to bail in time to let the remaining alumbradas *take the rap* for whatever crimes they had committed? They would know more soon, if they could get Sister Anna Teresa to talk. What he had learned from Faith would certainly help in having that talk, if what she was saying, if what he had been hearing from both women this strange night, were even true. Faith could not wait any longer for his response.

"I don't know how much of this you believe and I need you to believe it all. We were mismatched, but I do admire the man I met in your books. I still believe you are something of that man, and I've got to count on that being enough. Are you going to NY this weekend to confer with your brother?"

Tony nodded. "As a matter of fact I am."

"Well, then let me come with you. Let me confront Sister Anna at some point in the interrogation. Let me try to help you, not just for my own safety but because, whether you can stand me or not, I hope you know I never would harm another person, male or female, and I want to do all I can now to help."

"Why?"

"Do you think you Catholics have a copyright on guilt? If Marissa Hitzel or even that inane Monsignor Heamey are dead because of something I didn't figure out soon enough, I want to do what I can now to make sure no one else is harmed."

Tony thought of his own motivations, his own past, and realized that Faith's present explanation made as much sense to him as anything he had ever heard.

"You think you'll be safe here overnight? You've got deadbolts, right?" When she nodded, he added, "Good. I'll pick you up at eight."

Chapter 29

Sister Anna Teresa's real name was Debbie O'Reilly. She had grown up in small town Missouri, a little town near Hannibal called Monroe City, where she had been raised in the Catholic faith. Though she had told the Cupellis she had graduated from Temple, with a double major in English and Theater, she had really attended Smith for three years, with those same majors, but had never graduated. The one year she had earlier claimed in the MFA program at NYU was verifiable, but she had gone there under the false pretenses of being a college graduate and had been asked to leave when the truth was discovered. Since then, she had held various jobs, lived in a commune, and been in trouble with the law more than once for shoplifting, check bouncing, fraud, and, finally, bail-jumping charges.

The resume she had used to gain admission into the Carmelite convent had also been largely a fraud, framed around the lie of a life growing up in Pennsylvania. All this and more Tony learned for the first time when Mike caught him up on what had been discovered about the real Debbie O'Reilly. Since she was a clear flight risk, she was being held without bail, as the police had been able to convince a judge they had reason to believe she was involved in more than one murder.

The light blue prison issue jump suit that Debbie O'Reilly wore to her encounter with the Cupelli brothers brought out her blue-green eyes, but her long, probably shapely legs, were not done much justice. Her short, spiky, blonde-brown hair felt both appropriate, yet still unsettling, after the brothers had only seen her before in an entirely different uniform. If they expected her to seem worried or intimidated by them or by where she was, they were going to have to settle for another surprise. If anything, it was her lawyer, a short, slender man who seemed a little lost in his brown, three piece suit, who looked a little nervous, and seemed guarded in his diction and body language.

He was young, but no court appointed novice, rather from a top-shelf legal firm. Apparently, O'Reilly's family in Missouri—even after having fronted three years of Smith tuition with no degree resulting, and abiding the many false steps Debbie had taken since—were not yet ready to abandon their daughter.

"Thanks for agreeing to speak with us," Mike said to both parties. "Just curious—did you have a choice about giving up the habit for this lovely ensemble? And are you still claiming to be a nun?"

"Claiming, Lieutenant? Your brother can tell you, I'm sure, that you can't reverse Holy Orders. And, yes, I'd very much appreciate it if you addressed me still as Sister Anna Teresa."

Nothing in Debbie O'Reilly's confidence or calm seemed altered by her capture and delivery to Riker's Island. So there was no sense in hoping she would voluntarily reveal anything incriminating or important. With her lawyer present, there was no chance to intimidate, even if that seemed like a possible option.

Mike tried a different tract. "So, you probably know we know that you're wanted in two different states. The thing is, you've never been convicted of a crime, you've never robbed anyone of a large sum of money, even this latest charge of grand theft the nuns might be willing to dismiss if you are willing to return the stolen property. So, really, it would be in your best interest to help us with what you know."

"I help you, dear Lieutenant, and, magically, all my troubles are over? Including you find for me the gold cross to return to my sister Carmelites, since I never stole anything from them and never would."

"That's right," her attorney chimed in. "Sister Anna denies all guilt in this felony theft case, and, to any other crimes you stand ready to charge her within this jurisdiction."

"Still, if you could help us, Sister—" Mike tried to sound beholden.

Debbie O'Reilly laughed. "You want me to confess to being a thief and the mastermind of some strange cult that murders nuns, priests, and coeds? I could play that part, I'm a very good actress, but it would be just a part. Sister Maria really did commit suicide and I know nothing of who killed either one of those priests."

Tony pointed out the obvious omission. "What about Marissa Hitzel?"

"I don't know anything about her either," O'Reilly claimed, but with a bit of hesitation. "I was a cloistered nun, after all, how would I know what they were up to over at Holy Cross?"

Tony looked at Mike and Mike gave a subtle sign with his hand to his ear, like an old third base coach's signaling for the hit and run, to okay Tony's next move.

Tony knew it was legal for the police to lie to a prisoner and all the more for a civilian like himself. And he felt no guilt about lying now, since he was trying to save lives.

"It's all falling apart, Sister Anna," he began. "Look where you are. Here's the real test whether you really want a cross to bear. There's bound to be a few people in the system who won't think you're as swell as you think you are."

She laughed. "You're so flattering.".

"Listen up. Faith Covington is waiting to talk with us here now, if the police think it's necessary and you agree to see her. She's already told me about the times you skipped the convent and how it was you who handed her the 'original' Directives for her to authenticate. And all your other alumbradas have also been willing to sing pretty strong songs with real conviction, telling me in person about how you have been the ringleader all along, how you were the one who introduced the whole rosary choking move, and how you were the one who preached a kind of amorality that could lead to about anything. You might think we just think you're responsible for the two New York murders, but we've got it on pretty good authority, your own sister alumbradas, that it's been you really leading all along. So, if I were you I'd take any opportunity to help the police you can get, before the option isn't there anymore."

The lawyer balked. "I don't really think threats are appropriate, especially from a civilian. If you had any real evidence against my client, she'd be charged with something more serious than thieving a gold cross. I think we're done here."

"Wait. Wait a minute," Debbie O'Reilly requested, apparently more from anger than panic. "You know I'd call your bluff on Faith, so she must really be here. And if she's ready to give me away, if she's lost her cool. I bet you have gotten some of the others to 'cooperate' with you. If you believed them all the way, though, you wouldn't be here and you'd certainly have enough witnesses against me. So listen up, you'll want to take this down."

"No, Deb—Sister, I really think you shouldn't say another word." Sister Anna's flustered lawyer rose out of his uncomfortable seat to emphasize his advice as dramatically as he was able.

"Calm, down, this isn't going to be a confession. Poor Sister Maria Dolores really did kill herself. She couldn't take all the guilt over coming over with us. The Catholic Church brainwashes its women from day one and she never could overcome it."

"You expect us just to believe that?" Tony interrupted. "Nuns don't often commit suicide."

"Believe what you like," Debbie O'Reilly advised. "But after all you went through with the Church yourself, I figure you should know better than about anybody else how it can split you in half. Plus, if you think about it, any woman in the twenty-first century who voluntarily locks herself up in a cloister, in New York of all places, well, we aren't the most normal people to begin with, are we?"

"Fine, we'll call that one a suicide for now," Mike agreed. "What about the others?"

"I don't know anything about who killed those priests, except that it wasn't me. I was nowhere near either one of them the days they were killed. I was in the convent in Brooklyn when Monsignor Heamey was murdered and on a bus headed for Missouri for this more recent killing. But Marissa, those idiots—it was the first time I wasn't there to show them how to do the Saint Teresa Rosary, the first time they wanted to do it on their own. Haven't you guessed by now that it was Shanti and

Nancy on that tape, that those were the two women behind Maria Dolores and me? We had snuck them into the
convent and what you saw was a kind of 'training session' for them, but when they got on their own, well—"

Tony wanted to be sure. "You're telling us—"

"Yes, that's what I'm telling you. Marissa and Sally,
they were both reluctant to take the active part in that ritual, but those two, Shanti and Nancy, they just got a little
too enthusiastic. They didn't mean to kill Marissa, had no
reason to want her dead, maybe they just didn't think you
could actually kill someone that way. So if they're looking to blame me for her death, it won't hold up. My alibi,
as you call it, is secure for that night too. There's a whole
convent of nuns in Brooklyn, no matter how angry they
might be with me now, who can swear I was with them.
You know it isn't easy to sneak out of there. I only ever
did it about three or four times total, the first few with
Sister Maria covering for me, the last time not needing to
come back. But Marissa, that was all Shanti and Nancy.
And as much as I'm upset at them now myself, I'm pretty
sure they didn't mean to kill her. But you can do what
you want with that, except I'll also tell you poor Sally,
she'd never do the choker role, she was always a chokee,
so she was there, but she didn't kill anyone."

Mike and Tony knew that the woman who was telling them this tale was an expert liar, a first rate actress
and con artist, and maybe worse. But her testimony had
the almost certain feel of truth to it. Even if she were
somehow responsible for the murders, she had proof that
she hadn't actually committed them herself. What she
had given them was progress, but even if it was all true it
left two murders without solution or even a lead.

Mike proceeded to press her a little more. "Okay,
Ms. O'Reilly, I—" Mike began.

"Sister Anna, please," Debbie insisted.

Mike laughed. "Nah, I'm tired of that act. We wondered if you'd come clean on that, gave you every opportunity, but, you know, enough is enough. We've also found out how you were able to falsify a biography and the documents that pertained to it so you could get into the Carmelite convent. You're no more of a nun than I am. Impersonating a nun—I looked it up and you can do time for that one too."

"That was the easiest scam of all." Debbie laughed with Mike, almost as if she were relieved she would have one less thing to pretend. "I mean, who would want to pretend to be a discalced Carmelite, right? Who would want to lock herself away like that except a nun? No one ever suspected me a bit."

"And why did you do it?" Tony wanted to know. "To get in place to rob the cross? But if that, why wait so long? Did you just only recently find out where it was hidden? Or is that something you free lanced once you were in? Did you go in first just to hide out from the law?"

"No, not at all. I had other reasons."

"Those are reasons you'll want to share with us if you have any hopes of not spending the next several years in jail, that is, if you're cleared for all these killings in the first place," Mike informed her.

"You guys have been pretty good at figuring things out. Just keep up the good work. I've given you Shanti and Nancy. Find out if they have alibis for the night Marissa was killed. But I'm not giving you anything else, boys. I mean, you've got to have some fun for yourselves, right?"

Debbie got up from her seat, signaling to the other three men in the interrogation room with her that she was done. She blew Tony a kiss as she headed for the door. But just as she was about to be allowed to exit, she turned to him. "Oh, and you should really talk to Veronica Teuma one more time. If you can find her, that is."

The sham Sister Anna Teresa's laugh was a little colder as she and her reluctant lawyer left the Cupelli brothers to consider all that she had said and how much of it they could afford to believe.

Chapter 30

Mike, Tony, and Faith made an odd trio at the Neptune Diner. Mike had insisted they go there—his favorite Greek diner in Queens, not five minutes from his home—to confer after the morning at Riker's Island. While Faith could not officially be taken off the unofficial list of murder suspects, Mike and Tony had agreed it would do no harm to act as if she were in the clear with them—a place Tony sensed she belonged anyway—to see what help she could provide. She had expressed her disappointment in not having been allowed in to see Debbie O'Reilly, but had been briefed on what had taken place during the interview.

"Here's the thing," Mike noted as he cut into his dolmades. "If we sweat Shanti and Nancy, maybe we get somewhere on the Hitzel murder, whether accidental or not, but that still gives us nothing on the other three, right? Okay, and maybe we even take the first nun as a suicide, like fake-Sister Anna wants us to, though that's possibly because she did that one herself. That's the one she doesn't have an alibi for. But do we think she's good

as the overall ringleader and that Shanti and Nancy might
have done her bidding with the priests?"

"It's possible, but it doesn't make total sense," Tony
countered.

"How not?" Mike questioned, with half a mouthful
of grape leaves.

Faith spoke up before Tony could answer. "Well, for
one thing, I don't see Debbie O'Reilly as a leader. She's
an actress, a con artist, maybe even a little bit of a script-
writer, but I always had the impression she was getting
this material from someone with more experience, more
of a vision."

"So who did she get the original of St. Teresa's writing from to pass on to you?" Tony looked straight ahead
at Faith, who was across from him in the four person
booth, while Mike sat to her left. "Did she ever say?"

"No, that was going to be a secret till I was more
full-fledged. Or at least that's the reason she gave."

Mike made a gesture like a throwing up of his hands,
but mostly with his eyes, as he kept knife and fork on his
big white plate and now attacked a piece of roasted lamb.
"But she doesn't seem willing to spill that name. Whether
it's out of fear, loyalty, or co-conspiracy, we don't
know."

"One thing that's been bothering me, we questioned
Deb O'Reilly, on the whole—what did she call it? 'St
Teresa rosary' thing—and then she fled the convent and
we found Father Sweeney murdered, in the same style as
the St. Teresa rosary prayer group's ritual. But now
O'Reilly's bus ticket confirms she was already heading
west when the murder was committed. Still, it seems like
too big a coincidence."

"Because it probably is," Faith agreed, as she politely put down her spanakopita, whose cheese did not seem
to be upsetting her vegan sensibilities. "Maybe the killer

wanted you to look the wrong way, to see this as some ritual series of murders, while now you know, if you believe what you've been told, that the deaths of the two women were probably unrelated, and, possibly, neither was even a murder. So maybe the last priest was killed to blur the motive for killing the first one."

"That's pretty good, Faith. You just started on this amateur sleuth business and you're already thinking clearer than Tony." Mike still had his laugh available, especially in the service of chiding his younger brother.

Tony wasn't insulted, was instead happy to go along with Faith's premise. "Okay, and add to that the fact that the video of the choking rosary ritual was mailed to us, anonymously, maybe another way for the killer to get someone other than herself in trouble."

"And mailed from Massachusetts. You didn't happen to send that our way, did you Faith, you know, as a way to give us a heads-up to how wacko this whole group was?"

Mike nudged Faith with his right elbow as he said this, but Faith was used to his antics by now and gave his gesture no discernible reaction.

"I almost wish I had. But I had no knowledge those things were being taped, much less a copy to share with anyone. On the other hand, now that we know Debbie O'Reilly actually attended Smith for three years, we can guess she has some friends in Northampton and maybe in Worcester. And now that we know that Marissa might have died from an overly enthusiastic enactment of the St. Teresa rosary, maybe it really was sent by the killer to get us to look Sister Anna's way, or maybe it was sent from Worcester to have you look Veronica's way," Faith reasoned.

"Still, just because it was mailed from Worcester doesn't mean it couldn't have been mailed, say, by someone from, oh, I don't know, Northampton? But I bet you have an alibi for both the night Marissa died and for the time when Father Sweeney got it?" Mike questioned, semi-rhetorically.

"Yes, plus I was with your brother when Monsignor Heamey 'got it,' and I'm sure I was in Northampton also the night Sister Maria Dolores died, so that officially gets me 'in the clear,' doesn't it?"

"You're still good, I think, for diabolical mastermind of all the killings, though," Tony said in a tone that was mostly playful.

"Isn't that mistress-mind?" Mike corrected. "I want to be as politically correct as possible here."

"I grant that I am perfectly capable of having out-smarted the two of you for the past months," Faith agreed, "and I still admire the principles unearthed in St. Teresa's secret writings. But whoever has misused them to give a rationale for killing people is a kind of monster, and if I had been the so-called mastermind of the alum-bradas from the beginning, we would have had a thriving, open examination of all these principles, not a secret or-ganization infiltrating convents and allowing young, oth-erwise intelligent women to involve themselves in sick and dangerous behavior."

Faith's small speech certainly removed the light tone from their table, and maybe even made the brothers feel a little guilty for allowing their ever-present sense of humor again to intrude itself where it did not belong.

But Faith seemed to feel she had gone a bit too far in shaming them, so she said, "But thanks for the compli-ment."

"Okay, so where are we? Before the baklava platter arrives I want to know where we are," Mike announced.

"I'm ready to think it really possible the first death was a suicide, with a chance, though, that it was 'assist-

ed' by Debbie O'Reilly. Monsignor Heamey's murder—
the murder of someone we know was actively investigating the alumbradas—his has perhaps the most clear cut
motive, to prevent him from discovering anything more."
Tony was on a roll, but Mike slowed him down.

"But why murder?" Tony demanded. "Just because
he was going to question the legitimacy of some of what
they were up to? I mean, what was so important, so sacred about keeping it all secret? That points to some really nutty women, no?"

"Perhaps, but my suspicions about some of this being
bogus, about how small the network may really be, the
elements of fraud that Debbie O'Reilly brings with her,
there might be some motive there," Faith reasoned.

"In any case, Heamey, we know, was working
against the group." Mike nodded, toward Faith, who
seemed appreciative that he had not referred to the alumbradas as "your group."

"Okay, then," Tony came back. "Then we've got
poor Marissa Hitzel, maybe killed by the odd equivalent
of a hazing gone bad, or maybe that's a ruse to keep us
unaware of how both she and maybe even Maria Dolores
were executed for not 'keeping the faith.'"

"Either of those two seem possible to me," Faith
agreed. "Which leaves us still with no explanation for the
last priest, unless it was a random murder of a convenient
target, with a method that would throw us off the track
and make us suspect Debbie O'Reilly, since she had just
fled the convent after we saw her engaged in a similar
choking incident."

"But she was a chokee on that tape, not a choker,"
Tony advised. "And now that we know, or think we
know, who the chokers were, Shanti and Nancy, and
since Sister Anna has an alibi, why not suspect those two
of the Sweeney murder?"

Mike nodded, as he picked up his glass of Retsina. "Especially since them being on that tape shows they know their way around New York a little and are pretty good at sneaking back and forth."

"But why did they kill Sweeney then?" Tony wondered.

"It could be any number of reasons," Faith responded. "They could both be truly unbalanced fanatics who killed Maria Dolores when they discovered her treachery, killed Marissa when she somehow maybe showed she was having second thoughts, and killed Heamey even, when the opportunity arose to end the life of a real enemy to their cause."

"Well, were they in Northampton the night of the murder? Maybe they have an alibi for some event they attended in Worcester that same night?"

"They can't have an alibi," Faith interjected.

"Why can't they?" Mike wanted to know.

"Because I'm just remembering, they definitely did attend the Heamey reading. Both of them were excited about how well it had gone for 'our side.' I remember Nancy saying something a little snide to me at the reception about Tony, about maybe there being some hope for him yet after Heamey was so utterly defeated in the debate."

"That does it for me," Mike concluded. "We've got Sister Debbie's testimony about them killing Marissa—accident or not, it's negligent homicide—and then the body dump is also a felony of course. So we've got plenty to have the Worcester cops bring them in on. We'll bring Sally along for the ride, since she might be the most likely to have reason to support what O'Reilly's claiming. At the least we'll get them off the streets and make you two safer, and maybe we'll sweat them for these other killings. If we're lucky, Faith's right about there not

being much more of a network, and we'll have the alumbradas about shut down."

"I agree it's a good move to bring them in," Tony
agreed as the three took a look at the dessert offerings.
Tony surprised both Faith and Mike by passing on the
possibility of a sweet end to the meal. "But I still think
we're missing someone, the mastermind, the one Debbie
O'Reilly takes orders from and is still covering for."

Mike nodded. "Well, let's get all these girls in and
see if they don't know a little something about that too.
We can't afford to keep them on the streets when four
people are already dead."

A few minutes later, after Tony and Faith had said
their goodbyes to Mike and were headed to Tony's car
for the drive back to Northampton, Tony got a cell phone
call and had a brief conversation with someone before
starting the ignition on his Corolla. By the look on his
face, it was clearly not a casual call.

"That was Veronica. She's back. She says she needs
to talk. Says that it's urgent."

If Faith could have read the mystery of Tony's dark
brown eyes, she would have scanned a mix of doubt and
wonder, overcoming a slim remnant of hope.

"It's a good thing we just had a big meal. We can
just drive straight through," she assured him, with what
felt to him like the hint of a supportive smile.

Chapter 31

Though Tony appreciated Faith's willingness to hurry, he decided it was more prudent to call Mike immediately and let him know of Veronica's return. Mike okayed meeting with her, but suggested Faith not go along, so that Veronica would not get suspicious. Though Mike argued recent evidence did not point much to Veronica, especially since she seemed to have had nothing to do with Marissa Hitzel's death, the absence of a "mastermind" from their discoveries so far did not rule Veronica out completely.

Nor could Tony rule out the idea that Veronica—who was, after all, a practicing Carmelite, like St. Teresa herself—had only pretended to be an orthodox Catholic, in order the more freely to be a truly radical feminist. Tony had to discover if there was any real reason to suspect Veronica. And finding out why she had left in the middle of the semester, only to abruptly return, would be the first part of that discovery.

It was Saturday evening before Tony arrived at Veronica's home, after dinner, in the darkness of a cold, late

February New England night. He had told her he would
not arrive until after dinner, in part to make sure she
didn't have to be bothered with making him a meal. Over
the past week even food had somehow mattered less to
him than it normally did. He was looking to eat only
enough to sustain himself so he could be at his best while
trying to help solve this sad series of crimes committed
mistakenly in the name of God, like so many of the worst
sins of the past centuries, the Crusades, pogroms, Inquisi-
tions, by those of the Christian faith.

Veronica was dressed as conservatively as usual with
chocolate brown slacks and a modest light green sweater.
Around her neck she wore her usual brown scapular,
though its icon was hidden under the sweater. In her ears
were gold earrings, shaped like little crosses.

"When did you get back?" Tony asked, as he handed
Veronica his coat.

She motioned him into the living room as she walked
away from the door, before hanging up his coat in a hallway closet. When she returned, he was sitting at the long,
dark gray couch. She sat a comfortable speaking distance
away from him on that same sofa.

"I got back late last night and I have so much to tell
you," she began. "But don't you want some coffee first? I
didn't have time today to bake, so much catching up to
do, but I did stop at the bakery."

Veronica was talking to him as to a certain friend.
Tony thought it might be good to let the tone remain that
way and see where it took them, but he also felt almost
ethically bound to warn Veronica of all the reasons he
was there.

"No, nothing for me now, thanks. I guess I ought to
say I was pretty surprised when you left so suddenly."

"Tony, you sound almost suspicious. I don't understand. Why are you looking at me like that?" Veronica

asked, as she subtly moved inches farther from him on the couch.

Tony avoided the question momentarily by taking a quick look around the room. The walls were painted a faint grayish-blue and, to the left of the couch just above an upright, black piano, hung a traditional painting of the Blessed Mother holding the Christ child. Tony thought it must be new to the house since he had never noted it before. He thought to ask where the art work came from, but realized he would just be delaying the inevitable. Still, he hesitated.

"Tony?" Veronica prompted, with a look of worry in her dark brown eyes.

"Listen, Veronica, a lot has happened since you left. Angela and Teresa Sargento are in protective custody, Faith Covington has admitted her role within the alumbradas but is helping the police now to try to uncover all they can about the group, and Shanti Patel, Nancy Temple, and Sally McGuire have all been brought in for questioning, which may or may not lead to an arrest for the death of Marissa Hitzel."

"Those girls. Capable of murder? Can it really be?" Veronica seemed genuinely concerned, but still innocent of any possible suspicion about her own involvement.

"One of the things those young women told me was that Marissa showed you the original Spanish document of the Directives of Saint Teresa, and before I could even ask you about why you hadn't told us about any of that, you suddenly disappeared. Just where have you been the past two weeks?"

"B—but Tony, you can't possibly suspect me of anything. You had me help you when we went to talk to the Sargento sisters, I've been helping you all along, I—"

She seemed close to tears and certainly spoke with some real hurt in her voice. He wanted to draw closer to her and comfort her, but he knew he could not afford to trust her until she had given him satisfactory answers to his questions. First, though, he had to field one of hers.

"Tony, will you pray with me?"

"Pray, now? Now isn't the time for prayer, Veronica. I need to know where you were and why you went. And why you didn't tell me about knowing all along about that book."

"Just a single decade of the Rosary, Tony. The way St. Teresa taught us to pray." Veronica seemed insistent and this insistence frightened Tony.

"I don't carry rosary beads with me, Veronica. I'm not a priest anymore, remember? I'm not even what you'd call an orthodox Catholic anymore, okay?"

"That's a shame, Tony, but, still, I have rosary beads we can use."

She got up from her couch, went into her bedroom, came out with two pairs of Rosaries with large, dense, brown beads. As Veronica walked behind him, ostensibly to return to her seat, Tony nearly shuddered and looked to protect himself from an attack. She couldn't help but notice and quickly sat down, this time much closer to her visitor.

"What's wrong, Tony? You're acting very strangely. We don't have to pray now if you don't want to, but I thought it would be an ideal time, since what I have to tell you is so important to understanding all that has happened and so related to true prayerfulness."

Tony was too flustered to feel comfortable with her so near still clutching her rosary beads. So he anxiously restated his concerns. "Just tell me where you've been Veronica, and why, and why you didn't tell us you knew—"

"Knew what? You believe the testimony of young women you just told me will soon be arrested? You were with me the first time that foolish Teresa Sargento said she had proof of secret writings. Don't you remember how upset I was? Do you really think I was pretending? What possible reason would I have to pretend?"

"But you were so upset in the face of such clear evidence. It seemed almost like you were 'protesting too much' and I—"

"I was upset. Upset that you, of all people, couldn't see what I saw, that the 'Directives' had to be false, even if the evidence seemed to say they were true. That's why I left the country. I had to find out for absolute certain. And that's why I had you come tonight. Because I have."

Veronica was animated, but in a positive, almost exalted way, not at all like someone resigned to a truth she feared.

"You have what?

"Where have I been, Tony?" Veronica asked as she got close enough on the couch to touch him. "I've been to Spain. I went to track down Professor Villareal. It took more than a week, but I found him and I've spoken to him, at length."

"Why, why didn't you tell me where you were going?"

"I couldn't. As much as it pained me I had to lie even to my department, since I had no real justifiable reason to leave my teaching duties mid-semester on a wild-goose chase that might lead to nothing. I had them believe it was personal." She touched his hand, a light touch she immediately withdrew. "I knew you might also try to discourage me."

"Didn't you talk to Hank Gallagher first? Didn't he convince you of what Villareal had said?"

"Yes, yes, I did speak to him. He went over what he had told you about Professor Villareal, and I pretended to be satisfied, but then, without telling him or anyone else,

I went to Spain anyway. I just could not accept it. And I was right not to accept. St. Teresa must have guided me herself to find the professor."

Tony could not tell if he was about to hear the testimony of a woman in denial or the conclusions of an inspired detective. He wondered if he'd ever be able to read people properly. He was certainly listening intently now, though he didn't take his eyes entirely away from the rosary beads, which Veronica still clutched tightly in her hands.

"I found Professor Villareal at an old monastery in Segovia, where he was doing research and wanting to be as far from the U.S. culture as possible. At first he respectfully declined to see me and had the monks send me away, but I persisted and he gave me an interview."

"And?"

"And Professor Ernesto Villareal has never even heard of any 'Directives Toward the True Path of Glory' in English or in Spanish, and he hasn't seen Henry Gallagher in over a year."

She told him these last words with a look of happy triumph and vindication. But what she said made so little sense to him that he had to doubt it. Why would Hank lie?

What did Hank care one way or the other about St. Teresa? Why should Tony believe this woman he hardly knew? Where was the proof?

Almost as if reading his mind, Veronica added, "I've got a signed affidavit from Villareal, since I knew it might be important to your brother and his investigations. The whole thing has been an elaborate hoax."

"A hoax, b—but I—"

"I'm sure they can verify Professor Villareal's signature at Harvard or the police can do whatever they do. He reluctantly gave me a phone number where he could be contacted, actually where someone else could be reached who could then contact him, if they need to actually talk to him."

"But this is fantastical. It simply makes no sense. I mean, I guess it isn't beyond belief that Hank would play a prank on Faith Covington—he never liked her—but then to continue to lie about it when I asked him? I mean, it makes no sense."

"Well, that can all be cleared up later. The main thing is that now we have proof to combat this growing misunderstanding, this new branch of the alumbradas."

"But that's the thing. We've pretty much figured out that there is no big branch, just a twig at best. The nuns in Brooklyn, one of whom was a fake, and the girls at Holy Cross, plus Faith, that might have been the whole bunch, except maybe whoever was the leader of the whole group."

"B—but why?" Veronica stammered. "Now I'm confused all over again."

"You're confused? How do you think I feel? I'll have to go and hash this out with Hank. And, you know, it's still possible that Villareal is lying now because he doesn't want the truth about St. Teresa revealed."

"I'm sure he wasn't lying. Why would he? Why wouldn't he have just lied about the book being authentic in the first place, then?"

"I don't know. I guess because he knew someone else could eventually confirm its authenticity."

"Tony, no, I can't believe any of that," Veronica said, clearly disappointed in him for still holding out the possibility of the Directives being authentic. "What he told me is the truth. He's not even seen Henry Gallagher in over a year."

"But it makes zero sense." Tony was almost equally insistent. "I mean, how can Hank be mixed up in all this

alumbrada stuff? He isn't even religious. Maybe he's pro-
tecting someone. I mean, all the more, if this was just a
hoax to begin with, why are four people dead?"

Tony was shaking a little, when he stood up, to
leave. Veronica grabbed his arm and motioned for him to
sit back down.

"You can't leave yet."

"And why is that?"

"First, because you're too upset to drive. And next
because there's something I still need to explain to you.
You owe me at least that much after not trusting me all
this time."

*I still am not one hundred per cent certain I trust
you*, Tony thought to himself. Still, he sat back down and
listened.

"You're fluent in Spanish, aren't you, Tony?" Veronica began.

"Well, mostly, pretty fluent, but not like a native
speaker," he corrected.

"Well, you know what *dolor* means then, right?"

"Well, sure, pain or ache, like 'dolor de cabeza,' for
headache, right? It can stand for various kinds of pain.
It's a pretty important word for your pal Teresa, right?"

"Yes, a very important word, but maybe you don't
understand how important."

"I'm good at not understanding things, so clue me in,
but please hurry. I've got to get back to Northampton as
soon as I can."

"It's ironic," Veronica decided, with a voice that had
become calm and a little didactic. "Because you know the
nun who died was named Maria Dolores. And Dolores is
a popular name. Do you think very many people would
name their daughters 'Pains' or 'Aches'?"

"Well, the Spanish are a pretty somber lot, really.
After all, St. Teresa says if she can't suffer, she just wants

to die. So 'Pains' might be just the name she'd choose for a niece."

"You can be as glib as you like, Tony. It doesn't change anything. How would you translate, Maria Dolores, in reference to our Blessed Mother?"

"Oh, I see where you're going. That's usually translated 'Our Lady of Sorrows,' right?"

"Yes, and if you look at any standard Spanish/English dictionary, you'll see *dolor* is translated as sorrow or grief as well as pain or ache. The truth is that it's a word, like many, that really can't be readily translated from one language to another."

"Yes, but so?"

"Actually," Veronica said as if Tony had not said a word, "the seemingly same word exists in English, dolor, though it's listed in the dictionary as archaic. In English, it just means sorrow or grief, as if English speakers in the past knew that was the more accurate translation. And, as you say, it's one of St. Teresa's most important words."

"Where are you trying to take us, Veronica?" Tony asked, still with a kind of angry glibness, though Veronica might have recognized a bit of its edge already wearing off.

"*Dolor* may be one of the Spanish language's most important words. In Spanish it speaks to the human condition. *Dolor* is inescapable, whether it manifests itself as a headache or stomach discomfort or it lingers in how one never gets over the loss of a loved one or even a past love. It's the sorrow that has to come from the very finite and imperfect nature of our lives. When St. Teresa says she wants what is translated into English too often simply as 'pain,' she is really asking never to have absent from her the suffering that makes her human, her connection to all others. So, when she says, 'Let me suffer or let me die,' it isn't a sick call to always be in some masochistic state of enjoyment of pain, it's an acknowledgment of dolor, of being tied to all of us who also feel life's inescapable sorrow. What she is really saying, then, is that as soon as I don't share in that suffering, that sorrow, I might as well be dead. And when she says she loves Christ and wants to emulate him, marry him, it's not so she can suffer the awful physical misery of the cross that Christ willingly accepted, but more the fact that Christ, God-made-man, was willing to enter into all of the dolor of this world, that he had sympathy for our world-sorrow, and offered us salvation from that grief, salvation that comes from loving him, and from loving our neighbors as ourselves."

"So this whole case hinges on a misunderstood word, is that what you're trying to tell me?" Tony asked, still a little resistant, but noticeably less so.

"No, I'm saying the whole Spanish expression, '*padecer es vivir*,' 'to suffer is to live,' is not a glorying in pain, but a glorying in sympathy, in connection, in caring about others. Anyone who really understands St. Teresa, the Spanish, the human condition, has to know that there are no secret writings, that St. Teresa all along proved her love for human kind by how she was willing to embrace rather than try to escape dolor."

Veronica, mid-speech, had taken Tony's hands into hers, but there was no perversely strong grip, no intensity beyond the gentle, sure conviction of her words. She looked at Tony and saw the beginnings of tears in his eyes.

He looked away from her then at her again. "Dolor. How could I not know? My dad had a heart attack while you were away. But what does the physical pain of that, which he survived this time, compare to the overall ache I have over knowing he won't be long for this world? And from there, the pain and sorrow of knowing if we live long enough we'll lose all our loved ones. You knew the Directives had to be false, not because they were against men or against the patriarchal nature of the church, but because they emphasized pleasure in pain, pain for its own sake, not the redeeming power of a shared sorrow, a connection that is unbreakable."

"That's right, Tony."

"You knew St. Teresa's writings, really knew them, like none of these alumbradas ever could, so you knew while it was possible she could be a closet feminist, she could never be someone who turned her back on her co-sufferers. You knew and I should have known."

"It isn't too late to know, Tony. I pray and pray, and the farther I go toward St. Teresa's 'way of perfection,' the closer I get to total sympathy for all the suffering of the world, and farther from suffering for its own sake, or a meditative state that selfishly looks to a union only with the divine. Dolor, understanding dolor, guarantees our knowledge that there can be no union with the divine without sympathy for the human condition. 'Pray unceasingly' doesn't mean to lock yourself in a room and say words over and over again until they become meaningless. It means to try to unite with Christ in real love, a love that means nothing if it doesn't encompass the creation, every neighbor equally worthy of that love. One can't claim to unite with God who doesn't love all, and it is dolor that most unites us with each other, that is the starting point to a co-suffering that makes us able to love at all."

Veronica was now also tearful, as if the change in Tony's demeanor was almost too much joy for her to bear. She looked him directly in the eye and gently insisted, "Pray with me now, Tony. Pray for your father and for all parents. Pray for the victims of these killings and pray for the killer. Pray to thank God that we need no

self-torture to receive his love, just a sympathy for all he
suffered, gladly, for our sake. Then go and do what you
need to do."

The rosary beads had been placed on the blue, glass
coffee table. He picked up one pair and handed the other
over to Veronica. As they began to pray, he knew he was
too suffused with perhaps the truest dolor of his life to
have to worry about any physical strangling in this grief.

Chapter 32

When Mike received the information about what Veronica had discovered in Spain, he questioned his brother on what possible motivation Henry Gallagher could have had for not admitting the hoax to Tony when he first asked him about it. Still, though both brothers were confused, they agreed it was not a crime for Hank to have lied to Tony since he wasn't a police officer investigating a felony. Even if Mike had done the questioning, whether or not the "secret writings" were authentic or not had no provable bearing on any of the murders. So Mike agreed to let Tony handle the next interview with his boss, to see if another casual conversation, without police escort, could help them figure out why Hank had lied and whether it could possibly help them with any aspect of any of the murders.

Tony went ahead and called Hank up that same Saturday night, after leaving Veronica, and invited him over the next afternoon to watch together a few Marx Brothers movies that were going to be running on TCM, Tony finding it hard to believe that Hank had never seen *Mon-*

key Business. They were almost a half hour into *Duck Soup*, Tony in his favorite recliner and Hank an apple wood coffee table across from him on the old plaid couch. Tony furtively looked for signs of anything telling in Hank's demeanor, but he seemed to be his same old jokey, irreverent self. They were enjoying the movie, some Negra Modelo beer, and a nice variety of snacks when Tony tried to sneak the real reason for his invitation in as an overlay to the absurdity of Groucho's leadership of Freedonia.

"So, Hank, I know you love a practical joke, but I didn't think you'd snag me too," he began.

"What are you talking about?" Hank asked, seemingly a bit annoyed at being displaced from one of his favorite parts of the old flick.

"I mean, that whole elaborate story you handed Faith about those secret writings of St. Teresa being authenticated by Villareal. Turns out you haven't seen Villareal in over a year and he has no knowledge about any secret writings. I mean, 'what's up with that?' as they say."

Hank said nothing at first, looked back at the movie, but then reached for the remote, and flicked off the television. "How could you possibly have known that? Isn't Villareal still in Spain?"

"We tracked him down, Hank," Tony lied, leaving Veronica out of the discussion. "So, what's going on?"

Hank hesitated, reached into his pocket, but brought nothing out. "Man, I'm sorry about that. I really am. Kind of got myself into a mess and then couldn't do anything about it, really. It was just too big a temptation to screw with Faith Covington that way, you know. I mean, she hates my guts, thinks I'm way too old school to be chair of a department at a Seven Sisters place like Smith, but, practical thing that she is, she figured I was the guy who could find her an authenticator for something that old, so

I couldn't resist leading her on. And I knew Villareal would be on sabbatical this semester—I'd heard it from a mutual friend—so I knew no one could check on it any sooner than his return this summer. So I didn't see any real harm in it, just a joke on that stiff."

"Okay, I guess I'm buying that." Tony nodded before sipping his beer. "But why not tell me when you knew it was important to the investigation?"

"Well, you're going to like this answer even less, Ton'." Hank almost grimaced. "But I was pretty sick of you thinking you were a detective, missing time from school, and not leaving the police work to the police, so I figured I'd screw with you a little bit too, especially since I was pretty certain none of that nonsense could be any real help in finding out who killed anybody, since it was all so damn silly."

Hank spoke with conviction and even a bit of anger.

Tony recognized he was more than a little angry himself. "I never claimed to be some great detective. I was helping my brother out, in a way he thought made sense. And, believe it or not, there are some young women out there who have taken all this stuff really seriously, and some of the worst of this might not have happened if you hadn't assured Faith what she had was genuine."

"But it so clearly wasn't. I don't even read Spanish with any fluency, but from what I know about sixteenth-century manuscripts and paper, it was clearly a phony. Whoever did it didn't even go to the expense of trying to get as close to the real materials used then."

"All the more, then, why the hell didn't you tell me all this when I asked? I'm really surprised at you, Hank. This makes no sense to me."

Hank had nothing more to say. Tony looked at him, considered kicking him out of his apartment.

Hank seemed to read his long-time friend's body

language enough to ask, "You want me to leave, then? I can just leave."

Tony hesitated, looked around the room, then down at his friend's beer stein, which he noted was about empty. "No, man, we've been friends too long. I just want to understand this all, make some sense out of it. We need to talk this through. I must be missing something. Let me get you another beer and we'll talk."

Hank nodded and Tony went into the kitchen for the beer. Just then his cell phone rang. He fished the phone from his pocket to find Mike at the other end.

"Listen, Ton', something's come up, something pretty big."

"What, what's going on?" Tony asked.

"Well, I know you were planning to see Gallagher, but I think you'd better wait for me to get there."

"But he's here right now," Tony said, in a muffled tone, since the TV was no longer on and the distance from the kitchen to the living room was nominal.

"Well, okay, no problem, probably, but, well, we've done some more digging and it turns out Debbie O'Reilly had a few classes with your pal."

"Wow, yeah, that is interesting but, still, it doesn't prove anything," Tony responded, though without confidence.

"No, not much, but we've also had a chance to check her phone calls and they've spoken to each other, more than once, in the past few months, including a few calls after she got to her hide out in Missouri."

"S—so that means—"

"That means, and I don't know quite how or why yet, that your pal is mixed up in this thing up to his forehead. We still don't have enough to arrest him. It's no crime to know a suspected felon or to talk to her, but I think I'd better be there before we question him on all of it. Don't let on that you know any of this and you'll be cool for now, but I wouldn't turn my back on the guy, all right? I should be able to get to—"

"Oh, sorry, gotta go," Tony said as he got off the phone.

Hank was in the kitchen.

"You're not leaving, are you?" Tony asked.

"No, you said you wanted to talk some more. I just came in to refill the cheese straws bowl, if it's okay with you."

Tony nodded. "Sure, go ahead. They're right over there."

Tony really did not know what to do next. Almost in shock over what Mike had just told him, he was not thinking as clearly as he might have. Right after the men reentered the living room, still not able to believe that Hank was a threat to him or to anybody else, Tony blurted out precisely what his brother had told him to keep to himself.

"So, whaddaya hear from Debbie O'Reilly lately?"

Hank just looked at Tony, at first without responding, as if to think things through. "Sit down, Ton', and I'll explain everything," he promised, in the same sort of tone he used with his faculty when he was about to let them know something they were not going to like.

Tony sat back down on his recliner, nervously sipped from his beer, kept a wary eye on Hank, ready for about anything.

"It's just as well," Hank began. "That malarkey I just gave you made no real sense at all. Pretty soon you'd have come to that conclusion and would know something wasn't kosher. But I'm all packed and my plane leaves in about three hours anyway. I was going to make some excuse and leave soon. *Monkey Business* was going to have to wait for another day."

"Well, why'd you even come over then?" Tony wondered. "And where the hell do you think you're going?"

"That's top secret, Ton'. I shouldn't even have come, but I needed to know what you knew so far, whether anyone would come looking for me right away. I'm glad I did. I didn't figure on you finding Villareal, for one thing. But I knew that the police had picked up Deb, so I figured you'd make the connection sooner or later, and though I was almost certain she wasn't going to mention my name, I couldn't be absolutely certain. Who did tell you about me and Deb? Dean Athanason? That witch always had it in for me."

Tony was a little relieved that Hank had not overheard his conversation enough to realize it was his brother and the other police who now knew the connection. He wondered why Hank was so confident that Tony wouldn't just tackle him and prevent him from catching his plane, but there was still time to see how that would play out.

For now, he wanted to hear whatever Hank had to say.

Hank almost seemed able to read Tony's mind. He took out a .32 automatic, pointed it toward his old friend. "There's absolutely no way I want to hurt you, so please don't try anything silly, okay? I doubt you could take me anyway, but this makes all that moot, right?"

Tony was once again in shock, could not really believe any part of what was happening between him and Hank. "Yeah, whatever you say, Hank, you're the boss," he said, trying to sound calm.

Hank laughed. "Nice pun. In a few minutes ,the gun will be unnecessary. It was just a backup, in case you didn't sip your drink after I—"

"Oh, my God, you've poisoned me," Tony jumped

up in a panic and then seemed ready to leap across the low table onto Hank.

"Calm down and sit down, damn it," Hank insisted. "I didn't poison your beer, I just 'doctored' it, with some chloral hydrate, about fifteen minutes ago, when you went to the bathroom."

"Chloral what?"

"Hydrate. You know, the classic 'mickey,' but a mellow one, with just the beer chaser. You shouldn't even start feeling it for another ten minutes and you'll be out in maybe another twenty. I'll have to stick with you till you're asleep, so you don't try to call anyone until I'm gone. Since I've got to wait anyway, I'll tell you all you want to know, so long as you don't get frisky on me."

"Why bother? What's in it for you?" Tony asked suspiciously, as he started to notice or at least thought he noticed himself getting groggy.

"Well, for one thing, I think I owe it to you, I want at least someone who was a real friend to realize I wasn't just some kind of madman. The other thing, once you know the truth, and can pass it on to your brother, Deb will be a lot better off, since she didn't kill anybody."

"Fine, I'm listening and I'll stay put," Tony acquiesced, though he looked around his own living room for possible weapons toward a surprise attack.

Hank kept an eye on his friend's eyes, shook his head, but tried to continue. "It all started as—"

"You killed everyone, didn't you?" Tony broke in. "All four of the victims. But—but I still can't even half way figure out why."

"Will you just let me talk, goddamn it!"

Tony ignored his friend's angry request, in spite of the gun he was still pointing at him. "If you're killing people left and right, why would I believe you just want to drug me? You're some kind of maniac, someone I don't really know. You might as well shoot me—at least that would be quicker."

As Tony said these words he looked around for something to try to defend himself against the gun. He considered his beer stein itself, a pewter mug from England with his name engraved, a gift, he remembered sadly, from Hank himself.

But once again Hank seemed to know what he was thinking. "Please don't try anything heroic, man. This gun is actually loaded. Hell, don't you realize that if I had ever wanted to kill you, you'd be dead already? Like when I had Deb bump your car on New Year's Eve. She could have just as easily done something worse. She was up for about anything, but all I wanted was to make you think of the threat coming from New York, all the less suspicion on me. She was pretty pissed, though, that you left that party early. She was having a great time."

"How did she even know—"

"You don't even remember telling me you were going out with Isabel that night, do you? That's why you never suspected me of anything, until just now. But, really, I don't want to hurt you. The truth is I never wanted to hurt anybody, except maybe toward the very end. So, all the more, you should know you're safe. So no sudden moves, okay? Do you want to hear the rest of this or not?"

Tony, definitely beginning to feel the first signs of sleepiness, sat back down resignedly. "Okay, sure, tell me what the hell this is really all about."

"It was Debbie O'Reilly who blew up my second marriage. It started right in my office, I mean, it was like some fantasy come true for me. The sex itself was ridiculous. There was no way I could resist her, even if I had wanted to try. But it wasn't just sex. She's crazy smart too, and the only girl I ever met who was as equally disgusted by Catholics as she was by feminists. Two sides of the same goddamn coin, both as sanctimonious, both as ready to burn anyone not on their same stupid page."

Hank was getting worked up. The gun was unsteady in his hands, which made Tony all the more nervous.

"I'm still not getting it," he admitted.

"Just shut up and listen then. Debbie's a wild woman, sure, but she's an even better con artist. Once she left Smith, she was up to one con after another. She eventually showed up at my doorstep and we got right back to where we were before, except now I had no wife to slow us down. But she wasn't looking to be Mrs. Gallagher number three, at least not in this prissy little berg. She had this plan for stealing the Carmelite's gold cross, something I had told her about years before, since it always bugged me that a work of art like that, from the Renaissance, should be locked up with a bunch of nuns. And she figured, and figured right, that once she was in, it would just be a matter of time before she knew where it was hidden and how to get at it. She also figured that while she was at it, she could have some fun with the Catholics and the feminists at the same time. But she needed my help."

"So there never was any plan to kill anyone? This was all just a con gone bad?" Tony started to try to guess, even as he continued to survey his living room for a way to distract Hank.

"I'm getting to that, man. Yeah, she had been raised Catholic, had been abused by a nun who was principal at the little Catholic school she attended, but the church had just covered it all up, reassigned the witch to some other town. So Deb had it in for nuns ever since. Plus she had really gotten into this banned movie about St. Teresa of Avila that this British guy made. It portrayed Teresa as a sex-crazed masochistic maniac, and from there Deb researched her and got into all her writings and saw how easy it would be to fool people, especially Catholic feminist types, into believing that St. Teresa really was a masochist and a feminist who hated men. She put me to work on making an authentic-looking sixteenth-century document, which wasn't hard for me, though I had to hire a grad student in Spanish to translate what Deb came up with for the text. She already had her con set for getting into the con-vent. We laughed over that pun a bunch, I'm telling you, and she knew once she was in she could figure her way to finding out where the cross was kept hidden. You know, if she had kept this strictly to robbery, no one would have gotten hurt. But she was on a mission, was having too much fun with all that 'Do not fear the cross' stuff when she was planning on stealing it from them. And I had my own axes to grind with both the Catholics and the feminists, my last wife having been both, so, what the hell? I was willing to play along. Even if I hadn't been, Deb O'Reilly is a tough person to say no to. She's absolutely irresistible, I'm telling you, and not just in bed."

Tony should have let Hank go on, but he wanted answers to each murder. "Why did she kill Sister Maria?"

"She didn't. I told you, Deb didn't kill anyone. But that nun, that Sister Maria, she was, in her own way, as unstable as any of the civilians in this whole mess She was one of these Catholic feminists too. They want an equal place for women, but are supposed to toe the line about women's obviously secondary role in the church. Hell, that hasn't gotten any better since St. Teresa's time, so someone like that is conflicted right to the core. She had studied with Heamey a little at Loyola as an undergrad, though I suppose you already knew that. She was the easiest target for all this St. Teresa mumbo-jumbo and then those nuts from Holy Cross went for it big time too, and Faith herself, of course and Deb, who does have a big thing for S& M, believe me I know. She started with this choking rosary business and she filmed it for me secretly so I could get off on it too, though, I'll tell you, I didn't much care for that. Well, Sister Maria, she had second thoughts and all kinds of guilt and contacted Heamey. And he was investigating and was explaining to her why and how the document she had seen was a phony, which, by the way, anyone who knows anything about Renaissance documents would know, even hearing about it second hand, and the girl actually did kill herself, because she was so ashamed of what she had let 'Sister Anna' get her into."

"That's awful, but then why was Monsignor Heamey killed? That was no suicide."

"The guy was a really forthright, old school Jesuit son of a bitch—reminded me of Father Toohey from Cathedral, remember him? He somehow suspected that I might be involved in all this. I guess he was a way better detective than your brother or any of these local clowns, eh? His clue was an article I had written years before in a pretty obscure Renaissance scholarly journal about authenticating Renaissance documents, something that gave him at least enough of a clue to have a talk with me, since Sister Maria had told him about Sister Anna going off to Northampton more than once. That's the real reason he accepted the debate with you in the first place. Why else set himself up for failure like that, right?"

Tony nodded, while trying not to nod off. "That never did make sense to me."

"Well, I tried to reason with him before the debate, but he wasn't having any of it, so I met him in his hotel room after. I had snuck in through the service entrance of the place. He was on me quick and hard, made me feel like I was back in grade school at Holy Child and was being sweated for why I used my Propagation of the Faith money to buy candy instead of giving it to the poor. He told me I would certainly lose my job over this 'heinous hoax' and that I might even be guilty of negligent homicide for Sister Maria's death. I mean he was practically foaming at the mouth, and—well, I just saw my whole life, all of a sudden, down the tubes, no job, maybe jail time, if I didn't stop this guy. Half of it was fear, half of it was anger over this old priest jerk threatening me. I strangled him with his own damn rosary and—"

"We thought it wasn't his," Tony interrupted.

"He had found out where we were getting ours from, both our scapulars and rosaries, and he had them with him to show me he knew even that, and I just—I just, well, you know, before I was done he was dead."

"That's it, he was dead?"

"Okay, yeah, I was in shock, I felt awful. When I called you about it, I wasn't acting. I was freaked out, but I'm just trying to get this all in. I'd split right now if I thought you wouldn't call the cops on me, but I've got to stay till you're out. So let me tell you all this. I need you to know I'm not really some psycho serial killer—you, of all people, I need to know that."

"And Marissa Hitzel?"

"From what I heard from Debbie before she got arrested, that was an accident. Really an accident.

"And Sweeney?"

Hank hesitated, seemed to be choking up, but then continued in an informative tone. "With all this murder investigation going on, Deb and I decided the best way to avert suspicion was to make it seem like some kind of a cult fed series of murders. That's why I sent your brother the choking rosary tape, though I drove to Worcester before mailing it, figuring it might make you suspect some of those Holy Cross co-eds all the more that way. Deb was confident she could get away, so it was fine to throw suspicion on her because she would have the bus ticket alibi if she ever did get caught. So that would leave the other women as suspects, none of whom knew a thing about me. But, anyway, Deb was going to grab the cross and go and we thought she'd be safe stashed away with those hippies in Rutledge. I'm still not sure how you found her. I had no qualms about implicating the other girls, especially since two of them actually did kill that poor Marissa character. Hey, are you still with me?"

Tony was showing more signs of the effects of the chloral hydrate. But part of it was a ruse. He was still hoping to catch Hank off guard. He thereby tried to slightly slur his response. "Yes, I'm hearing you Hank. You can bet I won't forget a bit of this."

"The most ironic thing of all, of course, was Faith bringing me the Spanish phony document for authentication—me, who had made it up in the first place. Of course, Deb had something to do with steering her my way, but it still was just too funny, with her thinking she was so damn clever and superior all along. I thought I would be in the clear until Villareal returned. I knew he was inaccessible, plus no one would have a reason to suspect me of lying about the authenticity thing. I wanted to leave at semester's end, to alert no suspicion, but now that's out the window."

"But until you came here this afternoon and I told you about being onto the Villareal thing, you had no way of knowing anyone was wise, so how can you be prepared to leave so soon?

"I had my suspicions. I was being wary all along. I've got more than one friend at Holy Cross, and when I found out Veronica Teuma had disappeared, after talking to me about the authentication, I was worried about what she might be looking into or finding out. If she got a hold of the 'original,' which Deb had actually hidden, but hadn't even told me where, I knew the jig would be up. So I've been getting more and more nervous, of course, and I figured I'd better get out while I still could."

"So, where are you headed?" Tony asked. "I know you pretty well. Aren't you afraid I'll guess?"

"Your record as a detective is none to stellar, Ton'. I'm pretty confident you won't guess, and even if you do, by the time you're able to, I'll be out of reach."

"Sounds like the perfect crime. Were you able to sell the cross?"

"That was less trouble than you'd guess. There are many thousands of people who are very rich, which, as both Christ and Thoreau will tell you, means that most of them probably aren't very nice, and so when they can get their hands on something they want, they don't worry about what's legal, so long as they think they'll get away with it. I'll leave it at that."

"And Debbie?"

"The less I say about her the better. She didn't kill anyone and you can't even prove she stole the cross. No one has ever seen her with it, so she'll be out by and by."

"But what about Sweeney? That's the crime we couldn't tie to anything else. Don't tell me you killed someone exclusively to make catching you harder. How can anyone turn into a cold-hearted killer that quickly?"

Hank again hesitated and, when he spoke, it was with more agitation, though still full of his usual overlay of sarcastic irreverence: "You're the detective fiction fan. Isn't it in *Death on the Nile* where good ol' Poirot says once you take that step toward evil, that defining step, you're married to evil forever?"

"That's the book," Tony confirmed. "But damn it, Hank, that's just a book. These were people you actually killed."

Hank responded with rising anger. "Sweeney wasn't exactly random. I always hated him. He was a bastard to me at Cathedral, had the upper classmen on the baseball team haze me because I was the first freshman ever to play varsity and it actually put him on the bench. And the hazing got out of control because I fought the bastards. Sweeney actually felt me up pretty heavy in the boy's locker room. Even the guys that were holding me down told him he was going too far. Way too far." Hank seemed ready to explode. "And I never forgave that. Never. Plus, he didn't get any better with age. He was the same cowardly, moronic creep the day he died. I'd never have killed anyone if that Heamey mess hadn't happened, but since I'd already killed one priest, it was a lot easier to kill another, especially a piece of shit like Sweeney. If you'd only remembered a little better how much I couldn't stand that jerk, it might have given you a clue. I never told you what he had done to me, but you knew, at least back then you knew, how I hated his guts. That was a clue you missed. But you're not one ever to suspect your friends are you?"

Hank's biting sarcasm and anger, his growing-more-evident desperation, made Tony all the less ready to believe that Hank just wanted Tony to drink a sleeping potion so he could escape. He could have just not come at all, Tony reasoned. And now, he figured, it was just the sound of gun fire that Hank wanted to avoid, while still enjoying somehow letting Tony know, right before he died, just how completely he had miscalculated again. But what could Tony do now to prevent his own death or Hank escape? His only recourse was to believe his assailant's relatively benevolent intent, his only hope that he would indeed wake up, groggy but safe, in his recliner the following morning.

The intensity of their interaction had made Tony

oblivious to the scene outside the apartment, an oblivi-
ousness aided by Tony's curtains being drawn, as they
habitually were during movie watching. Both men reacted with surprise to the repeated loud ringing of the door-
bell. But Tony recuperated more quickly from this surprise, took the bell ringing as a tolling back to life,
grabbed his beer stein, and hurled it at Hank's head. He
missed high, but enough beer splashed into Hank's eyes
that the gunshot he may or may not have intended to fire
also went high. With the shot, the relatively cheap lock
on the entrance door gave way quickly to almost two
hundred pounds of energetically applied force as Mike
flew into the room. Though Hank had recovered enough
to have the draw on the lieutenant, Tony jumped more
athletically than he would have imagined possible, even
without being burdened by a sedative, over the coffee table and into a tackle of Hank, hard enough to dislodge the
gun from his hands. Mike quickly aided his brother in
subduing their adversary.

"I thought you were calling from Queens," Tony said
with grateful astonishment once his brother had Hank
cuffed. "Why didn't you tell me you were almost here?"

"You hung up before I could, plus I didn't realize
how important it was to you. Glad to see me for a change,
eh?"

"Yeah, yeah, it's a very good change," Tony decided, as he flopped wearily back into his recliner and waited for Mike to call for more police for Hank's incarcera-
tion and an ambulance for himself, in case his old friend
had been lying yet one more time.

Chapter 33

S o they found the 'Directives' in the convent?" Veronica shook her head, with disbelief.

Mike Cupelli chuckled, as he reached for a helping
of Maltese style potatoes with onions. "Yeah, 'Sister Anna' thought it would be a good joke to hide them there
before she split. O'Reilly decided to get a hell of a lot
more cooperative once we convinced her we had a case
on her for conspiracy to commit murder in the Sweeney
killing. She's ratting on that poor schmuck Gallagher after all, though he was ready to swear she had no
knowledge of his plans for Sweeney. Can you beat that?"

"And will the nuns get their cross back?" Faith questioned.

"Yeah, Gallagher had no love for the fellow they
sold it to. He'll get a slap on the wrist for receiving stolen
property or maybe he'll claim he didn't know it was stolen."

"How could he not have known?" Veronica protested.

"Rich guys with really good lawyers can do all sorts

of things the rest of us can't manage. But at least the cross goes back home either way. Will you pass the salad?" Mike requested. "Veronica, you're such a good cook I'm even having salad. Is that feta cheese in here?"

"Yes, and the croutons are homemade. Will you pass them to your brother, Tony?"

It was the Saturday after Hank's arrest. Veronica, Faith, Mike, and Tony were together again at Veronica's for dinner, but with circumstances a great deal altered since their previous dinner engagement there. Though a celebration of the capture of a murderer might have seemed a little macabre, what Veronica was really wanting to celebrate was the clearing of her favorite saint's name, and not even Faith was unwilling to share in that joy, since she had narrowly escaped the consequences of misreading that sixteenth-century Spanish woman's work.

"But what's going to happen to the students?" Veronica asked.

"Well, we sweated Sally pretty good and let her know we would go easy on her if she gave up her two nutty friends and, away from their direct influence, she got pretty damn cooperative," Mike explained. "Turns out it was Nancy who actually went too far and killed Marissa, but it was Shanti's idea to hide the body in the dorm, far away from their house. That hiding the body part is going to add some time to their sentence, but since the death, even from Sally's view, was totally a reckless accident, they'll probably plead out."

"And the Sargento sisters?" Faith asked.

"They had nothing to do with Marissa, not even the cover-up, according to all three of the others, so I guess they're in the clear," Mike noted. "Same goes for Faith here, for the same reasons, but I guess you already figured that part out."

Veronica was not quite ready to make light of any of it. "I'm worried about their spiritual well-being more even than the criminal charges. Have they all accepted the reality of having been duped? Are they all ready to understand what really happened to them?"

"Teresa needs some sort of therapy, that's pretty clear." Tony spoke up for the first time. "I think Angela's going to be fine. Sally too, once she's free and clear of all of it. Nancy and Shanti, I couldn't begin to say. They seemed like they were wedded to a kind of evil, regardless of where they got it from. I don't think the prison system is going to do anything to combat that."

"You'd rather we set them free?" Mike questioned.

"No, I'm not saying that." Tony shook his head in vigorous confirmation of his acceptance of the sentences awaiting Nancy and Shanti.

"So where was Hank Gallagher off to? Did he tell you that, too?" Faith asked Mike, who was sitting next to him at the table and who seemed to enjoy every bit of her gold-green focus on his responses.

"Albania."

"Albania?" the two women asked with equal surprise and almost in unison.

"Exactly. Who would ever suspect? He figured once he was established there, under some false identity, he could still have the run of Europe and even Asia at his leisure. You know he cleared over a million for that cross? You know how far a million—plus he had about twice that all together from a careful life of investing— goes in Albania?"

"I guess he doesn't get to find out now," Tony said, stating the obvious. "I'm just glad he still thought enough of me to just put knock out drops instead of poison in that beer."

"We're all very glad of that," Veronica came back

with something just as obvious, though Faith's responding "Amen" was certainly almost fully playful and only a slight touch ironic.

The rest of dinner and the time after were largely taken up with a further discussion of all the nuances of the case. Once Tony had been discharged from the hospital, where they had monitored the effects of the chloral hydrate on him very cautiously before discharging him on Tuesday, he had spent a day with the Northampton and Worcester police and the next two back in New York to make his statements and visit with his worried family there and was only now able to have a bit of a break. Still he naturally understood Faith's and Veronica's desire for the same closure that he and Mike now owned. Mike had come for the weekend and was staying with his brother, and he had suggested that Faith make the dinner at Veronica's a foursome, an idea that Veronica had no problem welcoming. The idea of Faith and Mike actually dating had not come up openly, but it was no surprise when Mike suggested Faith show him around the area, maybe take in a night spot or two. "If you actually have any around here," while giving Veronica and Tony some time to be alone.

It was time Tony put quickly to use. "I'm sorry I doubted you Veronica. Sorry about this whole mess."

"It was impossible to know what to think. I don't blame you at all, Tony, especially now that I think you understand what St. Teresa was all about and why I was so sure she could not have been the author of those awful 'Directives.'"

The two were again sitting on the gray couch, close, but not intimately so, each with a glass of Maltese Bajtra liqueur in hand. Tony had been thinking of Veronica a lot all week, so he was ready to go in the direction he could not take while there were others in the house.

"Where can we go next, Veronica? Is there any future for us? I know how adamantly Catholic you are, but—"

"Haven't I been thinking about these same things? Tony, I really feel you're ready to be in a truly committed and holy relationship, the way God intended. But you're an ordained priest, and as you know better than me, 'once a priest always a priest,' so that would seem to make a relationship between us impossible."

Tony put his liqueur down on the coffee table, looked at Veronica, whose dark eyes responded to his own. He sighed. "Knowing how happy we might be together, but having a belief in something that disables you from ever pursuing that happiness, is this really what's best, Veronica? Are you really going to pass up this chance we might have for happiness?"

"I'm not a saint, Tony, not at all. My feelings for you are as real as my sense that it should never be. I'm not as simple as my devotion to St. Teresa might have made me seem to you. I should say we can't ever be, but I won't. If you'll give me some time, time to pray, if you promise to pray too, maybe something...something...I don't know what, but something good could still come of this."

With those words Veronica touched Tony's hand, gave him a brief kiss on his lips, and left the room. It was Veronica's signal that their evening was over. Whether there would be other evenings was not up to Tony.

He drove back to Northampton in more vivid pain than he had suffered since the traumatic events of three years before. In some ways this pain felt even more powerful since, for the first time in his life, he knew that Veronica would be good for him and he for her, rather than just fulfilling some sort of ego-driven need or carnal desire. But if he wanted to come back to that kind of belief system, how could he allow himself to lead Veronica away from the very foundation of her own life long faith?

He beat Mike home by three hours, but he was still awake when his brother arrived, only a little tipsy and volubly happy.

"Who'd have ever guessed that kid could be so funny? I mean, she's a riot—zinging me as good as any Brooklyn paisana, but like with a totally different vibe than when I first met her. I think she actually likes me."

"What's not to like?" Tony asked and without a bit of irony.

"So you think there's something there?"

"What the hell do I know? I mean, even if there is, you live hours apart, 'two different worlds,' and all that but, hey, stranger things have worked. You've got a better chance than me and Veronica."

"Are you kidding me? That woman's crazy about you. I could tell it from way back, when I was worried 'cause I wasn't sure whether she should be a suspect or not. But that one's in the bag, man. And what a cook."

Mike seemed almost giddy, and it was with happiness for his brother's future. That alone gave Tony yet another jolt of what he now might call dolor.

"'Once a priest always a priest.' She quoted it for me, in case I had forgotten. She can't really go with me, much less marry me, because, to her, I'm still Monsignor Cupelli."

Mike listened to his brother, heard all the words, but in his happy state, seemed unwilling suddenly to shift to something that sad. He had to sit down before he continued.

"You mean to tell me that first, way back when, you couldn't really be with Maggie Rosario, because you were a priest and so couldn't acknowledge the relationship, but now, when the church has pretty much kicked you out, you can't be with someone because, magically somehow you're still a priest. I mean, that's nuts. This Veronica, I mean, Catholic or no Catholic, she's one smart woman, and you, you're no slouch with the brains, so there's gotta be something you can figure out, no? I mean, she's not gonna let something this good pass her by, am I right?"

Mike's whole speech, though totally in tune, in terms of word choice, accent, and emphasis with the way Tony had heard his brother speak for his entire life, was still completely distinct, since it was so clearly suffused with affection, regard, respect, and concern for his brother.

Tony remembered when he had told Mike that he might be poisoned, how Mike had first had to resist the desire to throttle Henry Gallagher, who tried to placate him with what turned out to be the truth regarding the chloral hydrate, but then how he had nervously awaited the ambulance, trying to keep tears from his eyes so he could feign a calm about how Tony was going to be, "Fine, you're gonna be fine, ace, I swear to God, I'm sure of it." And now, almost a week away from that crisis, Mike had not waned in that regard. It looked like his brother's happiness meant more to him even than his own.

Tony's own eyes welled with tears. He looked at his brother, who looked so much like him but had for many years been more adversary than complement.

Tony tried to sound upbeat, though the best he could get out was a sad chuckle. "If anyone had told me that you and I were going to be together, talking about our dates, like a couple of teenagers, and rooting for each other like a couple of saps, I'd have been sure he was *pazzo*, a first class nut. But here we are, brother, so I guess anything's possible with God. Anything."

Mike saw the tears, but ignored them, and knelt down beside his brother, who sat upright in his recliner. "And can you imagine how happy Mom would be, you bringing home a 'nice Catholic girl.' And who could be nicer or more Catholic than Veronica? And still a hell of a looker. Dad will be impressed, too."

After that, Mike got back into a standing position, only to bend down again, implant a kiss on his brother's forehead, and announce, "Hey, all this girl talk has me beat. I'll see you tomorrow morning. Oh, make that later this morning. Don't get me up before noon. Remember, I've got a gun."

Tony laughed at his brother's easy escape from what had just transpired. He sat still in his chair, reached for the remote, and turned off the TV he had not really been watching for the past hour. He picked up a copy, lying off to the right side of his recliner, of *The Way of Perfection*.

"Teach me how to 'pray unceasingly,' Teresa," he began, his first fully genuine prayer in many years, and the first of many more to come.

About the Author

Joe Benevento received a B.A. degree from NYU in English and Spanish (magna cum laude, Phi Beta Kappa), an M.A. in English from Ohio State and a Ph.D. in English from Michigan State. Benevento is Professor of English at Truman State U, where he teaches creative writing, American literature, and Mystery. He is the longtime, co-editor of the *Green Hills Literary Lantern.*

Benevento's poems, stories, essays and reviews have appeared in about 300 places, including: *Poets & Writers, The Chattahoochee Review, Pearl, Wisconsin Review, Inkwell, South Dakota Review, RE: Arts & Letter* and *Bilingual Review.* His work has three times been nominated for Pushcart Prizes. In 1991 he was featured in a special issue of *The MacGuffin,* "New Decade, New Writers.

Benevento's previous books include two novels, two full length poetry volumes, two poetry chapbooks, and a book of short stories. They are, *Holding On,* Warthog Press, 1996; *Willing To Believe,* Timberline Press, 2003; *The Odd Squad,* Behler Publications, 2005 (a finalist for the 2006 John Gardner Fiction Book Award); *My Puerto Rican Past,* Ginninderra Press, 2006; *Some of My Best Friends and Other Fictions,* Lewis-Clark Press, 2008; "*Tough Guys Don't Write,* " Finishing Line Press, 2011; The Monsignor's Wife, Moonshine Cove Publishing, 2013.